Turnabout

TURNABOUT

by Carmen Webster Buxton

Cracked Mirror Press
Rockville, MD USA

Note:
This is a work of fiction. All the characters and events decribed herein are entirely the product of the author's imagination.

ISBN: 978-0997989816 (paperback)
Copyright © 2017 by Karen Wester Newton

A Cracked Mirror Press Book

One

The first time Becca Sommers mentioned Spanish class to me it surprised me—partly because I didn't know Becca took Spanish, but mostly because she had just that moment slid her hand under my tee shirt and raked my chest hair with her fingernails.

"So, Jason," she said, moving her hand down to just brush against my belt buckle, "you have Walters for Spanish 3, don't you?"

My fantasy of dating the most popular girl in the senior class crashed and burned. And I stopped worrying about hiding my now-fading boner. "What?"

We were half sitting, half lying on Becca's frilly four-poster bed with Coldplay's latest release playing on her iPhone speakers. Becca had invited me into her bedroom under the assumption that I wanted to hear Coldplay. I wasn't about to correct her. Becca had her clothes on, except for the flip-flops she had slipped off earlier, but that wasn't saying a lot because her tube top showed a lot of cleavage, and her jeans couldn't have been any snugger and still zipped shut.

I had on much looser jeans and a tee shirt. My sneakers had hit the floor as soon as I sat down, and I never wore socks if I could help it. "Yeah," I said, disgusted. I should have known something was up when she asked me to come to her house after school. A girl like Becca Sommers would never go for a borderline nerd like me, no matter how well I kept my ownership of a flip phone and my passion for classic jazz a secret.

Her hand kept stroking me. I knew it was a trick, but I couldn't move. Like a deer trapped by headlights, I waited for the impact.

"Have you read the novel yet?" she asked. "In Spanish, I mean."

"Of course I read it," I said, irked out of my frozen state. "I had all summer to read it."

She gave me a pouty look. "It's not available in English. I checked eBay, even. Nothing." She leaned over me and smiled, shaking her head so that her blond hair whipped across my face. "Nada."

The test on our Spanish summer reading, a rambling family saga set during the Spanish Civil War called Sin Vergüenza y Sin Honor, was set for Thursday and today was Tuesday. That explained Becca's sudden interest in me. She had cut it pretty close.

A faint vibration shook the bed, and a grinding noise sounded over the Coldplay track. I glanced at the sound system to make sure it hadn't some how skipped or kicked up a few notches.

Becca frowned and scrambled from the bed to look out the window. "Oh, my God!"

I figured one of her parents had shown up. It looked like Becca wasn't supposed to have after-school company—not male company, anyway. I sat bolt upright and looked around for my shoes. "Who is it?"

"It's my dad." She looked suddenly pale.

I glanced out the window and realized Becca's room was right over the garage. The vibration had been the garage door opening. One look and my eyes opened wider. "Is that a cop car?" I jumped up and grabbed for my shoes. "Is your dad a cop?"

"Yes!" She looked around frantically. "We have to get you out of here!"

I pulled on my sneaks and ran a hand through my hair, then took a quick glance at Becca's full length mirror to see if what was left of my bone showed. Did I look like a guy on the make? Maybe, but mostly I looked like a scrawny bean pole whose clothes hung on him like they were still on the hanger. "Why? We weren't doing anything."

Becca grabbed my hand and ripped open the bedroom door. She dragged me into the hallway, but then gasped and dragged me right back into her bedroom. "Oh, fuck! He's already in the house."

"Why don't we just go downstairs?" I said. "What's he going to do shoot me?"

She stared at me with her eyes wide, her pupils dilated like a stoner's. "We can't take that chance—not after last time."

That got me. "What do you mean, 'after last time'?"

She shook her head and glanced around the room. "It doesn't matter. Get in the closet."

"I'm not hiding in your closet." I tried to sound indignant, but it came out more whiny.

She picked up my backpack and shoved it at me. "Get in the closet!"

"Rebecca?" a deep, masculine voice called. "Rebecca, do you have the TV on?"

I raced across the room. The closet was the wide shallow kind with a pair of doors that were each supposed to fold in the middle and slide along on a track, but both doors stuck after only a few inches and wouldn't budge.

"I'm in my room, Dad," Becca called. "I'm just listening to music."

I wedged myself through the gap and discovered why the doors were stuck. Clothes and shoes covered the closet floor so thoroughly that I could barely stand up.

Becca gave me a sharp shove and then pushed the doors shut behind me. "Watch out for the laundry chute in the floor." The whispered warning sounded eerily muffled in the enclosed space.

I found myself clutching my backpack and teetering in the dark, with only thin strips of light coming in through the slats in the doors. Soft fabrics brushed my face and hands.

I took a step, and my foot kept going. I had found the laundry chute the hard way. I flung myself sideways and nearly fell over, hitting the back wall with a muffled thump. I grabbed a jacket for balance and then bent down to check out the laundry chute as a way out. It seemed awfully small for an escape route, and I didn't want to risk getting stuck like Santa in a chimney.

I moved as quietly as I could to the far end of the closet, holding the hangers as I pushed the clothes out of my way, so that none of them scraped on the bar.

"Rebecca?" The deep voice sounded incredibly close.

The mattress springs screeched as if Becca had thrown herself onto the bed. "Yeah, Dad?" She didn't sound nervous. I wondered how many guys she had shoved into her closet.

The bedroom door creaked open. "Are you alone?" The voice sounded even deeper from up close. I could see a shadow as he moved across the room.

"Yeah," Becca said. "It's just me." The bed squeaked again. She must have sat up. "What are you doing home in the middle of day shift?"

The shadow shifted like her father was moving around. "Mrs. Chester called your mom. She said you brought a boy home with you."

"Mrs. Chester is legally blind—and a nosy bitch." Becca sounded annoyed more than worried. I could see where a nosy neighbor could cramp her style.

"Watch your language!" Officer Sommers was still moving around. His shadow kept coming back to the closet. "And just because she's legally blind and nosy doesn't mean she's wrong."

I fought the urge to hold my breath. The last thing I needed was to pass out from a lack of oxygen. Suddenly something blocked the light almost completely and the doors rattled in their track.

"What are you doing, Daddy?" Becca sounded suddenly anxious.

I tried to press myself backward into the far corner of the closet. You would have thought a girl with a four-poster bed would have a walk-in closet, but no such luck.

The doors rattled again. "Nothing," Becca's father said. "Just checking this door. It's stuck on something."

"Mom says I need to clean out my closet." Becca's voice held an edge of desperation. "Too many shoes."

For a moment I thought about trying to drop down the laundry chute, but I couldn't make myself move to the middle of the closet. If Becca's father got the doors open, I'd be right there in plain sight. Instead I pressed myself into the corner, willing myself to dissolve into the wall. Just then I felt an angry vibration from my pocket and heard an insistent buzz.

"What's that noise?" the deep voice demanded.

I dug frantically in my pocket for my phone, flipped it open and closed it instantly, but not before the luminous display had shown me that I'd hung up on my best friend Ryan.

Not good. Ryan would either call back or text me—and my phone couldn't be silenced without making more noise than either of those events. A desperate need to be somewhere else consumed me. The doors jiggled back and forth with an angry metallic screech. I heard Becca's father muttering under his breath. He might not like her swearing, but it was obvious where Becca had learned to use the f-word.

I closed my eyes and wished desperately that I held a communicator instead of a cell phone, so I could beam aboard my starship—or maybe I could tap my heels to go home. I wanted to be home. More than anything, I wanted to be home!

I twisted my body, trying to block the angry blows I was sure would rain down on me once Officer Sommers got the doors open. Or maybe it would be bullets. I twisted the other way. I had nothing—no plan, no escape hatch, no hope.

Dizziness struck me for a few seconds, and then suddenly I heard my little sister's voice say, "Jason Miller, what the hell are you doing?"

I opened my eyes to find myself standing in my own living room with my jeans down around my ankles.

Two

My first thought was relief that I was wearing underwear. My next was that this couldn't be reality. I glanced around, sure I must be hallucinating, but the living room looked like it always looked. Same olive green thrift shop sofa and battered brown leather recliner. Same ancient TV with, believe it or not, a digital converter and antenna instead of a cable hook-up. Just then our cat Sancho came up to me, rubbed against my bare leg, and purred. I could feel his fur and hear the rumble.

I dropped the backpack, tossed my phone into it, and pulled up my jeans. I was out of Becca's closet, back in my own home, and my belt had disappeared. How the hell had that happened? Had I somehow blacked out? Did I have amnesia or something? And what had happened to my damn belt? It was my least-favorite of the three I owned, but how it had gotten lost still worried me.

"Well?" Lorrie said. Her glasses had slid down her nose a little, which made her look more studious than she really was.

I couldn't let go of my pants or they might fall again, so I held them up with one hand while I retrieved my backpack. "None of your business."

She snorted. "It will be when I tell Mom you're running around the house naked."

"I'm not naked." My backpack buzzed. I could feel the vibration through the strap. "And if you tell her I was, you're worse than a snitch." I wanted to answer my phone, but I was running out of hands. I glanced around to be sure my belt hadn't somehow slipped out of the belt loops and fallen to the floor. No sign of it.

I headed for my room and started to throw the backpack down when it occurred to me that it seemed awfully light. I dumped it out on the bed. Nothing fell out except the phone I had just tossed in. Everything else was gone—my books, my brand new iPod Touch, and expensive upgraded earbuds. And of course, the belt.

Suddenly I clapped my hand to my back pocket. My wallet was missing, too. What the hell was going on? Had someone gone to a lot of trouble to get their hands on my learner's permit, my student ID, a condom I had been carrying around for six months, my house key, and four dollars? I opened my still vibrating phone and said hello.

"Dude," Ryan's voice said. "What's up?"

"Well, for one thing I've just been robbed."

MOM gave me a sharp glance as she passed Lorrie the mac and cheese. "Your whole wallet?"

Like anyone ever lost half a wallet. "My house key was in it."

The glance evolved into a frown. "Oh, Jason! Whoever finds it will have our address."

"Don't sweat it, Mom," Lorrie said. "It's not like we have anything worth stealing."

Mom turned on her. "You count your blessings! There are plenty of people worse off than we are."

But most of them didn't live in Bethesda, Maryland. Mom paid twice as much rent as our apartment would cost near her job in Laurel, twenty-five miles away, just so I could go to Clara Barton High School, one of the best public high schools in the country—at least that's what people said. I didn't have such a high opinion myself, but then I ate school lunches almost every day.

Living in Bethesda was the reason I didn't know anyone else with a flip phone. Mom couldn't afford anything more expensive. And she thought smart phones made for dumb people.

Lorrie dropped her eyes to her plate and scooped up a forkful of mac and cheese. She shot me a strange glance—half amusement, half triumph. You owe me, that look said. I realized she had distracted Mom on purpose.

"Don't forget to take the spare key with you when you go to work," Mom said. She seemed to have forgotten she was mad at me so maybe I did owe Lorrie. "I don't want you waking me up to let you in when you come home."

"Sure, Mom."

She gave me an anxious glance. "Are you walking to work, sweetie?"

I poured dressing on my salad. "No, Ryan's picking me up."

And then finally I would have someone to talk to about how I had gotten out of Becca's closet.

I certainly wasn't going to tell Mom how I had gotten into it.

RYAN beat both hands on the steering wheel and frowned at me. "What happened?"

I unhooked my seat belt and glanced around the tiny strip mall parking lot. No one was close enough to overhear us through the open windows of Ryan's Hyundai. "It's not going to change the third time I tell it."

He shook his head. "It's not possible. Becca Sommers lives in Briar Woods. No way you could walk from there to your place in less than half an hour. Even the bus takes fifteen minutes."

And I had left school with Becca at 2:30 p.m. and arrived home at 3:25. What's more, my phone showed less than two minutes between the two times Ryan had called me. I held up both hands. "Well, duh! I guess Scotty must have beamed me aboard." I wished I could stop thinking about that. How had I suddenly materialized in the living room? The front door had been locked and the deadbolt in place. I had checked. My house key was in my wallet, and my wallet was gone.

Ryan pulled out his phone and glanced at it. "Dude, you'd better get going."

I opened the passenger door. "Thanks for the ride."

He waggled one hand at me. "Any time."

I had just stepped out of the car when Becca Sommers came up to me and shoved a paper grocery bag into my hands. "I've been waiting for you," she said, in a tone just short of annoyed. "Take your things."

I pulled open the bag and looked in. My books, my iPod, with the earbuds still wound around it, one brown leather belt, and one canvas wallet.

"How—" I started to say.

"Sorry about my dad," Becca said in a rush. "But really, you shouldn't have left all that stuff in my closet. If Dad had noticed it, he would have known who to look for."

The condom wouldn't have helped my case. I swallowed and tried to think what to say. "Thanks."

She gave me a head-to-toe stare. "Good thing you're skinny enough to make it down the laundry chute."

Could I have fallen down the laundry chute, hit my head, and blacked out? There was an idea. "Uh—"

A crease marred her perfect forehead. "How did you do that without making any noise?"

How could I have? "Uh, I didn't slide. It was so tight, I had to wiggle down."

The crease disappeared. "Oh. Good. I thought for sure you were dead meat when Dad finally got the door open."

A horn honked behind her. She whirled, waved at someone, muttered a goodbye, and darted off.

"You had to wiggle down?" Ryan asked through the open car window.

"I made that up," I said, pulling out my iPod. It looked okay, which was a relief; it had taken me three months to save up for it, and a week to get all my music loaded onto it. "I still don't have a clue."

Ryan chortled and nodded at the iPod. "And now you won't have to scrounge yard sales looking for old-people music."

It was an old argument between us that neither of us was really trying to win. "I'd rather be addicted to Miles Davis than Beyoncé."

He pointed to the window of Jimmy's Java Joint, the Starbucks-wannabe coffee shop where I worked. "Dude, you'd better get in there or you won't have a job to support your jazz habit."

Ryan was right. I waved a hand and darted to the door to get inside before Ms. Dock-Your-Pay-Because-I-Feel-Like-It Assistant Manager spotted me. I had put the bag away in my locker and put on my apron and paper hat before she even saw me.

I tried not to think about my freaky teleportation, but on my break I stopped to open the brown paper bag to get my wallet. When I took out my belt, not only was it still buckled, the tip was still wrapped tight to the belt with a narrow strip of duct tape. That belt was way too big for me—one of Mom's thrift shop purchases—so I had taped the end of it to stop it flopping down like I had a tail.

Which meant that somehow the belt had come off me without ever having been unbuckled.

BECCA must have found another translator, because she didn't ask me about the book again. But Thursday morning a few minutes before the first period bell, Doofie Slater stopped me in the hall outside the school cafeteria.

"Hey, Miller, I want to talk to you."

Since he had his hand clamped on my shoulder I stopped. Doofie was the star of Clara Barton's championship wrestling team, and he had a build that showed it. "What is it, Doo-Doug?" No one ever called him Doofie to his face—not without paying for it.

"It's that test in Spanish."

What he was doing in Spanish 3 I'd never understand. He couldn't speak Spanish worth a damn, and he only needed two years of a foreign language to graduate. Maybe he thought a third year would help him with college admissions. "What about the test?"

He frowned and lowered his voice to a growl. "I didn't get a chance to read the book. When you take the test, be sure to keep your paper turned so I can see it."

I snorted. "And risk getting suspended? I don't think so."

His grip on my shoulder tightened painfully. "You're the only one who sits close enough to me. Do it, or you'll be sorry."

He wrenched my shoulder back, let me go, and stalked off.

I went to Chemistry and tried to forget about it, but I couldn't. Doofie had beat up three guys since school started, and it was just barely September. I really didn't want to be number four, but I didn't want to cave either. Letting him read my paper without being obvious would be tricky because I'm left-handed. I always turned the paper sideways, and *I* could barely read what I was writing, let alone a guy behind me. And having a suspension on my record would blow my scholarship chances out of the water.

Three periods later I got to Spanish, and saw Doofie already in his seat. He hunched over the desk, clenched his fists, and scowled at me.

"Señor Slater," Walters said. "Estás listo?"

"Uh." Doofie's lips moved as he repeated the words silently, and decided he he was indeed ready. "Si, Señor Walters."

"Bién." Mr. Walters moved up and down the aisles passing out test papers. "I will speak in English this one time so that no one will have an excuse not to understand. You have until the end of class to complete the test. When you finish, come up to my desk and turn your paper in. Then return to your desk and sit. You may read anything you like until the bell rings. When the bell rings, I will immediately collect any papers that haven't already been turned in."

Clear as always. Mr. Walters was a pretty good teacher. I bent my head over my paper, conscious of Doofie's eyes on the back of my head. He sat in the row behind me but one seat to my left.

I read the questions and made myself concentrate. After I did the first one, I felt something sharp poking into my back.

"Miller!" Doofie muttered the name like it was a curse.

Mr. Walters' head came up. "Did you need something, Señor Slater?"

Doofie shifted in his seat. "No."

Lucky for him the word was the same in Spanish as in English.

I made myself go back to the test. Doofie poked me a few more times, and then tried to read LaShelle Brennan's paper. LaShelle was a good student; she sat directly in front of Doofie, but she was as tall as him if not as wide, so I don't think he could see much. I noticed he knew better than to poke her with a pencil. LaShelle didn't take shit from anyone.

I shut out the worry and the distractions and made myself finish the test. Once I was done, I walked it up to Mr. Walters' desk.

"Graciás," he said as I put it down in his in-box. "No erés un hombre sin vergüenza, o sin honor."

I wasn't a man without shame or without honor? What did that mean?

I walked back to my seat in the full glare of Doofie Slater's angry gaze, sat down, and pretended to read my English book.

When the bell rang, Walters collected the few remaining papers, including Doofie's.

It was lunch time and everyone filed out in a hurry except me. I lingered, waiting to make sure Doofie had gone ahead. I was wondering if Walters would let me sit in his class for a while. I'd miss lunch, but so what.

Walters was already grading the tests; he didn't even look up. I grabbed my books and headed for the door to scope out the view from the window.

The corridor had emptied out pretty quickly as everyone hurried to lunch. But there, right across from my window, it looked like Becca Sommers was getting mouth-to-mouth while standing up. She had her back to the lockers, so I could see her face but not the guy's.

I knew I shouldn't stare, but I couldn't help myself. All I could think about was how close I'd gotten to being the guy with his tongue down her throat. I remembered how her nails had raked my skin, and how great it had felt.

And then just as I was thinking I should turn away before I needed to sit down, suddenly Doofie Slater's face appeared in the window, his nose only inches from mine and his teeth bared in an angry scowl.

Three

I wanted to run, but I couldn't move! When Doofie put his hand on the door latch, I gripped my side of it, trying to keep him from opening the door. I half turned toward the teacher's desk, but Walters wasn't there. My heart started to pound as I glanced around the room. I had just glimpsed Walters through the window in the door to the supply room when the door latch slid from my hands as Doofie forced it downwards and started to push the door open. I wished desperately that I had gone straight to the cafeteria, where there would have been too many witnesses for Doofie to beat me up.

Just as I twisted around to call out for Walters, the classroom warped. For a flash of a second, the desks and chairs, the walls, everything, sort of melted, like in that weird Dali painting of a watch draped over a landscape, and then everything dissolved into an odd pearly gray something—not quite a mist, but not solid looking either—that surrounded me. Then that disappeared and I was in a grassy meadow surrounded by sheep, and then that all melted, and I was in a corner of the school cafeteria with people milling all around me.

I managed to grab my jeans before they slid any farther than my butt and yanked them up to my waist. I put my books down and sank onto a bench at the nearest table. I had lost another damn belt, and this one actually fit.

But how had I gotten to the cafeteria? Where the hell was that meadow? And was I going crazy?

RYAN shook his head. "Dude, you must be going crazy."

I put down the bag of chips Ryan had bought for me and let out a strangled snort of protest. "If it's all in my head, then where's my belt, my wallet, and my cell?"

I was glad I had left my iPod in my locker. Mom was going to flip when I told her I had lost the wallet again, right after I said I'd found it. Not to mention I'd have to spend the rest of the day holding up my pants. But losing my cell was the worst because I couldn't afford another one.

Why had the cell phone gone this time? What was different about my jump from Becca's closet to home versus from Spanish class to the cafeteria? My phone had made it the first time. I remembered gripping it while I crouched in Becca's closet.

"I can loan you my belt," Ryan said. "I have an actual butt, and my pants will stay up better."

I ignored the slam and glanced around the still-crowded cafeteria. "I'm not going to exchange articles of clothing with you. That's how rumors get started."

Just about then Mr. Walters came up to our table and put a brown paper lunch bag on the table in front of me. "I believe you left these in my classroom, Mr. Miller."

I started when he came up, and then tried to look casual as I opened the bag. My belt had been unbuckled and neatly coiled into a tight circle so it fit into the bag. My cell phone sat on top of my wallet. So they had all stayed where I had been.

"Uh, thanks—graciás, Señor Walters."

"De nada." He gave me a peculiar look, almost a sardonic smile. "Next time, you should try *holding on to them*."

He walked away without waiting for me to ask what he meant.

It took me a moment to figure out that the emphasis was as important as the words. "He knows!"

"What?" Ryan twisted his mouth into a confused grimace. "Who knows what?"

"Walters knows about the jumping or teleporting or whatever it is." I pounded on the table. "Anything I was holding or touching jumped with me—my clothes, my shoes, my backpack—this time my books. Anything I wasn't actually touching—my skin wasn't touching—like my belt and the stuff in my pockets, stayed behind."

Ryan sat slack-faced for a second, and then he nodded. "Whoa! Mr. Walters could be your watcher or guide or something!"

Ryan watched way too much SyFi Channel.

I HAD to wait until after school to talk to Mr. Walters. I hurried, but he was locking his classroom door when I turned the corner to the south corridor.

"Mr. Walters!"

He looked up at my shout. "Yes?"

I ran the last dozen yards. "Can I talk to you, please, Mr. Walters?"

He glanced up and down the corridor. A few kids were getting stuff from their lockers, but no one was paying us any attention. Walters looked inscrutable for a moment, like he was making up his mind, and then he reached into his pocket and took out a three-by-five card. "Here. This is my address."

I looked down at it. He lived in a small townhouse development in my neighborhood.

"Come to see me this evening," Walters added. "I'll expect you at 8:30 sharp. Be on time." He frowned. "My daughter has homework to finish, and it's a school night."

I'd heard he was a widower, even though he wore a wedding ring. I'd never been to a teacher's house before, and I wasn't too sure I liked the idea. "I have a ten o'clock curfew on school nights."

"It shouldn't be a problem."

I hoped that meant whatever explanation he could give me wouldn't last long—not that it meant he kept power tools in his bedroom and it wouldn't take long to cut up my corpse. "Okay, I'll be there."

He nodded once and headed for the exit, giving me the briefest of glances over his shoulder as he walked.

I sure hoped I wasn't making a mistake. And I hoped Mr. Walters could explain what was happening to me.

"SPANISH?" Mom said, her forehead pleating into its semi-permanent crease. She leaned back in the recliner and unrolled some fuzzy yellow yarn. "Why would you need tutoring in Spanish? You've gotten an A every semester."

"Spanish 3 is a lot harder." I cast around for an excuse for sudden failure. Luckily, Mom didn't speak any Spanish that didn't come from the menu at Taco Bell. "The irregular reflexive nominative verbs are killing me."

Lorrie looked up from the TV long enough to give me a suspicious look, but fortunately, she hadn't had any foreign language classes yet.

"Where does Mr. Walters live?" Mom asked.

I'd written out the address for her because I knew she'd ask for it.

Mom glanced at the paper and stuffed it into her pocket. "Don't be late." She went back to looping yarn around her knitting needle. The sweater was for Lorrie, and it was half done. "School tomorrow."

Like I could forget. "I won't be late." I had a sudden sense of unease—a sort of tickle on the back of my neck, like the characters in horror movies must get when they realize the monster is right behind them. I wasn't sure why I felt the need to do it, but I leaned over and kissed the top of Mom's head. "See you later, Mom. Bye, Squirt."

Mom looked up, her expression confused. "Everything okay?"

"Everything's fine."

I hoped I was telling the truth. But nothing could be fine until I figured out why I kept winking out of reality.

A GIRL of twelve or so answered my knock. She looked a little like Walters—same brown hair, same straight nose, same square chin. But she had brown eyes instead of blue, and skin as smooth and soft as cream.

The girl at the door turned as soon as she saw me waiting on her porch. "He's here, *Daida*."

For a second I thought she had called her father da-da, but it was a different word. She said it with a strange inflection, too, a sharp emphasis on the first syllable.

"Come in, Mr. Miller," Walters' voice called. He stepped out of the kitchen drying his hands on a dish towel. "Have you finished your homework, Ruveka?"

The girl nodded as I stepped into the living room.

"Very well." Walters held up his left index finger. "One hour of television, and then bed."

Ruveka disappeared into a doorway, and Walters waved a hand at the sofa.

I sat on a futon sofa with oatmeal colored cushions. The furniture was a little better than ours, but not a lot. It looked like it came from a low end retail store instead of a thrift shop.

"Now," Walters said, sinking into a chair. "What did you want to talk to me about, Mr. Miller?"

I opened my mouth to ask him about the teleporting and realized I had no idea how to ask the right questions without sounding like a wing nut.

"Um, did you notice me waiting to leave your class right after the test this morning?"

He nodded. "I do seem to remember you standing by the door."

I couldn't think of a good way to ask him if he had seen me disappear. If I hadn't been so freaked out by what had happened to me, I would have given up and gone home right then. "When I left, you were in the supply room. Did you happen to see me leave?"

Walters must have been great at poker. His expression gave nothing away. "I did, actually."

I cleared my throat. "And *how* did I leave?"

He didn't say anything. Finally, he rubbed his eyes for a second, and then said, "I have a question first. What were you staring at in the corridor before Mr. Slater confronted you through the window?"

Now this was an easy question. I was pretty sure Walters wouldn't try to pin a PDA violation on Becca. "I was watching Becca Sommers make out with a guy."

Walters nodded. "I thought it must have been something like that."

What the hell did that mean? Did he think I was a perv or something?

Walters stared right at me. "You sort of faded around the edges for a second, and then you vanished entirely."

I sucked in a breath and held it. I didn't know whether to be relieved I wasn't crazy or scared by the fact that I had somehow teleported from one room to another.

"Your belt and the contents of your pockets hit the floor," Walters went on, "so I knew you must have made the Turn."

Funny how I could hear the capital letter T in turn just from the way he said the word. "The Turn?"

He nodded. "You're left-handed, right?"

I nodded.

"And you've obviously hit puberty so the testosterone is flowing." He gave me a faint smile. "I was glad to see you in the cafeteria. Not everyone makes a full Turn the first time."

Suddenly light-headed, I let my breath out with a whoosh. "It wasn't the first time."

His eyes opened wider. "No?"

"No." I could feel a ton of questions bubbling to the top of my mind. "What the hell is the Turn? And where was the meadow?"

"Meadow?" He cocked his head. "You Turned through a meadow? Were there any people there?"

"I didn't see anyone except some sheep." My hands itched to grab his shirt and shake the information out of him. "Where was I?"

Walters held his hands palm up, like he was pleading with me. "It's going to be difficult for you to understand."

I snorted. "More difficult than believing I can teleport from one place to another? I don't think so."

"Okay." Another pause, but this one was like he was choosing his words carefully. "The world we live in—the world we see—is not the only world there is. There's another version of Earth that shares the same space with us, but it has a different—a very different—history."

It would have sounded crazy a week ago, but now his story offered hope that I wasn't nuts. "Okay, but how and why do I keep going there?"

Walters shrugged. "I don't know how it works. The only part I know for sure is a man who's left handed and the right age can make the Turn from our world to theirs—and back again if he's lucky."

It sounded too easy. "Then why doesn't it happen to lots of guys?"

His shook his head in a gesture of frustration. "I don't know. No one knows. We used to compare notes about it. Most of us liked music—although none of us were musicians—but the only things all of us had in common were being male, being left-handed, and being scared out of our wits right after having or thinking about sex."

I tried to parse that sentence. "Who is 'we'?"

He ran one hand through his hair. "Let me start at the beginning—my beginning."

That sounded logical, even if I was in a hurry to know what the hell he meant. "Okay."

He took a deep breath and let it out. "I was five years older than you the first time I Turned. My girlfriend and I had gone camping. Right after we made love in our tent, I went out to use the porta-john and surprised a bear trying to break into our cooler. Just as I turned to run the twenty yards to my girlfriend's car, the darkness melted into a mist and then a different kind of darkness. And then I found myself in the car." He shook his head. "The doors were still locked. I was stark naked and didn't have the keys."

He'd had a bear, and I'd had Officer Sommers. But Walters had gotten laid, and all I had gotten was pissed off. "What happened to your girl-friend?"

"Nothing. The bear ripped the cooler open, gulped down our cold cuts and ambled off. Once I stopped shaking, I let myself out of the car, woke her up, and made her drive me home. We broke up the next day."

His first Turn had left him as confused as I had been. "So, when was the next time?"

He grinned, but not like he was really amused. "It was a few years later. I had stopped thinking about the camping trip. I persuaded myself I must have blacked out for a few seconds while I let myself into the car." His grin slipped. "Then when I was twenty-six, I took a vacation in Mexico. I was sitting in a pool-side bar watching an attractive young woman in a bikini rub sunblock all over herself when a couple of guys with handguns held up the place. The bartender pulled a shotgun. I was frantically wishing I had stayed in my room when the pool and the bar seemed to melt. All at once I stood in the middle of a market square surrounded by oddly-dressed women babbling away in a foreign language. A fraction of a second later I was standing in my hotel room and hearing the gunshots from downstairs."

The sequence seemed clear. I'd done it twice, myself, but only once with my eyes open. "So you get turned on, then you get really scared, and then it happens?"

He nodded. "I assume it's some combination of hormones and adrenalin. Some guys need to be really aroused and others just have to think about a pretty girl."

How did he know that? "What about the left-handed part?"

He lifted one hand as if to bat my question away. "Maybe our brains work differently. I tried to study the mechanics of it while I was in Dodomah, but I only got as far as gathering statistics."

He had said he would start at the beginning, but it felt like I had walked into a theater in the middle of a movie. "Dodomah?"

His eyes got a faraway look. He stared at a picture on the wall behind me, but I didn't think he really saw it. "On the third time, I only made a half Turn. I came out in the city-state of Dodomah. In the other Earth there are few nations as we know them but many, many city-states."

His story still wasn't making a lot of sense. "You mean you were there long enough to learn their history?"

He smiled with a strange kind of wry sadness. "I was there for almost eight years." He jerked his head toward the corridor where I could hear the muted tones of a TV. "Where do you think Ruveka comes from?"

I didn't know what to say. It seemed incredible. Even having had my mind twisted into a pretzel by the last few days, it was hard to swallow.

Walters seemed to know I was having a hard time with it. I could tell by the way he was watching me.

"So why did you tell me all this?" I asked. "Aren't you afraid I'll tell someone?"

That same sad smile came back. "I don't think you'll tell anyone—not anyone in authority. I never did." He set his shoulders like someone facing an unpleasant task. "And I'm telling you about this just in case you ever make a half Turn and end up there." He leaned forward, his gaze suddenly intent, and I knew that this was the important part. He had told me this whole long story only to get to what he really cared about. "If that happens, if you end up in Dodomah, I'm hoping you'll be able to find out what happened to my wife—and maybe come back to tell me about it."

I didn't know what to say. "Your wife?" I repeated, feeling like an idiot.

"Yes, my wife." His smile had gone, and now he just looked sad. "Ruveka's mother."

I cleared my throat. "I thought your wife was dead."

He nodded. "Quite possibly, she is." He stood up abruptly, like he couldn't sit still, and paced a few steps, back and forth. "Bejida was the Ocan Garun of Dodomah—like a general and a queen combined. Her lieutenants organized a coup to unseat her. The palace was under siege, and Bejida begged me to take Ruveka to safety, so I did."

"How?" I said. It sounded like something Ryan would watch on the SyFi Channel.

Mr. Walters' face twitched, like it hurt him to remember. "Fear wasn't a problem. I could hear the women outside screaming for Bejida's blood. Ruveka was crying in terror when I picked her up. Bejida hugged me and began to—to get me turned on. I told her to hold on to me, but at the last second, she said her duty to her people wouldn't allow her to leave them. Just as she let go, she and the rest of the room started to melt. A second later, Ruveka and I were alone in a gray mist."

"And then you arrived here?"

"Upstate New York, actually. It's where I'm from, so it was in my mind." He shuddered. "I came out on my grandfather's farm—except now an interstate runs through it. Ruveka and I were nearly killed."

It was hard for me to picture stuffy, respectable Walters popping into upstate New York from another universe. "How did you end up teaching school in Bethesda?"

His face got a funny look—not angry or anything, more cautious, or even scared. "As I said, I studied the men who Turned from our Earth. I discovered they had started arriving in Dodomah in the mid 1960s."

So it was a new sort of thing, then, not something that had always been true.

"Also," Walters went on, "younger men Turned much more often than middle-aged men, and they tended to arrive more from some places than others—possibly the ability to Turn runs in families. Over the years there had been more guys from this area than anywhere else on the East coast. So I got a job teaching in a high school and kept an eye on my left-handed male students, hoping to find someone who might Turn."

I was having trouble believing him. Oh, I believed he believed it. I just didn't think it was possible.

"You think I'm crazy, don't you?" Walters said.

"No," I said automatically. Not actually psychotic, just mildly delusional.

"Ruveka!" Walters called. "Would you come here, please?"

After a few seconds the girl appeared in the doorway from the corridor and frowned at him. "You said one hour."

He smiled and sat down again. "I know. I'm sorry. Tomorrow you may have two hours, and I'll do the dishes by myself."

Her expression brightened. "What is it, then?"

Walters nodded at me. "This young man wants to see what your mother looks like."

I expected the girl to fetch a photo album or a portrait or something, but she didn't. Instead she came over to where I sat.

"What's your name?" she asked me.

"Jason Miller."

She looked me up and down. "My mother's name is Bejida Urbi Siti. This is what she looks like." She suddenly placed her hand on my forehead. She had a cool touch, but after a second her hand seemed to grow warmer—or maybe it was my forehead that grew warmer.

Like a memory I had never had or a vivid daydream, a picture formed in my mind. In a huge hall lined with white marble pillars, a tall, black-haired woman in a red pantsuit stood in front of a large group of soldiers in drab gray trousers and even drabber jackets. The soldiers stood in formation and carried long, thick sticks that resembled rifles but the barrels looked too thick for real guns. They held the rifle-like things in front of them as if to salute the black-haired woman as she walked past. After a moment, I realized all the soldiers were women, too.

The black-haired woman turned and faced me. She smiled and held out her arms. I noticed first that her pantsuit was more of a tunic and really tight trousers than anything I'd seen a woman wear. Then I realized she was totally hot—liquid brown eyes, a wide mouth that needed no lipstick to look lush, and a figure that could have gotten her a contract modeling swimsuits any day.

Ruveka moved her hand away and the image vanished from my mind.

I looked at Walters and blinked. He looked the same as always—ordinary in a dorky sort of way. Shit, he had married out of his league.

"Thank you, Ruveka," Walters said. "You may go back to your program."

She headed for the door but stopped to give him a stern look. "Two hours tomorrow?"

He nodded. "Two hours tomorrow."

She gave a little skip, and waved at me. "Goodbye, Mr. Miller."

As soon as the door shut, I turned to her father. "How does she do that?"

He blinked as if he were suddenly tired. "I don't know. Many women can do it in Dodomah." He leaned back in his chair. "Things are different on Makoro."

"Makoro?"

"That's what they call their world. It just means Earth in their language."

I had other questions. "Why were all the soldiers female?"

Walters smiled, but it was a bitter smile. "Because there aren't enough men on Makoro. That's why they fight over those of us who make the Turn."

I WALKED back from Walters' place really slowly, thinking over what he'd said.

Could it be real? The idea of another version of Earth seemed impossible—something out of a made-for-TV movie. And even if there was another, weirder version of earth, how was it *I* was one of the guys who could go back and forth between the two without even trying? I'd never been special in any way before, and that wasn't how I wanted to start.

What I kept coming back to was, incredible as the story sounded, it fit what had happened to me perfectly.

So if it was real, the question most on my mind was could I ever learn to control this talent or curse or whatever. Walters didn't seem to think so.

He had Turned four times in his life, two full Turns and two half Turns, and only on the last one had he been trying to Turn.

I still had a lot of questions, but Walters hadn't wanted to talk anymore. I'd left shortly after he told me that ever since they'd had a devastating war a few centuries before, fewer than ten percent of babies born on Makoro were male, and even those died more often than the girl babies.

It sounded like a horny guy's dream, but Walters didn't seem that fond of the place, only of his wife. According to him, men in Makoro lived restricted lives locked away in heavily guarded quarters. There were no families as I knew them. Instead, five to ten women shared a single husband.

I didn't know whether to hope I Turned again or not. Clara Barton High School had more girls than boys, and a ten to one ratio didn't sound bad at all.

But the getting locked up part would definitely not be cool. I decided the safest thing to do was to not get scared and turned on at the same time. Which meant it would be best to avoid both Doofie Slater and Becca Sommers.

Four

"Jason!"

I turned from my open locker and found myself nose to nose with Becca Sommers. I backed up a couple of steps and almost bumped into Ryan, whose locker was only three over from mine. "Oh, hey, Becca."

"Do you think you could help me study for the Spanish test?" Becca gave me warm smile. "You're so good at languages."

I was good at Spanish, anyway. I'd never tried any other languages. "I have to work."

Her smile slipped a little. "All weekend?"

Only Saturday actually. I had my first in-car driver's ed session Saturday morning, and I had to work a full shift after that, but I was free all day Sunday. I wasn't sure I wanted to tell Becca that. It had been several weeks since I had made the Turn from her closet, and I'd been keeping my distance from her, trying to pretend it had never happened. "Most of it. Sorry. Maybe someone in your class can help?"

Her lower lip protruded in a deliberate pout. "No one in my class is as fluent as you are."

I wondered how she knew that since we were two periods apart in Walters' schedule. Before I could comment, she put a finger tip on my left wrist.

"Couldn't you find an hour to help me?"

I knew she was trying to play me. I knew she wasn't attracted to me for me. She wanted a conjugal visit that focused on verbs, not sex. But still, I could feel myself responding. It was like she exuded a scent I couldn't resist, no matter how hard I tried. "I guess I could spare an hour on Sunday afternoon."

Her smile lit up her face and made her blue eyes sparkle. She really was a pretty girl. "Perfect." She flicked the back of my hand in a gesture that might have been a high speed caress—or it could have been just carelessness. "How about the library at 2:30?"

A public place would be good—no need for her cop father to get worked up. And the library had decent bus service, so I could be sure I could get there and back. "Okay."

She gave me a cheerful wave, spun around, and strolled off.

I figured she was giving me a good view on purpose so I watched her ass sway without any sense of guilt.

"Dude," Ryan said from behind me, "you are so dead."

I knew he was right. There was no way I could avoid the turned on part. I would just have to be sure there was nothing scary at the public library.

WHY was it every driving instructor I ever heard of was an immigrant? At least Mr. Aiyuku's English was good, not like the woman who had taught the classroom sessions. She had called me Jay-sone Mee-lair. Mr. Aiyuku had a slight, rather odd accent but he was perfectly understandable. All too understandable sometimes.

"Shit!" Mr. Aiyuku slammed on the instructor's brake. "What the fuck are you doing? You almost hit that car."

I took my foot off the accelerator. So I had a problem with judging distance? I'd only been driving in traffic for ninety minutes. "I thought I had time."

He waited until I had pulled into the mall parking lot to really let me have it. "You think I went through hell in Rwanda only to die on a fucking street in this fucking town?"

I wasn't sure I believed the Rwanda part. He might be black, but he didn't sound African to me. "Sorry."

He waved a hand toward a far corner of the parking lot where the driving school had set up some orange plastic traffic cones to block out parking spaces. "Never mind. Let's work on your parallel parking."

I pulled up and tried to line the back end of the car up with the first cone, going over in my mind everything Ryan had told me when he was practicing parallel parking for his test. It was hard to see the cone because someone had run over it and the tip was bent over.

Mr. Aiyuku pulled out a pack of cigarettes and a lighter. I guessed he wasn't so worried about dying anymore. "We don't have all day," he said.

I pivoted the steering wheel, eased up on the brake, and let the car crawl backwards into the space. Just as my seat was even with the first cone, I started to straighten out. The car slid into the space nice and straight, and I never even touched the cones.

"Not bad." Mr. Aiyuku took a puff of his cigarette and put the window down to flick ash outside as he glanced at the dashboard clock. "Shit, it's not as late as I thought." He waved a hand. "Go ahead and pull into traffic again. We'll drive once around the mall, and then you can go."

"When is my next session?"

"You have to call the office to set it up." He pulled a piece of aluminum foil out of his pocket and stubbed the cigarette out into it. I guessed he wasn't supposed to smoke in the car. Good thing for him swearing didn't leave evidence.

I drove once around the mall, taking my time, because it wasn't two full hours yet, and I liked the sensation of being in charge. Except for a few sessions in an empty parking lot, Mom had refused to let me practice in her car until I had all three of the in-car sessions that came with my driver's ed course.

Mr. Aiyuku was getting antsy by the time we got back to the space reserved for the driver's ed car. A girl with dark glasses, a tweed jacket, and bright blue hair waited there with her log book in her hand.

Mr. Aiyuku got out when I did and looked the girl up and down. "You're not a doper, are you?" he said. "I don't drive with dopers."

She pushed the shades up on her head and glared at him. "Blue hair means I don't like to be constrained by arbitrary rules. It doesn't mean I use drugs."

Mr. Aiyuku asked to see her permit. I gave her another look while she pulled out her wallet. Kind of skinny. Not really pretty but definitely attractive. She wore her blue hair in a sort of funny cut—long on the sides and shorter in back. Her eyebrows were light brown and her eyes a color between blue and green. She barely came up to my chin, but she seemed taller because she was so slender. She wasn't totally flat-chested, but she was a long way from stacked. "First time driving?" I asked.

She turned the glare on me as she put away her permit. "No. I know how to drive, actually. I just need the certificate to get my license."

She sounded damn sure of herself. I had a ten minute wait until the bus was due, so I stood by the driver's ed car while Aiyuku checked the girl's log book and then told her to get in. The windows were up but I could see he was rattling on while she buckled her seat belt and adjusted the mirrors.

She gave him a brief glance and put the shades back on. Then she pulled the car out of the space, drove over to the traffic light, put on her turn signal, paused just long enough to be legal, and made a right turn on the red light, pulling into the far right lane with a smoothness I envied.

I sighed as I started for the bus stop. Even once I got my license, my chances of getting to drive anywhere were slim. I would have to pay for the increase in Mom's insurance myself, and I was short two hundred bucks.

For just a moment I thought about Ryan. His folks had given him the Hyundai on his sixteenth birthday—not a cool car, but it was brand new and all his. I felt bad for being jealous of my best friend. Ryan had stood by me since our first day in eighth grade gym class when I couldn't climb that stupid rope. It wasn't his fault his folks were so much better off than my mom.

It wasn't even his fault he was better looking than me. Allie Tedlock, the prettiest girl in our Honors English class, had asked him out for coffee the second week of school. Ryan was shy with girls, but he'd had sense enough to say yes. With me, whenever a girl seemed to show interest in me, it always turned out like it had with Becca—they wanted something besides me.

I climbed on the bus feeling sorry for myself. Fortunately, I had brought my iPod. I slipped on the earbuds, dialed some Coltrane and let the music take me away from Clara Barton HS, and driver's ed, and girls who were only interested in my brains.

I ALWAYS liked to start the day with a classic, so the next morning I rolled out of bed and put on Louis Armstrong's version of "St. Louis Blues." Then I lay face down on the floor and started doing pushups. "One." I gasped as I reached my peak. I kept going until I got to twenty-five, and then I groaned and let myself sink onto the floor. "Agh!" I lay as still as I could while the muscles in my arms and chest let me know they weren't happy. They hurt like hell. Not even Louis' upbeat tempo served to motivate me to move.

Finally, I rolled onto my back, and did fifty crunches, trying to distribute the misery. Somehow having my abs just as sore didn't help the agony in my biceps and my pecs. I sat up and leaned against my bed, trying to find a position where I didn't ache all over.

A series of rapid knocks sounded and then the door flew open before I could say anything.

"You're up." Lorrie stood in the doorway wearing a bathrobe over her pajamas. She glanced around my room like she expected to see something other than me half-sitting on the floor in just boxers and a tee shirt. Sancho slipped past Lorrie and padded across the floor to me.

I let him sniff my hand and then stroked his head. "Yeah, so what?"

"Mom's fixing breakfast." She sniffed like she felt ill used. "French toast."

That explained it. Sunday was the only morning that Mom actually cooked breakfast instead of just putting out cold cereal. Lorrie always wanted pancakes, but my favorite was French toast.

"Okay, I'll be there in ten minutes." I needed a shower.

Lorrie made a face, but it might have been the music. She had no taste. "What are you doing on the floor?"

I grinned at her. "Thinking of ways to torment my little sister."

She turned on her heel and walked off.

Once I made it to the bathroom, I pulled off my tee shirt and looked at myself in the mirror. Still skinny—twenty-five push-ups and fifty crunches every night and every morning hadn't had any visible effect. Of course, I'd only been doing them for three days.

I sighed and ran the shower. Mom looked stern when I rushed out of my room fully dressed several minutes later. A platter of French toast sat in the middle of the table next to a pitcher of orange juice and a bowl of blueberries. Each of our three plates had two strips of bacon—a major treat. Mom had gone to some trouble.

"Sorry I'm late," I muttered, reaching for my napkin. But by the time I had wolfed down seconds and asked for thirds, Mom was smiling.

"You were hungry," she said as she passed me the platter.

"Your French toast is the best, Mom." I gave Lorrie a mocking smile. "You should make it every week."

"Mom!" Lorrie's face flushed with indignation.

Mom shushed her. "What are you doing today, Jason?" She turned back to me as she stacked her coffee cup and silverware onto her plate. "Do you have homework?"

"Some." I debated how much I wanted to say about Becca. I decided it would be too much for Mom to believe I was tutoring Becca if Mr. Walters was supposed to be tutoring me, and I might need to go see him again. "I'm going to the library to work on a project this afternoon."

She looked pleased. "Will you need a ride?"

"Ryan's going to give me a lift there. I can take the bus home."

Mom got up and picked up her plate and the empty platter. She gave Lorrie a pointed look, and Lorrie stacked up her own dishes.

So far, so good. I swallowed my last bite, snatched up my silverware, plate, and glass, and took them into the kitchen.

All I had to worry about today was not letting Becca raise my testosterone level.

BECCA frowned at me. "How can *vista* mean getting dressed or wearing? I thought it meant to see."

Far from being turned on, I was getting annoyed at Becca. "Look, *vestir* is an irregular verb. In the present subjunctive, the e changes to an i."

Becca tapped her perfectly painted and probably fake fingernails on the library table. "Spanish is a pain."

We weren't in the quiet room, but I could see some library patrons giving us annoyed looks.

"Not as much of a pain as English," a girl's voice said.

I turned and found the blue-haired girl from driver's ed standing right behind my chair. "Oh, hi." As soon as I got over my surprise, I could feel awkwardness rushing in. "Hello again."

Becca glanced up and frowned. "Is this a friend of yours, Jason?" She gave the other girl a once-over that took in her blue hair, uncool tweed jacket, slightly grubby slacks, and hiking boots.

"Uh, not exactly." I cleared my throat. "We're in driver's ed together."

The blue-haired girl stuck her hand out to me. "Monica Martin. Nice to meet you."

Such old-fashioned manners seemed so at odds with the blue hair that I stared as I shook her hand and said my name.

Becca shook hands more gingerly and mumbled her own name. "We're studying," she added, in a pointed tone. "Spanish."

Monica Martin nodded. "I heard." She rattled off a few sentences in such rapid-fire Spanish that I had trouble following her. Her accent was so perfect that she had to be a native speaker. It surprised me because she didn't have any kind of Spanish accent when she spoke English.

"What?" Becca said.

"She said—I think she said—that she'd be happy to help us study. She was born in Costa Rica and lived there until this past summer."

"Oh." Becca looked less than thrilled. "Thanks."

Monica grabbed an empty chair from the table behind her and swung it around to our table. "What are you working on?"

"Irregular verbs." I had to make myself speak normally when I said it. Part of me wanted to push Monica away, and I didn't understand why. Then Becca turned to her and poured out some questions, and I got it. If Becca had help from Monica, she didn't need to suck up to me.

I hadn't wanted to tutor Becca, but now that I was doing it, the idea of being pushed aside annoyed me. It turned out I didn't need to worry. Even though Monica spoke Spanish fluently, she didn't know what the rules were. She knew the right way to say something without knowing how to explain *why* it was the right way. And she spoke so fast, *I* could barely follow her, let alone Becca.

Becca lost patience after the fourth time Monica corrected her. "This isn't helping."

"You just need to practice conjugating," I said. "You're okay on the vocabulary." I went over some of the verbs with her and had her repeat them back to me in all their forms and tenses. I had to prompt her a few times when she got them wrong.

"You should practice by speaking Spanish," Monica said. "That's the best way to learn it."

Becca shot her a sharp look, but Monica seemed oblivious.

Monica waited until Becca had finished all the verbs on my list before she said anything else. "It's after 4:00, and the library closes at 5:00. Do you guys want to get a soda or something?"

I hadn't realized the time. Sunday bus service to my neighborhood was crappy, and I had ten minutes until my last bus left. "Shit." I stacked my books together. "Sorry, Becca. I've got to go."

Becca didn't look at all heartbroken. "Thanks for the help, Jason." She stuffed her things into a tote bag and then took out a cell phone. "Can we give you a lift?"

I wasn't sure if she was calling a boyfriend or a parent for a ride, but either way, I wasn't interested. "No, thanks."

Becca drifted off, cell phone glued to her ear, and I found myself walking out the library door toward the bus stop with Monica right beside me.

"Where do you live?" Monica asked.

"Westmoreland Apartments," I said as we came up to the bus stop. "The 34 bus goes right past it."

She nodded. "So you go to Clara Barton, then?"

"Yeah." It seemed rude not to ask her any questions. "Where do you go to school?"

"I go to Clara Barton, too."

I was surprised, because I was pretty sure I would have noticed her. Plenty of kids dyed their hair bright colors, but hers must be very blonde for the blue to have taken so well. "Really?"

She looked away. "Yeah. I'm in the IB program."

That explained it. The international baccalaureate program was what made CBHS a magnet school—and what made it nationally ranked. But except for gym and stuff like that, the IB kids didn't mingle much with us regular kids. All their classes were in one wing.

I didn't know what to say. How nice that you're so smart? Or maybe, what are you doing slumming in the library with me?

"If you don't want to wait for the bus, I could give you a ride." Monica made the offer in a rush. Maybe she was covering the awkward silence, or maybe she wanted to say it in a hurry so she couldn't change her mind.

"Did you get your license already?"

She shook her head. "No, I take the test tomorrow. I have to call for a ride today."

"Where do you live?" I asked.

"Potomac."

I would never have guessed it. I had hazy ideas about girl's clothes, but I knew she didn't dress like her folks had a million dollar house—or maybe a multi-million dollar house. And she went to public school, even if she was in the IB program. "Won't it take awhile for someone to come from Potomac?"

She set her shoulders like she was confessing a sin. "Grandpa made me take the limo, and it's waiting nearby for me to call."

For just one second I was tempted. I had never ridden in a limo in my life, and unless I won a prom-season radio contest, I probably never would. But accepting a ride in Monica's limo could start rumors I didn't want to hear. I stalled while I thought about it. "You live with your grandparents?"

She shrugged. "I live with my grandfather and his second wife." She twisted her face into a grimace. "My parents are still in Costa Rica. They run an antipoverty program there."

I wondered what had made them move to Costa Rica—drugs, the Peace Corps, or maybe just the lower cost of living. The last seemed less likely if she had a grandfather rich enough to own a limo. But regardless of their reasons, her parents had sent her home to the States to finish high school. No wonder Monica didn't fit in.

I was trying to think of a polite way to decline her invitation when the 34 bus pulled up to the stop. "Thanks, anyway, but my bus is here."

I climbed the steps feeling a mixture of relief and guilt. I already had three strikes against me—no car, no cash, and a fondness for old-people music. Being friends with a misfit like Monica would be social suicide. Still, she must be lonely. And I had left her standing on the curb.

I tried to tell myself that it wasn't my fault, but I couldn't think of a convincing argument for being such a wimp, so I reached for my iPod, planning to lose myself in a little early Miles Davis. Just then the guy in the next seat looked up. I forgot all about Monica Martin and Miles Davis, too.

I was sitting right across the aisle from Doofie Slater.

Five

"Miller." Doofie clenched both his teeth and his fists when he said my name.

"Hey, Slater." I was tempted to ask why he was on the bus because I knew he owned a car, but I didn't. Whether he'd lost his license or his car, I didn't want to bring up what could be a touchy subject. Instead I decided it would be safest to pretend we were friends. "How's it hanging?"

He glared. "I flunked that test."

I cleared my throat. "Sorry." I glanced around. There were six other passengers, two men and four women, and one of the guys was pretty big. I didn't think Doofie would assault me in front of them. "So why are you in Spanish 3, anyway? You don't need a third year of a foreign language to graduate."

He grunted, stared out the window, and didn't say anything.

"If you think it'll help you get into college—" I started to say.

Doofie reached over and shoved me so hard I nearly fell out of my seat. "College? I hate school. Why would I want to go to college?"

Why go to college? How about for an education? Or maybe so he could get a decent job and earn a living. Or if nothing else, to meet some smart girls. "You don't plan to go to college?"

He snorted. "Not me. I'm not waiting four years to start earning money." He flexed his arm a few times, and his biceps bulged. "Besides, I've got talent."

I tried to imagine what talent Doofie thought he had. "Wrestling?" Light dawned. "You want to be a pro wrestler?"

Doofie curled his lip in a sneer. "Not an ordinary pro wrestler. Those guys are bogus. I want to be a looch a door."

It took me a second to put the three words together into one. "A *luchador*? You want to be a Mexican wrestler?" Why he thought the Mexican wrestling circuit was less fake than regular wrestling I didn't get. How did wearing masks over their faces make them somehow more honest?

He nodded, his face lighting up with real enthusiasm. "Lucha libre is awesome!" He rattled off some details of fights he had seen, including the names of the wrestlers and their most famous moves. He knew their real names as well as their stage names, and even the patterns on their masks. For a few minutes, he actually sounded smart—except of course he couldn't pronounce any of the Spanish words correctly.

I could see why Doofie wanted to learn Spanish, but it was equally clear he was missing the point. "If you're taking Spanish to actually learn the language, why cheat on the exams? Getting a passing grade doesn't mean you can speak Spanish."

He got a stubborn look. "I'll get it eventually. But it's not easy, not like math."

Now that surprised me. I never would have picked Doofie as a math whiz. "But you're tanking your grade point for nothing. Why don't you drop the class while you can and just buy that language software they sell at the mall? It's supposed to be really good."

His eyes narrowed as if he suspected me of having some kind of hidden motive for making this suggestion. "Software?"

"You have a computer, don't you?"

He frowned, still looking for obstacles that weren't there. "Yeah."

The bus turned the corner to my street, and I got to my feet. "It's not cheap software, but it's supposed to work." I swayed a little as the bus pulled up to my stop. "Good luck with it, Slater."

I got off the bus feeling pleased with myself. If I could keep Doofie off my back, I'd have eliminated half the Turn equation. A convertible with four girls in it pulled up to the stop sign at the corner, giving me a moment to check out the occupants.

I certainly didn't want to eliminate the other half.

"SO, today makes one month exactly," Ryan said, pulling the Hyundai into the first empty parking space on the block. We were a good four blocks from school because only seniors could park in the school lot, and all the close streets were permit-parking only during school hours.

"One month since when?" I asked, grabbing my backpack from the back seat.

Ryan grinned. "Since your first trip to the Twilight Zone—also known as Makoro."

"Let's not talk about it." I had managed not to think about it much for the last three days—not since I had seen Doofie on the bus.

Ryan reached for his own backpack and opened his door. "Man, I am so glad I'm right-handed." He waited for me to get out before he clicked the key fob to lock the door. "Especially now that I've got a girlfriend."

Yet another thing for me to be jealous about. He and Allie were dating seriously now, even making plans for Homecoming. Next thing I knew, he'd get laid before me, too.

Before I could comment, a car slid into the space behind us. I felt it more than heard it, and when I turned to look I knew why. It was a red Prius, and those hybrid engines didn't make much noise. I looked at the missing front plate and realized it must be brand new; it still had paper tags.

The driver's door opened, and Monica Martin got out.

"Hello, Jason." She gave Ryan a quick glance. "Who's your friend?"

I introduced Ryan, who was looking the Prius over.

"New car?" he asked.

She nodded. "I just got it yesterday."

She'd already passed her test and been given her own car. I still had my last in-car that afternoon—not that I was in a rush to get my license. I needed sixty hours behind the wheel to even take the test, and no one was going to give me a car when I passed. "Grandpa wouldn't spring for a Lexus, huh?"

I felt like a douchebag as soon as the words were out of my mouth. Monica had never said anything to make me feel bad. Why did I need to make her feel bad?

She gave me a hard look. "As a matter of fact, he offered any car I wanted. I chose this car because it's better for the environment."

Now I wanted to slink away, but I brazened it out instead. "How did you get your hours so fast?"

She waved a hand. "I had my learner's for several months before I took the classes, and I drove a lot in Costa Rica."

I wondered if her getting her license was legal. And I wondered how old she was.

"It doesn't look as dorky in red," Ryan said. "Did you get the backup camera?"

She nodded. "It makes parallel parking a lot easier."

The sense of relief in her voice made me feel better. At least parallel parking was one area where I did as well as anyone.

Monica walked with us as far as the back entrance to school. The IB corridor let out there, so she peeled off and went in that way while Ryan and I kept walking up the sidewalk.

Ryan gave me a sideways grin. "New girl in the picture? You gave up on Becca Sommers?"

I snorted. "First off, I never had a shot with Becca Sommers—and I'm not even sure I wanted one. Second, it sounds like Monica's grandfather is filthy rich. I doubt he'd let me near her."

Ryan let out a crow of laughter. "So you'd like to get near her!"

I sighed. Why was it once a guy had a girlfriend, he liked to make jokes about his friends and girls? "I don't think Monica *likes* me. She's just lonely."

Ryan shook his head as we went through the front door. "With girls, that's the same thing."

THAT afternoon I decided Ryan was right. I was waiting at the bus stop, chilling to Ella Fitzgerald's "Autumn in New York," when a red Prius pulled up, and Monica let down the driver's side window.

I glanced inside. The Prius was empty except for her. "You sure you don't mind? I need to get to the mall for my last in-car."

She glanced at the dashboard clock. "When do you need to be there?"

"Not till 4:00." It took two buses to get to the mall from school, and I hadn't wanted to cut it close.

She smiled. "Mind if we stop by my house first? I have something I need to take back to a store, and it's at home."

My odds of being on time were better in a private car, even with a detour. "No problem."

I climbed in the front seat and spent a few minutes checking out all the instruments on the dashboard. One display showed her current gas mileage, another revealed that the electric engine was doing most of the work. I moved from there to watching Monica.

She drove very well, changing lanes smoothly and with an unconscious ease. "Where's your friend?" she asked, her eyes still on the road.

"He has SAT class on Wednesdays."

She sniffed as if to suggest disapproval. "Test scores are meaningless."

I knew she wasn't stupid. Maybe it was idealism. "They might not tell whether you're smart, but they have a lot to say about what college you can get into."

She didn't argue. We left Bethesda and headed out River Road toward Potomac. There were plenty of well-to-do neighborhoods in Montgomery

County, but Potomac was where the big money was—big cars, big houses, and big yards.

Monica drove the Prius past the newer subdivisions—the ones where the lots were only an acre—until we were in old Potomac. Not just huge lots, but the occasional estate with brick walls around it and a gate across the driveway. People in old Potomac didn't just have live-in nannies. They had staff.

Sure enough, Monica reached up and clicked a remote clipped to the sun visor. She slowed the car as we approached a driveway and drove through the now open iron gates.

"Yikes," I said under my breath as we pulled up in front of a three story brick mansion.

"Indecent, isn't it?" Monica sounded dead serious. "A whole village could live here, but it's just Grandpa and his wife—and now me. Unless you count the cook and the chauffeur. They live over the garage."

She parked the Prius in the circular drive, right beside a gleaming black convertible.

"Whoa!" I said as I spotted the rearing horse emblem on the hood. "Who drives a Ferrari?"

Monica got a peculiar expression, half amusement, half something else. "My grandfather's wife." She shut the door a little more firmly than was necessary. "Come on. Do you want a soda or something?"

Or what? Perrier and lime? Maybe a champagne cocktail? "Sure." Curiosity consumed me as I followed her up the porch steps. I had never been in a mansion.

The front door had a security camera and a key panel. Monica pressed her right index finger to a screen, and keyed in a code to unlock the door.

I followed her into a marble-floored foyer and gazed up at the enormous crystal chandelier hanging from the two-story ceiling. Monica kept walking, and I hurried to catch up as she went through an open arched doorway into a big room furnished like a den or a family room—if the family was really well off. At the far end of the room, a long counter separated the family room from a huge open kitchen full of gleaming appliances. A round table with four chairs occupied a nook with a bay window between the two rooms.

"The funny part is, Dolores doesn't cook," Monica said, opening the refrigerator to indicate a door full of bottles—sparkling water, spring water, flavored water, and diet sodas. "Help yourself."

I grabbed a bottle of sparkling water. I'd never had any before. "Who's Dolores?"

Monica took a diet soda. "Grandpa's wife." She nodded at the bay window. "That's her."

I looked out the window. The backyard had a pool with a sort of greenhouse around it, to make it a year-round pool. An extremely attractive woman in an extremely small bikini half-reclined on a lounge chair and leafed through a magazine. She had long black hair and golden skin. "Holy shit! That's your grandmother?"

"Step-grandmother." Monica made a face like the soda was sour. "And she's older than she looks."

Since she looked thirty-five at most, that didn't bother me. "Wow."

"Yeah." Monica put down her soda. "Would you wait here a minute? I need to get something from my room."

I said okay and stood drinking my fizzy water while I took in the rest of the den. A flat screen TV on the wall was bigger than any I'd ever seen in a sports bar. Lighted glass cabinets full of expensive-looking Chinese vases took up another wall. A long slab of black marble served as a mantel over the enormous stone fireplace. The room was so big I counted three sofas and six upholstered chairs, and it didn't seem crowded.

"Who the hell are you?"

I jumped and almost dropped the bottle of water. I hadn't heard anyone come into the room. "Jesu—um, sorry, you startled me."

The man looked about sixty to me, but I've never been good at judging old people's ages. He had silver hair, going thin on top, and a beaky nose. He glared at me with open hostility. "Who are you and what are you doing in my house?"

"You must be Monica's grandfather," I said, trying not to let my voice break as I held out my hand. "I'm Jason Miller, a friend of Monica's from school."

The hostility in his expression eased as he shook hands. He had a darn firm grip for an old guy. "Frank Martin." He looked me up and down. "So, you're another IB kid?"

"Uh, no, I'm not in IB." I wondered whether it was worth it to mention I had two honors classes on my schedule. Probably not. It didn't take that much effort to get into honors classes. That was why I was in them. They helped my transcript without cutting into my work schedule like IB or AP classes would have.

"Grandpa!" Monica sounded annoyed as she strode into the room, a tiny shopping bag from a high-end jewelry store in one hand. "Are you interrogating Jason?"

The old man's face broke into a smile that surprised the heck out of me. He looked suddenly nice. "Hello, Princess." He gave her the same sort of quick once over glance he had given me. She still wore her school clothes, and her jacket. "What are you up to?"

"I'm taking the tennis bracelet back." She picked up her purse. "And I don't have time to argue about it. I promised Jason I'd get him to his driver's ed session."

Mr. Martin frowned, his face going back to the angry, accusing frown he had worn before she came into the room. "A sixteenth birthday present from your grandfather is supposed to be special."

She came over to kiss his cheek. He was as tall as me, so she had to stand on her tip toes. "The Prius was special enough."

His face softened again. He hugged her, and kissed her forehead. "Drive safe."

She laughed over her shoulder and then waved for me to follow her. "I always do."

"Pleased to meet you, sir," I said, deciding against shaking hands again.

He nodded, but I couldn't really say he looked pleased to see me leave with his granddaughter.

I waited until the car was through the gates and on the road before I asked Monica any questions. "So, how do you get along with your hot step-grandmother?"

She gave me a quick, sideways glance. "She's not so bad. She doesn't try to tell me what to do."

I could see where that would be a prime requirement with her. "And you've got your grandfather wrapped around your little finger, right, 'Princess'?"

Her mouth curved in a satisfied smile. "I'm lucky. Grandpa blew it with my dad, and he knows it. He's trying really hard not to aggravate me."

I laughed. "What a sweet deal!"

Her smile faded. "It should be. But I miss my folks." She darted another glance at me. "How do you get along with your parents?"

The question took me aback. I wasn't used to girls asking me about myself. "It's just my mom, actually. My dad skipped out on us right after the divorce."

She shot me another look, sympathetic this time. "That sucks."

"Yeah."

"So," she said, "single mom means no car, no college tuition, no spending money?"

She had scoped it out in a flash. Well, I had known she was smart, so I shouldn't have been surprised. "I have a job."

She nodded. "Good for you. Where do you work?"

"Jimmy's Java Joint." Would she show up there some time? Did she really like me or was it just that she hadn't made any friends in the IB set? Maybe the other IB types were so driven they didn't have time for the new kid.

She slowed down and signaled for the turn into the mall parking lot. "You're kind of cute, Jason. Do you have a date for Homecoming?"

I hate those kinds of questions. 'Do you have a date?' could mean someone was going to ask you out, or it could mean they were just nosy. "I can't afford Homecoming."

She slid into a space and put the car in park. "You could go with me," she said, turning to face me. "We won't have to rent a limo because Grandpa will let me use his."

Even without the limo rental, the tickets weren't cheap. I'd have to use my savings and wait to get my license. But Monica seemed to like me even though I had been something of a jerk with her. How often did a guy get a chance to go to a dance without risking rejection? "Sure, I'd like to go."

Her face lit up, and I realized she had been nervous. "Great! How about if I get the tickets, since I asked you?"

"I'll get the tickets," I said, overcome by machismo. It came to me that I'd be really short on cash if I bought two tickets, so I let go of machismo. "You can pay for dinner."

She nodded. "It's a deal."

It didn't sound terribly romantic, but maybe she had a practical streak. After all, she hadn't grown up rich, even if she was living in a mansion in Potomac now. I suddenly realized I wasn't sure whether I should kiss her or not.

Monica solved the problem for me by pointing at the clock on the dash. "Aren't you supposed to be there at 4:00?"

I looked at the display. It said 3:58 for one second and then clicked over to 3:59. I grabbed my backpack. "Thanks for the ride."

She smiled. "No problem. Happy to help."

I dashed out and headed across the lot to where the driver's ed car was parked. I could see Mr. Aiyuku pacing back and forth and smoking.

I had a date for Homecoming. I hoped my suit still fit. I hadn't worn it since my grandmother's funeral in January. And then my quandary came to me. Should I buy a corsage to match Monica's dress or her hair?

Mr. Aiyuku didn't give me time to think about it. As annoyed as he was at my being almost late, he still demanded to see my permit before we got into the car.

I pulled out my wallet, and when I opened it, a shiny foil packet fell out.

Mr. Aiyuku snickered as he took my permit and checked off something on his checklist.

I could feel my face turning red when I bent down to retrieve the condom. When I shoved it into my front pocket, I remembered a small hole had started in the bottom of that pocket. With my luck the condom would fall out in the middle of my in-car and drop to the ground when I got out of the car. I stifled a sigh but didn't do anything about it. I could always get another condom from the big bowl in the school nurse's office.

After Mr. Aiyuku gave me my permit back, I put my wallet away, and we got in the car. He began scanning the checklist. "Lots to do today," he muttered as I put the car in gear.

We started with changing lanes, making left turns, and passing slower vehicles. We had trouble with the last one because no one was driving slower than me until I came up behind an old lady so short I could barely see her head.

"Oh, fuck it," Mr. Aiyuku said after I managed to pass her. "You only have an hour left. Take the next right."

I put the blinker on and then glanced ahead. "But—but that's the on-ramp for the Beltway."

"I know that." He stubbed his cigarette out in the piece of aluminum foil he always carried. "But you need highway time. Turn right."

I eased the driver's ed car into the angled turn and tried not to panic. "But it's rush hour."

"Rush hour?" I could hear the sneer in Mr. Aiyuku's voice. "You call this rush hour? You haven't seen everyone trying to get home in Kigali when the traffic lights aren't working."

I was tired of hearing about Kigali and worried about merging into highway-speed traffic.

I needn't have worried. When we came around the curve to the Beltway, cars and trucks crawled along, bumpers practically touching, like a parade of armored snails. I had to fake-smile and wave at a woman in a silver minivan to get someone to let me in. But I could see flashing blue and red lights on the other side of the highway, so I figured things would get better soon.

They did. As soon as we passed the accident, everyone speeded up.

"Idiots," Mr. Aiyuku muttered. "Get your speed up!"

I stepped on the accelerator and watched the needle climb past sixty. I had never driven so fast. It felt great. Everyone was whipping past me, so I pressed the accelerator harder. Mr. Aiyuku didn't say anything when I hit seventy. The rush was as strong as when I had watched Monica's hot step-grandmother sunbathing. The thought made me grin. I imagined that instead of a battered driver's ed car with an extra foot brake I was at the wheel of Dolores Martin's black Ferrari—with Dolores in the passenger's seat. She wore her bikini and oversize sunglasses, and the wind whipped her long black hair back behind her.

I let myself enjoy the fantasy for a few minutes. Just as I imagined reaching for the gear shift and getting Dolores' left knee instead, Mr. Aiyuku brought me back to earth.

"We'll go up a few exits and turn around and take surface roads back to the mall." He waved a hand. "Be sure to look ahead. Get the big picture."

I nodded, trying to concentrate on the road instead of my daydream. Things looked okay at the moment, although the traffic on the overpass ahead of us came to an abrupt stop with a screech of brakes and a loud crash, followed by the wrenching sound of steel tearing as a big black SUV slammed into a tiny red Honda.

"Glad that's not us," Mr. Aiyuku said.

And then everything seemed to happen at once. On the overpass, a huge dump truck full of scrap wood rear-ended the SUV and pushed it into the Honda. The Honda hopped backwards like a billiard ball in a trick shot gone sour. The little car's back wheels jumped over the low railing as the SUV kept moving. The Honda teetered for maybe half a second, and then it started to fall right into my lane.

At that moment, Mr. Aiyuku and I both slammed on our respective brakes, and the junk in the back of the dump truck burst into flames. The driver's ed car slowed, but I could tell we wouldn't be able to stop. Time froze as we went into a skid, and chunks of burning debris rained down from the overpass onto the road. One thought popped into my head.

I was going to die a virgin.

And then, lightning fast, I knew what would happen. I put one hand on my belt. Wherever I was going, I wanted to be wearing pants when I got there.

Six

Mr. Aiyuku and the car melted swiftly into a pearly gray mist. All at once I was in a sort of alley with a high wall on one side and a shorter building on the other. I waited for the alley to melt, too, but instead I dropped on my butt before I could straighten up from the sitting position I had been in in the car.

"Shit." I sat up and looked around. The walls on either side of me were brick, but the pavement I sat on was flagstone. Where the hell was I?

I heard a door open, and I turned to see a woman coming into the alley. She looked white or possibly Latina, and she wore a blue-gray outfit, not quite a pantsuit, but definitely matching. Ruveka's image of her mother came to me. This woman was older but her clothes looked similar.

The woman's eyes opened wide when she saw me. She looked up at the far end of the alley and then back to me, and then she said something I didn't understand.

"Sorry." I shook my head as I got to my feet. "I don't speak your language."

Her jaw dropped, and then she said something else. I didn't recognize it either, but I was pretty sure from her tone it was a curse word. She ran over to me and started to pull me toward the door.

I was pretty sure I was on Makoro and not just in Afghanistan or China, and somehow it didn't seem like a good idea to let myself get dragged into someone's house the minute I got there. "No, thanks." I pulled hard and got out of her grasp. "I'll be going now."

I started for the alley entrance, and she followed, grabbing me by the arm and trying to pull me back. I wrenched free and then ran as fast as I could.

I stopped when I came into the open. Wherever I was, it wasn't Afghanistan.

I stood at one end of an open square, like a small park, bounded by roads full of traffic and sidewalks full of pedestrians, and all around us was a city. The shorter buildings were mostly made of pale pink brick, with the taller ones made of glass and steel or something equally shiny. Very tall buildings towered over me, many of them mere spires, not usable space. Women walked or rode on bicycles or drove some sort of hovercraft-like cars with no wheels. The effect was a combination of Chicago and the Emerald City with maybe a touch of Disney World.

I saw old women, middle-aged women, young women—a few of them totally hot—and even some girls, but no men. I should have been overjoyed to be without male competition, but somehow it really creeped me out.

The woman chasing me grabbed me from behind and said something as she tried to drag me backwards. Two women walking nearby stopped and pointed at me. "*Keesai!*" they shouted. That made other passersby stop and stare in my direction. A crowd gathered swiftly.

I didn't know what to do so I just stood there.

And then two women in identical black outfits pushed their way through the crowd. They both wore a silver hawk emblem on their right shoulders, so I figured they must be cops or soldiers.

The taller one said something to me that sounded like a question and ended in the word *keesai*.

I shook my head. "Sorry. I'm not from around here."

She pulled a gun from her belt. At least I guessed it was a gun, although it didn't look like any weapon I had ever seen. She said a few words in an authoritative tone, and all the bystanders stepped back a pace, even the one who had grabbed me.

It looked like I was getting busted just for being male, and so I lost it. "Fuck this!" I shouted, and then I ran, shoving an old lady out of my way as I tried to cut through the crowd.

I got about four steps and then something hit my back, and I could barely move my feet. A few seconds later the old lady I had shoved tackled me, and I went down like a quarterback who had held on to the ball too long. My head hit the pavement, and when I came to, I was trussed up in a sort of straitjacket and being carried by the straps. I tried wriggling, but my legs seemed paralyzed. Four women in black were carrying me toward a silver hovercar. When we got close, I could feel the tremendous rush of air that held it a foot or so off the ground. Someone opened the hovercar door, and the four women slung me inside like a bag of mulch.

I spent the next half an hour face down on the back seat, wishing to God that I had been born right-handed. I had no clue where we were going, but having been tied up like a dangerous mental patient wasn't a good sign. In my head, I just kept asking why this was happening to me. It occurred to me that if I had wished myself home when I was in the driver's ed car,

I might well have gone there. I tried wishing to be home. I closed my eyes and thought about Mom, and Lorrie, and Sancho, but when I opened them, nothing happened—no melting, no mist, no meadow, just the same light gray seat and darker gray door.

Finally the women soldiers hauled me out and half dragged me up some steps. They took the straitjacket off. I could stand okay now that whatever it was the woman on the street had fired at me had worn off.

I found myself walking along in what appeared to be a public hall in front of a line of women in black uniforms. They all had the same silver hawk emblem and they all wore sidearms, so I figured it was a group of cops or a group of soldiers. A few more of them walked in front of me. Their boots clicked on the marble floors, and everyone we met moved out of their way.

They might have taken the straitjacket off, but it was still clear I was a prisoner. Whenever I tried to lag behind, one of the storm troopers behind me would give me a shove to walk faster. When I tried to veer left or right a little, another trooper would nudge me back in line.

Finally we came to a tall doorway where two women with red sashes over their black uniforms stood like they were on guard. We had to stop while one of the storm troopers held out something that looked vaguely like an old-style PDA or a Blackberry. The guard checked it and passed us on with only a nod and a curious glance at me.

We went through the doorway and came out in a long windowless room with a large oval table. Several people sat at one end, four women and one man.

I studied the guy first, since he was the first man I had seen. He looked about Mr. Walters' age. He had gray streaks in his brown hair, and a receding hairline made even more noticeable by the weird way he had trimmed his sideburns into points. He wore a knee-length robe over his other clothes, and his eyes bored into me like I was his long-lost son.

"Sprechen Sie Deutsch?" he said, his tone eager.

I shook my head. "Sorry."

He let out a sigh. "I had hoped." He had a German accent—not old-war-movie German, but softer. He got to his feet and came closer, looking me over again. "American?"

"Yeah," I said, glancing around the room.

The women were watching us. The woman in the chair nearest his seemed about his age, or maybe a tad younger. She wore her black hair pulled back from her face in a single braid. They all looked vaguely Middle Eastern or maybe South American—brown or black hair and dark eyes.

"So where am I?" I said.

"Makoro—another version of the Earth." He gave me a suspicious once-over glance. "You seem very calm. Most men are more disoriented when they first make the Turn."

"It wasn't my first time." I decided against mentioning Mr. Walters' hot wife until I knew more about where I was. "I'd seen it before, but only for a few seconds."

His eyebrows shot up. "Really?" He glanced at my waist and smiled. "Yes, I see you still have your belt." His voice sounded suddenly eager. "Do you mean you can Turn at will?"

I shook my head. "Not that, no. The first time I Turned through Makoro while I was wishing myself home, so I ended up at my house. This time I thought I was going to die, and all I thought about was getting away."

His face fell. Before he could ask more questions, the woman with the braid broke in with a few curt sentences.

The man blinked and gave me an odd look, part pity and part disgust. "They want to know how old you are."

"What?" I tried to figure out what I should say. Why did my age matter so much that their first question was how old was I? Should I tell the truth? Lying could cause problems. For one thing, I'd have to remember my answer. For another, I looked my age. They might not believe me if I said I was radically older or younger. Besides, I didn't know which would be best to say. "Sixteen."

His eyes started to smile, like he was relieved, but he stopped himself and instead he just said one unfamiliar word.

The women didn't look nearly as pleased. She asked another question.

"When is your birthday?" the guy said.

Something made me nervous. I would actually turn seventeen in March, but I just had a feeling that the younger I was, the better off I was. "I just had it two weeks ago."

After he translated my fake birthday information, the women started to talk to each other and pretty soon it turned into an argument. I could tell because they kept talking louder and louder.

"What are they saying?" I asked the guy.

"They're quarreling over who gets to foster you." He jerked his head toward the woman with the braid. "The Ocan Garun wants it to be an Omdur household because she's in that clan."

I digested this. I wished desperately that I had pressed Mr. Walters for more information, but he hadn't wanted to talk about his wife or the life he had Turned away from. Still, I was pretty sure he had said his wife was an Ocan Garun. "What's your name?"

"Max Omdur Schwartzenthaler. What's yours?"

"Jason Miller." I waved a hand around the room. "Where am I? In what city, I mean?"

"It's called Egume."

So I wasn't in the same city Mr. Walters had been in. Dodomah, he had called it. It still didn't feel safe to mention what he had told me.

The Ocan Garun turned her head and asked another curt question. Max answered her at length, and it seemed to me his answer included names. I was pretty sure I heard him say Joshua, Hobart, Matt, and David, along with some other stuff I couldn't follow at all. The Ocan Garun looked pleased and turned back to the table.

"What was that about?" I asked.

"She wanted to know who else in Egume could speak your language."

I wondered how many guys from the real world were in this city. But more than anything I wondered what would happen to me now. "So what does it mean to foster someone?"

He shrugged. "It means they'll have custody of you until you're seventeen and old enough to marry into a household. They have to feed you and clothe you and keep you safe."

The final task sounded ominous. "Safe from what?"

Max grinned, but he didn't looked amused. "Safe from other households."

Now that sounded weird. How could a household be a danger? "What constitutes a household?"

He hesitated before he answered. "A basic household is five to ten women, and all their children, plus a husband if they can get one. But when the daughters grow up, sometimes they form a second generation household with everyone in the same house."

I wanted to ask a lot of questions but the Ocan Garun had run out of patience. She stood up and said something that sounded like an edict. The other women sat, grim and stone faced, but none of them said a word.

"Looks like it's decided," Max said.

I really wished I spoke the language.

THE second hovercraft-car had smoked windows, but as I was sitting up, I could see out pretty well. They hadn't let Max come with me, although it had seemed to me he had wanted to. Instead two cop-soldiers rode in the back of the hovercar, one on either side of me.

After a few minutes we left the skyscrapers and spires behind and came out in an area that reminded me of a Middle Eastern city—two- and three-story houses that edged the streets, with no yards or park space between the houses, and a sort of tall minaret for each house, each one with a colorful banner flying from its tip. All the windows were tall but narrow, and the ones on the lower levels had bars on them. The streets rambled like they had been laid out by someone who was drunk, with hardly a straight line in sight.

It was just getting dark when the hover-car pulled into an arched gate-way and paused while the gate opened. The gate reminded me of Monica's grandfather's mansion, but instead of coming out into open space we drove through a long archway. The hovercar waited while another gate opened, and finally we arrived in a courtyard enclosed by the house itself. The second floor had a sort of balcony all around it, overlooking the flagstone and grass courtyard. It reminded me of a Roman villa or maybe a Mexican hacienda. Even in the twilight I could see the bright red and orange flowers blooming in the flower beds. The ground floor rooms had doors and windows that opened onto the courtyard, and unlike the windows that faced the street, these were large and mostly open; light from them shone onto the grass and flagstones.

My guards opened the door for me just as a group of people came out from the shadow of a doorway into the lights of the courtyard. Most of them were female—gray-haired women, middle-aged women, and several girls. A few of the girls were my age, and a few looked older, maybe twenty-ish. There were two boys who looked eight or nine, and several school-age girls. I counted heads—seven middle-aged and older women, three young women, three girls about my age, and six younger girls, for a total of nine-teen females. At the back of the group I finally saw a man.

He wore a loose shirt, trousers, and sort of knee-length vest trimmed in blue and green. He was taller than anyone else, but not by much, and his hair and his well-trimmed moustache had gone salt and pepper.

The older of the gray-haired women started talking to the guards who had brought me. The other females all stood and waited while the man stepped forward, but the two boys pressed their way toward me until the man waved them back.

"Welcome to our home," he said to me, a trace of a drawl in his speech. After a second he held out his hand, like shaking hands was habit he had forgotten. "My name is Hobart Omdur Anderson."

The women and the boys watched as I shook his hand. The girls were kind of cute, especially one auburn-haired girl who smiled at me.

"Jason Miller," I said as I let go of his hand. "Where are you from?"

"Fort Stockton, Texas." He said the words without any sadness or nostalgia, like Texas was just up the road. "How about you?"

"Bethesda, Maryland."

He shook his head. "Never been in Maryland. Never been farther north than Amarillo." He glanced around at the house, or maybe it was the city he was thinking of. "It's fall now, but the climate is mild all year round. You'll like it."

I swallowed, suddenly homesick. "How long have you been here?"

His expression stayed serene. "Twenty-four years, next month."

It rocked me to think he had been here longer than I had been alive. I swallowed again. If I wasn't careful, I would cry right in front of all these women. "Did you ever try to go back?"

His eyes crinkled at the corners as he looked around the courtyard again, a glint of stark humor in his eye. "Kind of hard to do. The one thing I never had to put up with here was any kind of danger."

I smelled the sweet fragrance of the red and orange flowers, and then I looked straight up at the pearly gray minaret silhouetted against the charcoal sky where a few stars were already out. The flag was missing from the tip, but a red light on the top blinked like a radio tower. I felt a little like I was in a military base. Short of a tornado or a missile strike, I was sheltered from harm.

"Come and meet my family," Hobart said, holding one arm out toward the eldest of the women, who had finished talking to the guards. "This is my senior wife Adeola Omdur Hamad, my other wives, and my children."

The gray-haired woman nodded like she understood she was being introduced. She looked older than Hobart by several years, maybe pushing sixty, while he might be forty-five or fifty at most. The other gray-haired woman was about Hobart's age, and the other five wives looked fortyish.

Hobart rattled off everyone's name and their relationships, but I didn't pay attention except to note that the women's last names sometimes varied but everyone's middle name seemed to be Omdur. And of course, I did notice the three girls my age. The redhead's name was Teleza, and like all the other females who were way younger than Hobart, she was his daughter. I wasn't entirely clear which wife was her mother except I was pretty sure it wasn't Adeola, as the senior wife didn't seem to have any children. I thought Teleza was the prettiest girl, but that might have been because she smiled the most.

Teleza's two closest sisters were Panya, who was five months younger, and Ulu, two months older. Hobart must have been busy that year. Panya had night-black hair, thick and straight, and dark eyes, while Ulu's shoulder-length hair was wavy and honey-brown. The girls didn't look a whole lot alike, which I guess came from having different mothers—although Panya and Ulu's mothers were sisters, as were Adeola and two of the other wives.

"And these are my sons," Hobart finished off, indicating the two boys with a brief gesture. I noticed they wore their hair the same way as his—really short, but trimmed to a point in front of their ears, even though they were too young for sideburns. "Kafele is nine," Hobart said with pride, "and Gyasi is eight."

"Now ya'll have met everyone," he added, the drawl growing more noticeable the longer he talked. "Let's go inside and have something to eat."

My stomach growled, but I didn't like the idea of going into the house. Somehow the outside seemed safer.

Adeola said something, and Hobart looked me up and down.

"Adeola says you look tired." He gave me a sympathetic grin. "Would you rather just have a tray in your room instead?"

It sounded better. I was hungry, but I was also freaked out, and I didn't want to sit down and eat with a bunch of strangers, no matter that three of them were very pretty girls. "Yeah, I would. Thanks."

Hobart said something brief, and Adeola took it from there.

She rattled off some orders. The two youngest women disappeared into the house, and the two boys tugged on my hands.

"Kafele and Gyasi will show you to your room," Hobart said. "I'll come along to translate."

We trooped along, the only four males in the place. The boys chattered away in their own language as they led the way through the courtyard and toward a doorway.

Hobart grinned when I asked him what they were saying. "Gyasi is explaining that you'll be staying in his bedroom, but he doesn't mind giving it up to room with Kafele because he was lonely after he moved out of the nursery. Kafele is asking if you like to play games and do you fence."

"Fence?" It took me a second to make the word into a verb that didn't involve stolen goods. "You mean like with swords?"

Hobart's grin widened. "Of course with swords. Do you know any other way to fence?"

It surprised the heck out of me to think these people practiced what I thought of as an archaic sport. "I don't even know anyone who fences."

Hobart's eyes gleamed like he was amused. "It wasn't big in Texas, either. But it's popular here, along with a form of martial arts called *jin-weh*. They're both good exercise, and it never hurts to have a clue how to defend yourself."

That comment surprised me even more. "You said you'd never been in any danger here."

"I haven't." He slapped me on the shoulder. "The threat isn't death but kidnapping. You need to get used to the idea that you're a valuable commodity."

Now that weirded me out. A valuable commodity—like gold or diamonds. I looked around as Hobart opened a heavy steel door, and I stepped inside. I saw a short corridor with four doors, two on each side, and a stairway that led up to the second floor. All the inside doors were made of steel, too.

It looked like I was getting locked into a vault with the other treasures.

THE small room that had been Gyasi's was simply furnished—a comfortable bed, a night table, a tall chest of drawers, a lamp, and bars on the windows. That first night I went to bed in my clothes because I was afraid to take them off. I lay in the dark staring at the ceiling and missing my mom and my sister and wishing I had been holding my iPod in the car so I could at least listen to some music.

I figured Mom would assume I was dead. If the driver's ed car had crashed, it might well have burned up. Mr. Aiyuku might be dead for real. Would the police have been able to tell her whether I was in the car or not? My wallet and my cell certainly were, and probably there would have been traces of them left.

I tried to think of a way I could Turn back to my own world. The turned-on part wasn't a problem. I'd proved I could do that just by thinking about girls, and there were plenty of girls around to think about. But I'd need to be good and scared and that wouldn't be so easy to do.

I rolled over as I thought about it, and I heard something crunch in my jeans' pocket at the same time I felt a coolness against my thigh. When I slipped my hand into my pocket, my fingers found the hole in the bottom first, and then closed over a familiar foil packet.

I pulled it out and held it in front of my eyes. It must have been touching my skin through the hole. Of all the useless things I could have brought with me, a condom seemed high on the list.

I put it back in my other pocket and went back to thinking about the real world and feeling sorry for myself. A minute later, from somewhere above me, I heard a lock click.

I got up and went to the door. The bottom of the stairs was right outside my door, and when I opened it and looked up, I saw a woman cross the landing to the door I knew was Hobart's. It was Adeola; she wore a bathrobe over a longer red nightgown that looked a lot flimsier than the robe. I pulled back and watched through the crack in the door. Adeola knocked, and in a moment Hobart's door opened, and she disappeared from view.

I went back to bed. It looked like Hobart wasn't sleeping alone. Quite possibly he never slept alone.

This world might look like mine, but it was really different. A household like this one would never have existed on the Earth I knew. Sure we had polygamists, even in America, but the guys with multiple wives were more likely to lock the women up than the other way around. It struck me all at once that there could be more than two Earths. Maybe there were dozens—hundreds—thousands! The thought made my head spin. I decided not to worry about any other worlds unless I ended up in one of them—and right now that didn't seem likely.

I tossed and turned on Gyasi's comfortable bed until finally I went to sleep. The last thought to drift through my mind was to wonder if Monica Martin would find another date for Homecoming.

Seven

I woke with a start, convinced I had had a bad dream, but not sure what it was about. I sat up and glanced around the unfamiliar room in confusion. The bars on the windows brought it all back to me.

So it hadn't been a bad dream. I really was locked up in a house in Makoro. A sudden urge to cry almost overwhelmed me. Would I ever get home? I shut my eyes for a minute, and thought about Mom and Lorrie and our apartment. It was a school day. I should be getting up, doing my workout with maybe some Charlie Parker playing in the background for motivation, then taking a shower. If I were home, Mom would have yelled my name by now, to make sure I was awake, and to remind me to eat breakfast. Lorrie would have beaten me to the breakfast table even though her school started after mine. And Ryan would have called to let me know if he could pick me up or not.

A knock on the door made me jump. "Come in."

Hobart stuck his head in the door. "Are you up?"

I slid my feet onto cold tile floor and stood up. "Yes."

"Good morning." He came into the room carrying a bundle of clothes. "I thought you might like something clean to wear." He glanced at my rumpled jeans and tee shirt. "And then the girls can wash your things."

I looked at the pile of Makoron clothes. Other than being a little brighter colored, they didn't look that different from what I wore back home. "Okay."

He set the bundle on the foot of the bed. "The bathroom's across the hall—hell, ya'll know that." He cocked his head. "Should I come back to take you to breakfast?"

I thought about the huge assembly of people in the courtyard the night before. My face must have shown my dismay because Hobart laughed. "Don't worry. I can have someone bring you a tray again. How's that?"

"Thanks," I said, suddenly conscious that my stomach had no qualms about being in Makoro, only about being without food. "That would be better."

He nodded. "Be sure to let me know how the clothes fit."

I had a more important question. "Do they have anything like radio stations here?"

He laughed. "I should have thought of that. I remember when I was your age I couldn't go more than a few hours without listening to rock. I still remember the day Lennon was killed. I was crushed when I realized I would never get to meet him."

I didn't mention that I rarely listened to musicians who were still alive, let alone still recording.

Hobart pointed to a recessed panel on the wall above the dresser. "That's the radio console. We have premium service—thirty channels."

He showed me how to work the console, and then he left. I tried all thirty channels, but I couldn't find anything I liked. I hadn't expected to understand the lyrics, of course, but the music itself was weird. Some of it sounded vaguely like the soundtrack from a Bollywood musical, and some of it was more like new age mixed with harp music, but none of it sounded anything remotely like any kind of jazz. I gave up and turned the thing off to get dressed.

The shirt Hobart had brought wasn't that different, but the pants were weird. They had a button fly instead of a zipper, and the waistband had a row of buttons to fasten it snugly instead of loops for a belt. There was also a knee-length, open robe—no buttons, hooks, or sashes—in bright blue. I wasn't sure if it was supposed to be like a jacket or what, because the temperature was warm enough not to need it. But Hobart had worn a sort of robe the night before and this morning, so maybe it was more of a fashion statement.

I had just finished dressing when there was a knock at the door. Hobart came in with one of his older daughters, a black-haired young woman who carried a tray of food. I was disappointed it wasn't the redhead. Hobart called this girl Zuwina.

She put the tray down and frowned at me, then said something to Hobart.

"Zuwina wants to know why you're not wearing your *thrya*," Hobart translated. "She picked it out for you."

I looked down at the blue robe I had left on the bed. "I don't need it, and I feel silly wearing it."

He laughed and translated my answer to her. "You'll get used to it." He glanced around the room, saw my jeans and tee shirt, picked them up, and handed them to Zuwina. "We'll go get our own breakfast if you have everything you need."

I could smell the aroma of some kind of egg and cheese dish and something that wasn't quite coffee. My stomach would growl in a moment. "I'll be fine, thanks."

I ate all alone, sitting on the bed. Somehow it made me less homesick than sitting at a table would have. After I had finished, I put the condom in the inside pocket of my jacket and hung the jacket and my belt up in the closet. I didn't want to let go of everything that reminded me of home.

A little while later, Hobart came back and offered me a tour of the house. It seemed like a good idea, so I said yes. It took a while because the house was huge, two stories plus an attic. Unlike the men's area, in the main part of the house the bedrooms were all on the second floor, and we didn't go in them, although Hobart let me look inside and told me who slept in each room. I noticed there were steep, narrow stairs from the second floor to the attic, but Hobart didn't mention them, and we didn't go up them.

The common area rooms were on the ground floor, and the rooms for eating and sitting had been built to hold a crowd. The minaret, on the other hand, was more of a glorified flag pole than a real tower. It didn't seem to have any usable space, as there was no way to enter it that I could see. I wondered if I could find a way to climb to the top of it. If I jumped, I would be darn scared on the way down. On the other hand, I might not Turn, and then I would probably break my neck or end up crippled. I gave up on that idea, but I kept my eyes open as we went from room to room.

One of the smaller ground floor rooms was the schoolroom. Hobart explained that after age ten the girls went out to school, but no one in Egume let boys leave the house just for school. Teleza's mother was holding class for the two boys and the two youngest girls when Hobart and I went through on our tour.

Walking from one unfamiliar room to another and seeing so many strangers I kept expecting to wake up and find I was indeed dreaming. I pinched myself just to make sure, but it didn't help.

After the tour, Hobart told me the first thing to do was for me to learn Neluan.

"Great," I said, fed up with not knowing what anyone was saying unless Hobart chose to translate for me.

"Let's get a place set up for you in the gym," Hobart said. "We don't want to get in the way of the regular classes."

We moved some chairs, a bookcase, and a desk from the schoolroom into one corner of the gym, and then Hobart took out a kid's book and showed me the Neluan alphabet. I'd never had to learn a new alphabet, but at least it wasn't like Chinese or ancient Egyptian, with pictograms instead of letters. We spent a solid two hours going over the Neluan alphabet, and then Hobart started teaching me a bunch of nouns.

It turned out that Neluan had words we didn't have in English. Hobart translated the words for father, daughter, son, husband, and wife easily, but he had more trouble with the word *haru*.

"It's what my wives are to each other," he said.

"Do you mean the relationship that exists between them" I asked, "or the word they call each other?"

He shrugged. "Both."

Similarly, he had trouble explaining the word keesai.

"It means stranger," Hobart said. "You and I are considered keesai."

That made no sense to me. "But how can you be a stranger when you live here and have several wives and children?"

Another shrug. "I don't know why, but the word can mean a man you don't know, or it can mean a man who came here from another world."

I took notes better than I ever had in school, just because I was desperate to know what everyone was saying.

The second day Hobart started on some verbs and simple sentences. I worked at it, but it was frustrating. Just as Monica Martin had been fluent in Spanish without being able to explain the rules of it, Hobart wasn't good at explaining the syntax of Neluan. I actually missed Mr. Walters.

The boys joined us that afternoon, and watching them have their fencing lessons was more fun than struggling through a dense language with a bad guide. Hobart showed me some fencing basics, but it was all I could do not to stab myself in the foot.

The third morning Teleza showed up just as Hobart got the books out. She slipped in through the steel door of the gym and stood there waiting.

Hobart smiled when he saw her and signaled with a 'come closer' gesture. "Teleza is off school today, so I thought she could help us. She has *kayel*." As usual, he slipped between Neluan and English with perfect ease.

Teleza walked across the room and waited a few feet from my desk. The dark green of her shirt made her hair seem redder, and her pants were tight enough to make me take notice.

I didn't mind her joining us in the least, but I was curious. "What's *kayel*?"

"It's short for *kayel gazan*, which translates as openness of mind." Hobart jerked his head at me and said something to Teleza.

She stepped up to my desk and put her hand on my forehead. I managed not to pull away from her, and sure enough, all at once I had a vision in my head of Adeola's household sitting down to dinner in their enormous dining room, which I had seen but never eaten in because I was still eating in my room or the gym. In Teleza's vision, Hobart had a central place, with Adeola beside him, and assorted wives and offspring grouped at four tables laid out in a hollow square. The oldest daughter Zuwina was serving food with help from her sister Panya. In a second I realized Teleza was serving, too, and I was seeing everything from her point of view as she moved around the room offering a basket of bread.

The family seemed sociable but organized. It looked like Zuwina was in charge of the workers, as she directed Teleza and Panya and then took her place across from Adeola. The younger kids were intent on their food, but the older ones talked across the tables and called out to other family members.

It reminded me of Thanksgiving dinner in one of those Hallmark Hall of Fame TV movies my mom liked to watch. I'd never had much extended family around—none since my grandmother died.

Teleza moved her hand and the picture vanished, just like turning off a television. It dawned on me that I should act surprised.

"Shit!" I hoped I sounded convincing. "How does she do that?"

"It's not a rare gift here. Women have been able to do that for as long as Makorons could write." Hobart was watching me closely, so maybe I wasn't a good liar.

"But how does it work?" I asked.

He sort of grimaced, like he didn't like having to explain. "I have no idea. This world has its own rules. It'll be easier if you just accept them and don't worry how things work."

His reluctance only made me more curious. "But why is Makoro so different?"

He let out a sound that was half annoyance and half amusement. "It just is. Before the Great Folly and the Rage, Makoro's past was more like Earth's past. Men were in charge, and women stayed home. If anything, they advanced a lot faster than us, because they had modern weapons and mechanical vehicles four hundred years ago, when America was just a bunch of British colonies."

It sounded more interesting than learning a new alphabet. "What were the Great Folly and the Rage?"

He tapped one of the books. "You can read about it once you know the language. The Folly happened during a war hundreds of years ago. Some scientists tried to manufacture biological weapons to kill enemy soldiers. They created a virus that killed a lot of the men, but not the women."

"How many is a lot?"

"Most of them. Only one man in ten survived."

It sounded a lot worse than the Black Death.

Hobart was still talking. "But it was a lousy weapon. It didn't recognize friend from foe. After it spread, it damn near destroyed civilization. This world has been trying to recover ever since."

The thought made me shiver. I could have already been exposed to a killer virus.

"The virus doesn't seem to work on men from our world," Hobart said, like he knew what I was thinking. "That's why we usually have more sons."

Except Hobart only had two. "You have six times as many daughters as you do sons."

"True," he said. "But then my father had five sisters and no brothers."

So maybe the virus wasn't the reason for his lopsided family. "What was the Rage?" I asked.

He grinned, but it was a grim sort of grin, with his lips pulled back to show his teeth but no humor in his eyes. "The Rage was women's answer to what men had done. Within thirty years of the Great Folly women ran every government in the world. In some places they took over peacefully, others not so peacefully."

I tried to imagine a world-wide holocaust that killed close to half the population and couldn't do it, so I went back to the immediate question. "So, how many of your wives and daughters have *kayel?*" I asked, pronouncing the word carefully.

He smiled at my efforts, a genuine smile this time. "Four."

And yet somehow it was the hottest girl in the house who was helping to teach me Neluan. Not that I minded.

A thought suddenly struck me. "Can she see anything from my mind when she does that?"

He shook his head. "Nope. *Kayel* is strictly a one-way street."

I was glad of that.

We settled into a pattern. Hobart would go over some words, and Teleza would illustrate them for me. I got to see the city of Egume through her gift. Her life didn't seem that different from mine back home except there were no boys in it—other than her brothers—and nothing like dating. I saw scenes from her going to school, hanging out with her friends, driving a hovercar, and swimming in a lake at what seemed to be a summer camp. That last one was quite a shock because with no boys around, they didn't need swim suits. All the girls swam naked. It sure made that lesson fun for me.

Hobart must have realized I was getting turned on because he pulled Teleza's hand away from my forehead. "That's enough of that one."

Teleza laughed, and we moved on to some less exciting verbs.

When Kafele and Gyasi came in for their fencing lessons, Hobart suggested I practice Neluan with Teleza.

"Ya'll will learn it faster if you speak it for real," he said. "And if ya'll can't figure out what she means, she can show you."

"Okay," I said. "I mean," I smiled at Teleza and spoke in careful Neluan, "Very well. Let us go."

"We go," she said, and took my hand.

We went into the courtyard and sat down on a bench. Teleza clearly took her task seriously, because she promptly started pointing at things and asking me to name them. I knew a few words like sky, flower, and bird, but not bench, wall, door, or countless others. I felt like I'd walked onto the set of Sesame Street. I learned a lot of words though, including the name of the minaret-like tower which was called a *janullo*. After I diligently practiced my new vocabulary, I tried to make conversation in Neluan.

"Do you like school?" I asked, figuring it was safest to stick to the present tense.

She nodded and rattled off a couple of sentences of which I caught only the words 'the,' 'of,' 'more,' and 'less,' and then she laughed at my expression.

"Too fast," I said.

A mechanical sound made me look up. A ways above us, well above the flag that flew from the top of the *janullo*, I could see something hovering overhead that might have been a helicopter.

Teleza grabbed my hand. "Come!" She said the one word and then she jumped up and ran for the sheltered space under the second floor balcony.

I let her drag me along, but as soon as she stopped, I pulled myself free of her grasp. "Why?" I asked in Neluan.

She pursed her lips in frustration, and then put her hand on my forehead. I had a vision of a copter-like vehicle swooping down into the courtyard while female commandos leapt from it, snatched me up, and dragged me off into the sky.

It made my head reel for a couple of reasons. First I hadn't realized Teleza could communicate images she had never actually seen. Second, in her vision I looked a good deal buffer than I actually was. In fact, I looked just a tad like the 'after' guys in the Bowflex commercials. And third, I hadn't really believed Hobart's warnings about kidnapping.

Teleza moved her hand and my head cleared, but she wouldn't let me go back to the bench until the hovering vehicle moved away.

It came to me then that I wasn't just imprisoned in the house. The whole damn world was a prison for anyone with a Y chromosome.

I LIKED my lessons with Teleza. Hobart let her teach me more and more—whenever she wasn't at school or doing chores. I spent mornings with him and afternoons with her. Afternoons were more fun.

Teleza had a killer smile, and I could bring it out just by using a new vocabulary word correctly. On the other hand, I could get a hearty laugh by pronouncing it really badly. Teleza laughed a lot, but not in a mean way.

The only thing was, aside from missing Ryan, my family, and decent music, I was getting cabin fever from never going anywhere outside the house. I wanted out.

"Don't you ever leave the house?" I asked Hobart one morning after my language lessons. I said it in Neluan, and I was proud of my accent after only two weeks of practice.

He answered in the same language. "Every now and then." He gave me a measuring glance, like he expected me to wig out or something. He started up the stairs toward his own suite, and I followed because I had nowhere else I wanted to go.

"When?" I asked.

Hobart switched to English, maybe because he thought I wouldn't be able to follow the conversation—or maybe to be sure I understood. "There's an Omdur Assembly every few months. I go to those, if our household is attending." He opened his door and glanced around like he was checking to see if it was tidy.

An assembly sounded interesting. I recalled the Ocan Garun was in the Omdur clan. "What happens at an assembly?"

He made an abortive gesture, not quite a shrug, and advanced into the room. "Not that much, usually. A lot of it is just recordkeeping and socializing. But if there's any issue up for a vote, Adeola goes, because she's the senior wife for this household and casts our vote. I like to go because it's a chance to see other guys—in person, not just on the phone."

He used the English word even though the Makoron device was more like talking over the net through a laptop than using a cell or a landline phone. He flopped down at his desk, which stood in a bookshelf-lined alcove that was almost a small library.

I was wondering more about something else—specifically, how had I ended up here in the same household as Hobart? "Are any other guys from our world in the Omdur clan?"

"Just me and Max." He lifted his brows. "You remember him—the Ocan Garun's husband."

Now that surprised me. Adeola and his other wives all seemed quite fond of Hobart, but the Ocan Garun had spoken to Max with all the affection of a drill sergeant giving orders.

I must have looked shocked because Hobart chuckled. "Don't worry about Max; his other wives are much nicer."

That was another shock. It occurred to me that Mr. Walters has always used the singular when he talked about his wife. "Even the Ocan Garun doesn't get a man all to herself?"

A strange expression crossed Hobart's face—not disgust, but maybe fear or anger. "No, and the only Ocan Garun to ever try that found out her mistake the hard way."

His tone made me glad I had never mentioned Mr. Walters. It occurred to me that Walters had used the same words for the world and for the city leader that Hobart did, so wherever Dodomah was they probably spoke Neluan or something close to it. "So what does this world look like? You've never shown me a map of Makoro."

Hobart squinted like he was thinking about it, and then he pulled a book from the shelf behind him. He laid it down on his desk and flipped it open to a double-page map of the world as I had never seen it.

The resemblance to the Earth I knew was there, but subtly. The Americas were most recognizable, even though instead of the isthmus of Panama joining the two continents, a hundred miles of ocean separated them. Africa had the same horn shape at the south end, but the northern half was flatter and partly missing. I could identify Europe because Scandinavia looked the same, but instead of an inland sea, the Mediterranean formed the western end of a large ocean that separated Greece from a huge land mass that kind of looked like Asia. I could tell India at least, but Australia seemed to be attached to Southeast Asia.

I had never expected Makoro to be so different from my earth. "Holy fuck!"

Hobart didn't seem shocked by my language. "Kind of brings it all home, doesn't it?"

I nodded. "Where are we?"

He pointed to an area on the east coast of North America, roughly where North Carolina should be. "Here's Egume."

I leaned over to study the markings on the map. Egume seemed to be about a third the size of Kansas, with the city itself being more or less dead center in the pale blue area outlined in black. Just north of it was a slightly larger pale green area labeled Dodomah.

Most of the map was the same kind of patchwork—small areas colored and outlined. The whole world was made up of countries no bigger than Belgium.

"So where do they speak Neluan?" I asked.

Hobart's hand waved from the Rockies to the Atlantic coast, including a peninsula that sort of looked like Florida, but it was half the size. "Here, wherever there were other Nelu colonies centuries ago." He ran his hand down the western coast. "They speak Kechuan here, in the part that was never conquered."

It rocked me to know I was somewhere where I not only had no clue how things were, I had no clue *why* they were that way. I swallowed and nodded at the patchwork world. "So, are all these other city-states the same as Egume?"

He cocked his head. "How do you mean?"

It frustrated me to be so ignorant that I didn't even know where to start asking questions. "Do people live in the same kind of households?"

Hobart's eyes squinted as he looked me over, like he was assessing my reasons for asking. "No, not all of them." He held his hand over pseudo-Europe. "It's not that different here, but here," he swept his hand across the sea I had no name for to cover pseudo-Asia, "here young women fight to join households—literally fight, with knives, fists, whatever. Over here," his hand flitted to flat-topped Africa, "the virus hit harder. They have even fewer men. When a boy baby is born, the government takes him, raises him if he lives. He spends his whole life in a virtual prison making deposits for the state-run sperm bank."

It sounded like a weird life. "You mean without women?"

His expression got grimmer. "You ever see a cow hooked up to a milking machine?"

I had a vague memory of my geography class in fourth grade. "Just in a movie."

He tapped the map. "Well here it's not cows, and it's not milk they're after."

The mental picture wasn't pretty. "So, you're telling me I'm lucky to have landed here in Egume?"

He shook his head. "I wouldn't say you're lucky to have made the Turn. But I'm telling you it could have been worse."

He turned like he wanted to make a call, but he didn't do anything. I realized he was waiting for me to leave, but I didn't feel like being polite. "So, how do you call someone on that thing?"

He shook his head. "First you have to be authorized or the phone won't work for you." He glanced over his shoulder at me. "And then you have to know someone to call."

And I didn't know anyone I could talk to but him and Max. I gave it up and left. I went back downstairs to the gym and stood by the window and looked out at the street. The traffic moved briskly, pedestrians, hovercars, and bicycles. Everyone I saw was female, in a hurry, and free to go where she liked. Hundreds of years ago some guys had fucked up this world, and now I was paying the price for their stupidity.

That night I put the radio on before I lay down to go to sleep. I had found a station that wasn't anything like jazz, but at least it sounded closer to pop than to Bollywood. When I closed my eyes, I could almost pretend I was back home. It wasn't any worse than the time Mom had drunk most of a bottle of wine and gotten out her Abba collection.

I thought about my life at home and compared it to my life in Makoro. I had less responsibility here, and less work, but I couldn't go anywhere outside one very large house. At home I had spent my time resenting the fact that I was surrounded by people with more possessions than me, without ever realizing that I still had my essential freedom.

I slipped out of bed and went to the window. Instead of a busy street, my room looked out on the courtyard. The moon was up, a white disc just above the blinking red light at the tip of the *janullo*. The sky and the moon were the most familiar things in Makoro, even though the moon's craters looked subtly different. What came over me abruptly was a sudden sympathy for Monica Martin. She had been raised in one world and then transplanted to another. I knew now how painful that could be.

And then I noticed a shadow in the window across the courtyard from mine but on the second floor. Someone was standing in that window looking in my direction. It had to be a woman, since all the males were housed in my wing, safe behind our barred windows and steel doors. I counted windows from the corner and recalled my tour of the house. It was the room Teleza shared with Panya and Ulu.

Whoever it was couldn't be looking at the moon because it was on the wrong side of the sky to be visible from that window. No, whoever it was was looking at my window.

I hoped it was Teleza.

Eight

"Why can't I go to the Assembly?" I asked. I said it in English, because I was fed up with speaking nothing but Neluan. "You're taking Kafele and Gyasi, so it must be safe."

Hobart slipped an ankle-length, short-sleeved, red *thrya* on over his shirt and trousers and studied himself in the full-length mirror on the wall. "You're only a ward of this household, not part of it. That means you're not officially in the Omdur clan." He spoke in Neluan.

I could understand him just fine. I was eating my meals with the family now, and I could follow most of their conversations, except for the occasional word or phrase. But I wasn't in the mood to cooperate, so I answered in English. "It's not fair."

He grinned, but he kept speaking Neluan. "The *Wahlau* holiday is coming up in less than two weeks. We're having company for that. You'll get to meet new people then."

The *Wahlau* holiday celebrated friendship, and Adeola had invited another Omdur household to visit that day. It was the only time since I had arrived that a large group of outsiders had been invited into the household. Even the older girls who had jobs didn't bring friends to visit without asking Adeola's permission first.

Having company wasn't the same as getting out of the house and looking at something other than the same old walls, the courtyard, and the view from the gym windows. I looked around at Hobart's bedroom. The huge bed had a sort of gold satin tent over it, with the sides tied back with silk cords. The alcove with his desk and bookshelves was bigger than Gyasi's whole room. Hobart had a sitting area, too, with a gas fireplace, a sofa, and a really comfortable armchair.

Hobart dropped the red *thrya* to the floor and took a blue one, shorter but with long sleeves, from his walk-in closet. He slipped it on and turned so he stood at an angle to the mirror. "What do you think?" he asked, still in Neluan.

I was tempted to tell him it made him look fat. I had never watched a guy try on clothes before, and it creeped me out to see a straight man his age pay so much attention to what he was wearing. "It's okay."

Hobart must have decided he liked the blue *thrya* better, because he headed for the door. He left the red one on the floor. I knew someone would hang it up for him. Just as Teleza's mother taught the children, Panya and Ulu's mothers cleaned the house and did the cooking, with help from the girls.

I followed Hobart through the dimness of the corridor, down the stairs, and into the sunlight of the courtyard. Three hovercars stood parked by the gate. I had known the family owned three hovercars, but I had never seen them all at once because they were garaged in a nearby alley.

Adeola waited beside the first vehicle, her eyes following Hobart as he walked toward her. When she reached out to put one arm around him, I saw she was wearing a sidearm. A quick glance around confirmed that all the women and the older girls were armed.

It freaked me out. I watched as Hobart entered the first hovercar, and then Kafele got in the second car with his mother, and Gyasi got in the third with his mother. Adeola rattled off names, directing the others where to ride. Most of the remaining women and girls distributed themselves into the three vehicles, leaving me standing there with Adeola, Teleza and her mother, and Panya and Ulu.

Adeola spoke to Teleza's mother. "Be sure you *az shukar* the locks as soon as we're through the gates."

I didn't recognize all of the Neluan words, but the meaning was clear. The household was circling the wagons.

Teleza's mother obviously understood. "Of course."

Adeola nodded once, a curt gesture. She glanced at me. "You will stay in your quarters until we're back, Jayzoon." She said my name with that same odd inflection everyone but Hobart used, but with a dose of stern authority that even my mother had never used.

I didn't say anything. Arguing wouldn't get me anywhere, and I didn't feel like being polite.

"I will see to it, Adeola," Teleza's mother said.

Adeola got into the driver's seat of the first hovercar. I heard the door locks thunk, and then all three hovercars lifted with a loud rush of air and started for the gate.

They whooshed through almost soundlessly, and then the gates clanged shut.

Teleza's mother touched the screen on her portable console, a sort of tablet but with more controls, that interacted with the house's systems; her fingers moved in a rapid pattern. "You girls all have your assignments," she said, dashing my hopes for some time alone with Teleza.

The three girls went in one door, and I started for another, but Teleza's mother caught my arm.

"Come to the kitchen, and I'll get you something to eat," she said to me. "And then you can go to your room or the gym."

That was one consolation. I would have the whole of the men's wing to myself. I could work out or even wander around Hobart's suite if I felt like it. Or I could stand in the gym and stare out the windows at the traffic in the suburban street next to the house like I always did when I felt like I was in jail.

For a second I considered telling Teleza's mother to have one of the girls bring my food, but I wasn't sure it would work if they had chores. Besides, I would have more food choices if I went to the kitchen myself. It was three hours at least until dinner time, and I knew I would be hungry before then.

I followed Teleza's mother into the huge kitchen. Rows of pots and pans hung from the wall above the stove, and a long counter separated the kitchen from the equally large dining room. It reminded me of Monica's grandfather's house, only bigger.

Teleza's mother went into the cold storage unit, a sort of walk-in refrigerator, and came out with a platter of leftover leg of lamb. "Would you like some bread and cheese with this?"

"Sure," I said as she sliced the lamb.

When she put out a loaf of bread, I made myself a sandwich, which made her smile.

"That's a *cruzca* way to eat. Hobart likes to do that with cold meat, too."

I wondered whether *cruzca* meant peculiar or maybe convenient. I'd have to look it up. "It's called a sandwich."

She just shook her head like it was too much trouble to learn a new word, but she got me a glass of juice and a tray, so I could take my meal back to my room and eat when I was hungry.

She also followed me through the courtyard, and I heard the steel door to the men's wing lock as soon as I went through it.

Gloom overcame me as I let myself into my room. I locked my door just for spite, but I was feeling sorry for myself in a big way until I turned and saw Teleza standing next to my bed.

"Hello," she said.

I nearly dropped the tray. "What are you doing here?"

She smiled at me and took two steps to take the tray from my hands and put it on the dresser. "I wanted to be alone with you. We've never been really alone."

It was only sort of true. We had spent a lot of time alone, but we were always in the courtyard or the sitting room or somewhere where people could walk in on us any time.

I cleared my throat. "Was there some reason you wanted to be alone?"

She lifted her face to look at me. "Do you like me, Jayzoon?"

It sounded like a trick question. "Sure. I think you're nice." And hot, but I didn't say that.

She put one hand out to touch my cheek. "We're going to be married soon."

Whoa! "I-I—uh, is that certain?"

Something very like a frown darkened her expression. She dropped her hand. "Don't you want to be married to us?"

The plural pronoun still sounded weird. "Well—"

She cut me off before I could go any farther. "Don't you want to be married to *me*?"

Substitute 'go to bed with' for 'marry' and there was no question. "Sure."

The frown eased, and a smile dawned, lighting her face and giving her a kind of glow. "I like you, too. A lot." She stroked my face again, and this time it sent shivers of anticipation up my spine. "I never met anyone like you before in my life." She glanced around the room. "Is the door locked?"

I nodded. Suddenly my heart was pounding in my chest.

She took a step closer. Her hair smelled like flowers. "No one can ever know," she whispered.

"Know what?"

She started unbuttoning her shirt—slowly, not like she was in a hurry. "I wish I was stronger," she said, "but I'm not. It's not fair that I see you every day, but I can't really touch you."

I stared at the strip of flesh that showed as she opened her blouse wider and wider. Wild thoughts flew through my head. Did I really want to do this? Would I get into trouble?

I stared as Teleza undid button after button, and I swallowed hard when she got to the last one. Ever so slowly she let the shirt slip from her shoulders. She didn't have anything on under it.

I didn't give a damn if I got into trouble. At least for once it would be worth it.

TELEZA had all her clothes back on before I did. "That was nice," she said.

I hoped it was. It had been great for me, but I wasn't entirely sure I'd done everything right as far as she was concerned. "It was wonderful."

She smiled and slid across the bed toward me, waiting until I had slipped on my shoes before she kissed me lightly. "I had better go now." She touched my lips with one fingertip. "Remember! Not a word to anyone."

I had a flash of memory—hiding in Becca's closet while her father rattled the doors. Maybe I could set something up where Hobart got mad enough to scare me into Turning?

"You won't tell, will you?" Teleza sounded as scared as I had been in Becca's closet.

"I won't tell." I felt like a douchebag for giving her a promise, knowing I'd break it if doing so would help me get home. I stood up and pulled my shirt on over my head, partly so Teleza wouldn't see my expression.

When I could see again, she had started for the bedroom door. She unlocked it and started for the corridor.

It occurred to me that if I watched her, I could learn the code that opened the outside door without setting off the alarm.

"Wait!" I said, rushing toward her.

She stopped right by the door, one hand on the latch and a pleased smile on her face.

I looked from her hand to the keypad she was ignoring. The outside door had a five-key cipher lock like a secure facility would have had in the real world. "What are you doing? Don't you know the code to open the door?"

Her smile fled as she stared up at me, her eyes widening. "I know it's locked, but you can open it from this side. You must be able to open it, in case there's a fire!"

"Sure, I can open it, but it'll set off an alarm. Hobart told me that the first day."

Her eyes widened with fear. "What?"

"You can't open the door when it's locked or it sets off the alarm."

She put one hand over her mouth. "Oh, no!" She glanced around wildly. "I have to get out! Mother will notice if I don't get my chores done."

I wasn't sure what would happen if someone found out what we'd been up to, but she was so terrified I didn't have the heart to ask her. "Get ready to run."

She looked blank.

"I'll push the door open," I said. "You run like hell for the nearest doorway and disappear as fast as you can. When your mother and your sisters show up, I'll say I was feeling cooped up and needed some air."

A smile of pure relief broke across her face. She reached up to pull my face down and gave me a swift kiss. "Thank you."

"No problem." I put both hands on the latch. "Ready?"

When she nodded, I pushed hard.

The door flew open, letting in the late afternoon sunshine and a warm breeze. An ear-splitting racket rent the air, and all the birds in the courtyard shot upward, flapping their wings like the devil was after them.

Teleza ran, her long hair flying out behind her, and her arms and legs pumping like the same devil was after her. She had barely ducked into the laundry room when her mother raced into the courtyard from the kitchen. A moment later Panya and Ulu rushed out of the sitting room door and almost collided with Teleza's mother.

"What's wrong?" the three of them all said at once.

"I'm sorry," I said. "I felt sick. I needed some air."

Teleza's mother frowned at me, but she pulled her PDA out of her pocket and did something that silenced the screech of the alarm.

"What's wrong?" Teleza burst out of the kitchen, sounding genuinely breathless, like she'd been running hard.

"Nothing," her mother said. She slipped one hand onto my forehead in a maternal gesture. "You don't have a fever, Jayzoon."

"I feel better already," I said. "Maybe it was something I ate?"

"Next time, open a window," Teleza's mother said, a frown hovering over her face.

"I'm sorry I disturbed everyone," I said. "I didn't know the noise would be that bad."

"Maybe you should lie down," Panya said. "You do look flushed."

I wouldn't let myself meet Teleza's eyes. "I think you're right, Panya."

"Go back inside then," Teleza's mother said. "And I'll reset the lock."

I apologized again, and ducked back inside, leaving the four of them standing in the courtyard. A second later I heard the lock thunk behind me.

Once I was back in my room, I ate my sandwich, and then I leaned back on my pillow and stared at the calendar on the wall where I had marked off every day since I got to Makoro. Fifty-seven days since I had Turned. Here in Egume, where there were thirteen lunar months, it was the middle of *Okello*. In Maryland it would be the last week in November. At Clara Barton High School, homecoming was over. Probably we'd lost the game—our football team sucked—and most likely Monica had found someone to take advantage of a free limo ride and gotten a date.

But had Ryan and Allie done it that night? Was I first to get laid or was he? Even though I might never see Ryan again, it bothered me not to know.

Teleza's mother came and got me at dinner time, and the five of us ate at the kitchen table. I tried not to stare at Teleza, but it was hard not to, now that I knew what she looked like naked.

Teleza's mother locked me up again after dinner, but I didn't mind so much this time. I lay on my bed and thought about how great the day had been. After a little while I tried to sleep, but then I heard the gates clang. When I opened my eyes the lights of three hovercars swept across my wall. Adeola and the others were back from the Assembly. I smiled to myself and reached over to the bedside table where I'd left the torn foil wrapper from my one and only condom. I couldn't bring myself to throw away anything from home—well, not something so inoffensive. I had buried the used condom in the trash can to be sure no one ever saw it. But the scrap of foil had been with me for months and I hated to part with it, even if it was useless and would get me into trouble if someone found it.

Or would it? Teleza had never heard of condoms. She hadn't even thought about birth control until I mentioned it. And as terrified as she was that someone might find out about us, she hadn't given a thought to the risk of getting pregnant.

I slid the remains of the foil wrapper under the mattress. I could hear Gyasi and Kafele chattering away outside my window. It sounded like they'd had a great time at the Assembly.

I'd had a pretty good time staying home. Sex was a lot more fun with a girl in the room.

THE effects of getting laid lasted three days. After the third day, I went back to lifting weights to make myself less restless. It made me good and tired, but I was still on edge.

That night at dinner, I noticed that Hobart kept watching me. Whenever I turned my head, I'd catch him staring, and then he'd look away.

After the girls had cleared the table, we all sat and drank cups of hot herbal tea. It was Teleza's turn to help with the dishes, so I watched her heft trays and wipe down the tables. Once she dropped a fork and bent down to pick it up, giving me a great view of her ass when she did it.

As soon as Hobart got up to leave, everyone else stood up. Before I could go two steps Hobart caught up with me and put his right arm around my shoulder.

"Did you enjoy dinner?" he said, steering me toward the door to the corridor.

"Sure," I said as we stepped into the hallway. It was raining so no one used the courtyard shortcut. Kafele and Gyasi ran ahead of us; Gyasi was pretending he was a hovercar, and Kafele was pretending he was too old for that kind of game.

"So, Jason," Hobart said, and it occurred to me he was speaking to me in English for the first time in days, "care to tell me what else—or rather who else—you've been enjoying?"

I swallowed but didn't say anything. How had he found out?

Hobart tightened his grip on my shoulder and then held out his left hand. When he opened his fist, there was the crumpled foil wrapper I had hidden under the mattress.

"In Egume," Hobart said, "people think it's good to turn the mattress every week or so—makes it last longer."

Whoever did that chore—it would never be Hobart—had found the wrapper and given it to him—or to Adeola and she'd given it to him.

"They don't have condoms here," Hobart said. "Not much need, really. Married women use birth control when they need it, but not condoms."

He looked a little worried, maybe even annoyed, but in spite of his grip on my shoulder, he was far from angry—nothing like Becca's father rattling the doors of her closet. So much for using Hobart to scare me into Turning.

"To repeat myself," Hobart went on when I didn't speak, "which of my daughters got lucky?"

My head reeled at having this discussion. "Does it matter?"

He sighed and let go of me. "Of course it matters. If nothing else, I need to know who I should chew out."

The world was spinning. I'd gotten laid, and it was the girl who was getting blamed for it.

"I suppose I could lecture them all," Hobart said. "But then they'd all know what happened."

"Teleza," I blurted out. "But it wasn't her idea, it was mine."

He nodded. "I suspected it was her after I watched her drop that fork tonight."

It took me a second to figure out he meant Teleza had dropped the fork on purpose. The idea made me feel pretty smug.

Hobart frowned. "I was hoping it was Zuwina. That would have been one less problem, anyway."

I guessed he meant that Teleza was too young to fool around. I certainly had never paid much attention to Zuwina, even when she was home, which wasn't often. Adeola spent a lot of time giving her lessons on household management or something.

"In less than a year you'll be old enough to get married," Hobart said. "The Council has confirmed my daughters as a household, and they have first dibs on you, but you have to keep it in your pants until then."

My heart caught in my throat. They planned to marry me off to Teleza *and* her sisters and no one was asking me what I wanted.

"Don't look so scared," Hobart said. "None of my girls would ever hurt you. You like them, don't you?"

"How—how many?" I croaked. Hobart had twelve daughters. The youngest was six and the oldest was twenty-three. All of the three oldest girls worked, Zuwina full time, and Bolade and Jumoke in internships after college classes, so none of them were around as much as the younger ones. "How many of your daughters do you mean?"

He flinched a little at my tone. "Just the six oldest ones." He turned his head away like he didn't want to look at me. "That way we'd have room to add an unrelated woman or two to the household if we needed to."

I didn't even ask why they might want or need to do that. I could barely breathe.

"Are you okay?" Hobart asked.

"Yes." I wasn't though. I had six intended brides. I tried to imagine what it would be like to have them each come in turn to my room every night. My head reeled at the thought. Teleza was totally hot, Panya and Ulu were cute, and none of the others was exactly ugly, even if Zuwina seemed on the severe side sometimes.

Maybe Hobart was right and I was lucky to have Turned here?

It could have been a lot worse.

IT was only two nights after Hobart found me out that I was interrupted as I got ready for bed. I had just pulled off my shirt and tossed it on a chair when a knock sounded on my door.

The men's wing was already in lockdown so I figured it had to be one or both of the boys. Hobart would doubtless have company by now.

I started to yell for them to come in, then realized the automatic lock on my door would have clicked only a few minutes before, so I went to open it.

Zuwina stood there in a long gray bathrobe. Her black hair, which she usually wore pinned up, was down around her shoulders and her feet were bare.

I felt my jaw drop. "What are you doing here?"

She pushed the door open the rest of the way and stepped past me into the room. "I'm restoring *haru.*"

I had no clue what she meant. I also felt a little awkward with no shirt on, but I didn't want to look shy by putting it back on. "What?"

She turned and pushed the door shut, keeping her hand on it until the lock clicked. "I'm here to restore *haru.*" When I didn't say anything she made an impatient tisking noise with her tongue. "First Mother told me what happened between you and Teleza."

I gritted my teeth at the idea that Adeola and the rest of the household were talking about me and Teleza. "It was none of her business."

Zuwina's eyes opened wide. "How can you say that?" She crossed her arms over her chest, which made her bathrobe gape a little, and I saw that she had a lacy black nightgown on underneath it. "First Mother is within her rights to insist that *haru* be restored. I will be senior in our household, and Teleza should never have tried to deprive me of my place."

I knit my brows, trying to figure it out. "So *you're* mad at me because I had sex with Teleza?"

She snorted. "I'm angry at Teleza for not honoring her obligations. She should have been fifth for you, and not first."

It occurred to me that they were assuming I had arrived in their house as a virgin. They were right, of course, but it still annoyed me. "And that's it? There's no problem because of my age?"

Zuwina waved one hand. "That's a consideration, of course. First Mother has already appealed to the Ocan Garun to declare you legally of age. Once that happens, we can hold a proper wedding."

"How—how long will that take?"

She seemed unconcerned. "A few months, perhaps."

"A few months?" Somehow it sounded awfully soon. They might actually hit my real seventeenth birthday in March.

She nodded. "In the meantime, we must work on restoring *haru*."

I cleared my throat, which seemed suddenly dry. "And how do we do that."

She pulled off her robe. Static electricity made the nightgown cling in nice ways, hugging the curve of her hips, and the round, perfect mounds of her breasts. "By having sex." She looked me up and down. "Take off your pants."

I didn't like her tone, but the sight of her body under her gown made it difficult for me to care. I had started to undo my pants buttons when I remembered I had used my only condom. "Oh!"

Zuwina was watching me. "What's wrong?"

"I don't—" I started to say. "I mean, should we use some, um, protection?" I wasn't sure they called it that. AIDS and other STDs didn't seem to be a problem here. And Hobart had said there were no condoms.

One corner of Zuwina's mouth pulled up in a near sneer. "You don't need to worry. I've taken care of that."

My only qualm evaporated. Zuwina stepped closer. Her hands reached out to stroke my sides.

"I thought I would have to wait almost a year for this," she said. "In a way, I'm glad Teleza was so weak."

I wanted to say that Teleza hadn't been weak, she just liked me a lot, but I couldn't make myself string the words into a sentence.

And then Zuwina moved one hand down to my waist and undid the last button on my pants. I wrapped my arms around her and pulled her close against me, feeling the smooth sleekness of her nightgown against my skin.

Makoro wasn't such a bad place.

WHEN I woke up the next morning, Zuwina was gone. I sat down to breakfast in a thoughtful frame of mind. Would everyone know what had happened? If Adeola had given permission for Zuwina to visit me the night before, then she must know, but who else had she told? I glanced around the dining room. Adeola was deep in conversation with two of Hobart's other wives. Panya and Ulu were busy clearing empty plates and platters from the tables. No one was paying me any attention.

No, wait! Bolade, the second oldest daughter, was smiling at me in an inviting way from her place beside her next younger sister Jumoke. Had Zuwina told Bolade we had slept together?

I finished my food, and waited for some sign that she knew. Sure enough, Bolade made a point to brush against the back of my chair on her way out the door. She didn't say anything to me when I looked up. She just lifted her brows and gave me an even warmer smile, then left the dining room without a word.

I had lessons with Hobart that morning—the history of Egume. It wasn't too bad since it started with the Great Folly.

"So no one bothers to learn what happened before the plague hit?" I asked Hobart.

He looked up from his book. "Most of the records from before then were lost in the Rage."

I cleared my throat. "Speaking of rage, why is Zuwina so mad at Teleza?"

Hobart froze for a second, and then he shut his book. "It's because of *haru*."

I didn't get it. "But doesn't that just mean they'll all be my wives?"

He shook his head like I was being dense. "It's not really to do with you directly. *Haru* is the relationship between the wives in a household—even one without a husband. When households form between unrelated women, the order of *haru* can be affected by income, social status, even education. But when *haru* are sisters, the order is usually determined strictly by age."

I finally got it. "So Zuwina is in a snit because she thinks Teleza was trying to make herself my senior wife?"

Hobart nodded, something close to a smile on his face. "Adeola assured her that won't happen. Zuwina will get over it eventually. Sometimes it's rougher when all the wives in a household are sisters. That's why we might invite another woman in later, if things get tense."

I wondered about it all day. I was half expecting a knock on my door that night, but when it got late and Zuwina didn't come, I took off my clothes and climbed into bed.

Almost at once a knock sounded.

I got out of bed and debated, then grabbed a robe from the closet just in case.

When I opened the door, it wasn't Zuwina standing there, it was Bolade.

"Oh!" I must have looked surprised because she frowned. "Come in," I said at once.

She stepped through the doorway. Like Zuwina she had come barefoot, and wearing a robe and a nightgown, but her robe was pink and white flannel over a pink cotton gown. "You must have known it was my turn."

I felt pretty dumb for not figuring it out. "Sure I did. I was just surprised because you're here so late."

She flushed and looked mortified. "I forgot the door code, and I had to find Adeola to ask her what it was."

I pricked up my ears at this mention of the code that opened the door that Hobart's wives used to visit him. They always came in the upstairs door from the main house. "I can never remember numbers myself."

She nodded. "Words are easier. Numbers are too difficult."

I was trying to think of a way to find out about the code—how many numbers it was, for instance—when Bolade slipped off her robe, and then pulled her nightgown over her head and let it follow her robe to the floor. She stood there naked, with her head tilted to one side while she looked at me.

All I could do was stare. I hadn't realized she was so stacked under the prim clothes she wore to class and to work. She had long legs, a slender neck, a great tan, and no tan lines. I licked my suddenly dry lips.

"Are you ready?" she asked.

And just like that, I was.

THE next day I felt great. I had had sex three times with three different girls, and it wasn't anywhere near my seventeenth birthday yet. Besides, if last night had been Bolade's turn, then tonight Jumoke would visit me, then Ulu, and then it would be Teleza's turn again. Sex with her had been nicer—not that I minded having to sleep with the others, too.

I spent the day in a pleasant fog. Hobart seemed annoyed with me, but I didn't care.

"Pay attention, will you!" he almost yelled at me in *jin-weh* class. He always used a long stick as a pointer to tap whatever body part needed adjusting, and now he rapped it against my shoulder blades harder than he ever had.

I flinched and tried to make myself care about the proper way to punch and kick the air in front of me.

"That's enough," Hobart said with an abrupt gesture. "Your mind's not on this exercise."

I stopped where I was and tried to get my breath back. "Why are you so mad at me?"

He glared for a moment, then looked away. "I shouldn't be. It wasn't your idea to put *haru* before the law any more than it was mine."

I had that familiar feeling of not knowing what the hell someone was talking about even when I understood the words. "What does that mean?"

Hobart sighed, and tapped the long stick on the floor. "It means Adeola values *haru* more than staying legal. You're our ward, and she shouldn't allow the girls to sleep with you before the wedding." He looked away again. "For one thing, Panya is too young."

I had been so focused on Teleza coming to my room again, I hadn't thought about Panya. "She's only five months younger than Teleza."

"True," Hobart said. "But five months is a lot at her age. And she's shyer than Teleza, and not as mature."

I couldn't think of anything to say to that, so I said nothing.

Hobart started for the door. "I'm going to take a shower. You can amuse yourself."

I lifted weights for a while, and then when I was good and tired, I followed Hobart's example and took a shower myself.

I didn't see Teleza that afternoon; she kept to her room. I saw her at dinner, but she was serving, and she didn't say more than two words when she passed me the platter of chicken kebabs.

Jumoke, on the other hand, chatted away and kept smiling at me. I was glad I had figured out the taking turns thing, so her attention didn't make me paranoid. I smiled back, but I wished Teleza was next in line instead of Jumoke.

Sure enough, Jumoke appeared at my door as expected. It went okay. I enjoyed myself thoroughly, and I was even sort of used to having a woman sleep next to me all night. Makoro seemed like a wonderful place.

The only thing was the daytime hours dragged slowly, because I could hardly wait for the nighttime. I couldn't concentrate on any studies, and Hobart didn't try to make me. Teleza and the other girls, on the other hand, had exams, and were very busy. Teleza barely said a word to me that day. I hoped she wasn't jealous.

When I opened my door that night and saw Ulu standing there, I felt almost guilty for noticing that her golden brown hair gleamed like amber in the lamplight, and her skin glowed with a beautiful creamy luminescence.

Ulu seemed less pleased with the circumstances. Her expression could only be called pained. "I have a history exam tomorrow," she said, stepping into my room. She wore striped pajamas with no robe, but she had encased her feet in wool slippers. "Can we get this over with quickly?"

Her tone stung. She sounded like I was a dentist or something equally less welcome. I tried my best to make sure she was as turned on as I was, but I wasn't sure I succeeded. She slipped out of bed just as I was drifting off to sleep, and I heard the upstairs door click a minute later.

It was still sex, so I wasn't complaining, but I was really glad Teleza would be coming to see me the next night.

But when I opened the door the night after Ulu's visit, it wasn't Teleza standing there, it was Panya. Her black hair hung down on her shoulders and gleamed in the light from my bedside lamp. She wore a high-necked but rather thin white nightgown that set off the blackness of her hair and showed how nice her shape was.

It took me a second to notice that her eyes looked suspiciously wet. I realized she was about to cry.

Nine

I didn't know what to say. "Uh, hello."

Panya bit her lip.

"Uh, where's—" I stopped, not sure what was good manners in this situation. "Um, is it your turn? I thought Teleza would be next."

Her eyes welled up even more, and her lower lip trembled.

"Come in," I said, suddenly aware that one of the boys could come into the hallway at any moment.

When I stepped back, Panya advanced into the room with tiny, timid steps.

"Teleza—" She swallowed, wiped her eyes, started over. "Teleza doesn't get another turn. Adeola said we should each have one turn before the wedding, to restore *haru*, but Teleza already had hers."

Damn! Tonight was it, and then I'd have to wait months to get laid again. Oh, well. At least I'd have a steady supply after that, and Teleza would be back in line again. "Oh, I see."

She looked down at her feet.

"What's wrong?" I said.

She lifted her eyes. "It's not that I don't like you. But I'm not—not ready to—"

I got it. She looked so scared, it was difficult for me to be turned on anymore. Besides, I had really wanted Teleza. "Don't worry about it. We don't have to do anything."

She opened her mouth in an O of surprise. "We don't?"

I put one arm around her. "Of course not." I walked her toward the door. "You run on back to your own room, and everything will be fine."

She stopped in her tracks. "But I can't go back to my room. Adeola scolded Ulu for not staying the night. I have to sleep here."

I looked her slender body up and down. There was no way I was sleeping next to her all night with nothing happening. I sighed mentally, but tried to speak cheerfully. "You can have the bed. I'll sleep on the floor."

She gave me a happy smile and hugged me. Feeling the warmth of her body through the thin nightgown, I was tempted to change my mind, but I resisted.

I got the extra blanket out of the closet and curled up on the carpet. It would be a long night; I had really been looking forward to Teleza's visit.

Panya slipped out the next morning, and I took my usual shower before breakfast.

I glanced around at the four tables as I ate my porridge. Everything looked normal. Gyasi and Kafele were quarreling over which of them got the last mango slice, and the little girls were either talking among themselves or intent on their food.

Ulu had just finished serving thick hunks of crusty bread while Panya was still passing around bowls of honey mixed with melted butter. Panya smiled at me while she held the bowl out for me, a warm, grateful smile.

"Thanks," I said, returning the spoon. I glanced over at Zuwina, who sat in her usual place across from Adeola. She smiled at me, too, but her smile held more self-confidence than warmth.

I wasn't prepared to smile back at Zuwina, so I looked away, and somehow my eyes met Teleza's. Teleza looked mortified for a second, and then her eyes dropped to her lap.

I noticed she hadn't eaten more than two bites of her porridge. Adeola turned her head and said something to Teleza, and then Teleza got up and went into the kitchen. She came back with the teapot and poured some tea into Adeola's cup, and then she sat down without a word. Hobart asked her some questions about school, which she answered so quietly I couldn't hear her.

I munched my bread and honey and tried to figure it out. After everyone had finished and Hobart had risen to signal the end of the meal, Teleza jumped to her feet and darted out of the room.

I followed her into the corridor. "Teleza!"

She turned, and I saw her eyes had welled up. She looked as sick at heart as Panya had the night before.

"What's wrong?" I asked. "Are you mad at me or something?"

She shook her head. "I can't speak to you alone. First Mother has forbidden it."

"What?"

She put one hand over her mouth for a second. "I'm so sorry." She swallowed. "I shouldn't have done it. It wasn't good *haru*. I knew that. I deserve to be punished."

"Punished?" I said.

She nodded. "Even after the wedding I won't have a turn for months—until Zuwina decides to forgive me."

"Zuwina decides?" Zuwina got to say whose turn it was, not me. That did not sound good.

"Of course." She let out a profound sigh and darted off.

I went looking for Zuwina and found her in her room. The door was open, and she was putting papers and gadgets into a sort of briefcase. She looked up when I stepped into the doorway, and a slow, pleased-with-herself smile spread across her face.

She had nice, dark eyes, and white, even teeth. When she straightened up, I couldn't help but notice that her tunic was open a few buttons.

"Hello, Jayzoon."

"Hello." Somehow, now that I had seen Zuwina naked, it was difficult not to think of her that way.

"Did you want something?"

I remembered Teleza's distress. "Uh, yes, I did. I wanted to ask—" I stopped.

She lifted her dark, arched brows. "Yes?"

"Um, is it true you told Teleza she wouldn't get to—uh—to have a turn spending the night with me after we—" suddenly I wasn't sure what pronoun to use. "Um—"

Zuwina laughed. "Did I tell Teleza that even after our wedding she had to wait until I felt *haru* had been restored before she was allowed to share you?" She nodded. "Of course I did."

Her calm self assurance irked me. "Don't I get any say in that?"

She opened her eyes wide. "Don't be silly. What does a man have to do with *haru*?"

"But—but I'm the one who's being shared!"

She reached over and patted my face. "I know that, silly one. But I'm the one who'll be your senior wife and first mother to all our children." She twisted her face into a thoughtful scowl. "I think we should have a child right away. This year isn't a good time for me, but Bolade will be finished with school and could take a few years off. She might even decide she likes being house bound."

I goggled at her, but she just looked me up and down.

"I have to go to work now," she said. "Why don't you spend some time in the gym and build up your strength?"

I stood there with my mouth open while she brushed past me on her way out the door.

Sex every night or not, I wasn't happy.

I thought it over as I lay in bed that night—alone at last. Did I want to stay in Makoro and turn into another version of Hobart, amusing myself all day and letting six women take turns entertaining me at night? It sounded like a great life, put that way, but I didn't think I'd like it.

For one thing, Zuwina would make all my decisions, even whether—or rather when—to have children. And she seemed to want that to be soon. I tried to imagine myself living as Hobart lived—always staying home, only leaving under armed guard, letting Zuwina tell me and everyone else what to do. I wasn't sure I liked the picture,

If I wanted out, I had to get out soon. Once the wedding happened, I'd never spend a night alone, and a daytime escape would be too risky. If I got out into the city in the daytime, I'd be caught right away.

Besides, if Zuwina had her way, I'd be a father before I knew it, and the last thing I wanted was to run out on a kid the way my dad had run out on me.

I started watching the household routine, trying to figure out everyone's role. I discovered that Adeola set the schedule. She left for her high-powered job in the city right after breakfast and came home right before dinner—we always waited if she was late. No one ever sat down at the table until she was home, not even Hobart.

About three hours after we ate, Adeola would sound the curfew bell. Then she'd make a circuit of the house, checking the front gates to be sure they were locked. Finally, she would check all the doors and windows that opened onto the courtyard. The men's wing windows didn't have locks, but that didn't matter because of the bars on the outside.

Hobart was always in his room well before curfew. Adeola might be making his decisions for him, but he didn't seem to mind. During the day, he spent a lot of time with the two boys and the younger girls, but when the older girls came home from school and later when Zuwina and the others came home from work, Hobart always greeted them and asked each of them about her day. When Adeola came home, Hobart met her, too, greeting her just as affectionately as he did any of the others.

I had everyone's schedule scoped out, but I still couldn't come up with a plan for how not to turn into Hobart. Then one night at the dinner table Zuwina started talking about how she wanted to remodel the house to make new quarters for me. She had clearly spent some time thinking about how that could be accomplished in a way that gave me enough space, even though she had never mentioned it to me. She went on and on about it, but she never once asked my opinion.

Adeola merely nodded at Zuwina's description of her plans, even when it became clear that Kafele and Gyasi would need to move into the small room I now occupied, and their current room and part of the gym would become my new suite. Both boys looked glum.

"We'll have to find an architect," Adeola said. "I've seen houses where they tried to skimp on remodeling to start a secondary household. It never works."

"I don't need a lot of room," I said. "I'm fine where I am."

Zuwina paid no attention. "Who did the house we visited last *Wahlau*? She did an excellent job, whoever it was."

Adeola nodded. "I agree. I'll have to ask."

Hobart shot me a sympathetic glance. "Don't worry about it, Jason. Weddings bring out the side of women's nature that likes to rearrange things."

Zuwina sniffed and lifted her chin. She glared in Teleza's direction. "I believe in order and protocol."

Gyasi stood up. "Why do you want to take our room? You have your own room, Zuwina. You're the only girl who does."

Zuwina stiffened; her jaw clenched in indignation. "It's not for *me*. Once Jayzoon is a married man, he'll need proper quarters."

"I don't need more room than I have now," I said.

She turned her head to glare at me. "I know what's due to my husband, even if you don't."

Adeola stood up. "Enough. No more quarreling. I will find an architect, and then Zuwina and I will discuss our plans with her. Until then we won't speak of this."

No one said anything for a moment, and then Hobart turned to Kafele and started to talk about fencing.

I went outside and stood in the middle of the courtyard and looked up at the stars.

They were beautiful—sparkling white diamonds on black velvet. The night air smelled of flowers and fresh-baked bread, and the fountain trickled pleasantly. I found Orion's Belt in the sky, a familiar touch that made me homesick.

The sky might be open and free, but I wasn't. I was stuck in this house spending every day of my life with nineteen females—two of them very bossy—three guys—none my age—and no decent music.

It seemed like spitting in the face of good luck, but I had to get out. Not even sex every night was worth living the rest of my life inside these same four walls and taking orders from a woman who acted like I was a toddler and she was my nanny.

The only thing was, where could I go?

I SPENT some time online looking up information about what was around the city of Egume. The rest of the State was mostly agricultural, with numerous towns and villages scattered throughout, but there were wilderness areas. In the foothills north of the city, where a mountain range formed the border with Dodomah, there didn't seem to be any towns or even farms.

I decided the best thing to do would be to get out of the city at night and hide in a rural area during the daytime, trying to work my way north at night. If I could manage to reach the mountains, I might be able to find a situation where I could scare myself into Turning without actually killing myself.

I had to find a way to escape the men's wing first. The downstairs door opened onto the courtyard, and one on the second floor led to the hallway to the women's bedrooms. I had asked Hobart what the key codes were to open the cipher locks, and he'd looked me right in the eye and said he didn't know.

But even if I did get out of the men's wing, all the doors to the street were kept locked, and keys were in short supply. Even the older girls had to ring to get in when they came home from school. I needed some way out of the house that wasn't a door.

One night, about eight days after Panya had visited me, I let myself out of my room. The upstairs door opened every night and every morning; I just needed to find out how. Fortunately, all the corridors had night lights for safety reasons, so I didn't have to turn on a light. I crept up the stairs, headed for the broom closet between the door to the main house and the door to Hobart's suite.

Just as I stepped up to the closet, the lock on the door to the main part of the house clicked. I ripped open the closet door and whacked myself in the head trying to duck inside. I stifled a curse and ducked under the shelf as I jumped into the closet and swung the door shut behind me.

I managed to catch the bucket on the floor before I knocked it over, and I crouched there, my heart pounding, praying that whoever had opened the door hadn't seen me. The closet had no keyhole, so I was totally in the dark. I cracked the door open a tiny bit and saw a flash of blue going past me. I opened the door a little wider and saw Teleza's mother knock on Hobart's door. She was wearing a filmy sort of nightgown that would have made me check her out if I hadn't been scared shitless.

Hobart opened the door, wearing nothing but loose pants that looked like pajama bottoms. When Teleza's mother stepped into his room, he slipped an arm around her as he closed the door.

I figured they were set for the night, so I opened the closet door enough that I could see to explore the enclosed space. The shelf held cleaning supplies, the space under it, mops, brooms, a bucket, and a step stool. I rearranged things so I had more room and made myself as comfortable as I could on the stool. I propped myself against the wall and closed the closet door almost all the way, leaving just a tiny crack so I would hear when Teleza's mother left Hobart's room.

Sitting in the near darkness reminded me of being trapped in Becca Sommers' closet while her father rattled the doors. I had been scared then, and I was scared now, but for totally different reasons. I figured if Adeola or the other wives found me, I'd be locked up even tighter, and lose my only chance at getting out.

"SEE you at breakfast, sweetie."

I sat up with a jerk, wondering if Mom was talking to me or to Lorrie, and realized abruptly that I'd been dreaming of home, and in fact it wasn't my mother talking but Teleza's, in Neluan instead of English.

A crack of light poured into the closet as I leaned over to peer through the door. I bumped a broom handle and it fell. I caught the broom right before it hit the wall. I heard a door close, and then saw another flash of blue as I pressed my eye to the crack in the doorway. Having waited all night to watch Teleza's mother work the door lock, I didn't want to miss it.

Her hand poised over the keypad and then swiftly keyed the code. I mentally repeated the pattern to myself—one, one, five, three, two. I wasn't sure that's what she had pressed, but if it wasn't exact, it was close. The ease with which she did it reassured me. It didn't look like they changed the code often because she hadn't stopped to think.

As soon as she was through, I dashed out of the closet and down the stairs. I was just about to turn toward my own room when the door to the courtyard opened at the end of the hallway. I darted across the corridor to the bathroom. Unlike Hobart, the boys and I had to share a bathroom, so I did have an excuse to be out of my room.

I had made it to the bathroom door when Adeola's voice came from behind me.

"You're up early, Jayzoon."

I glanced over my shoulder. "I didn't sleep well." I turned back to the bathroom. "Sorry, I've got to—" I stopped when I realized I didn't know the Neluan word for taking a leak. I'd have to ask Hobart that one.

Adeola laughed and started up the stairs. I let myself into the bathroom. I really did have to pee, but it was difficult to do it while I was still shaking.

I SPENT the rest of that day making plans and looking for supplies. I figured with everyone planning for *Wahlau* in two days, they'd be too busy to worry about what I was up to. Scavenging proved difficult, though, because everyone I met kept asking me if I needed anything. I did, but except for some food, it wasn't anything I could ask them for.

After dinner I walked back to the men's wing with Hobart. As usual, Kafele and Gyasi raced ahead of us through the courtyard. Hobart watched them with an affectionate grin.

"Doesn't it bother you that both your sons will be married off as soon as they turn seventeen?" I blurted out.

He turned toward me and gave me a long gaze, and then he shook his head. "Nope," he said in English. "It's what they expect—what they look forward to. This world has its own rules." He nodded at the two boys as they disappeared into a doorway. "That's why they go to assemblies, so they can meet other families, maybe make friends—with girls as well as boys."

He seemed so truly okay with the situation that it made me wonder if I could ever feel that way. "But don't you ever wish you were back home with just one wife that you cared about?"

One corner of his mouth pulled up in a lop-sided grin. "Son, I was lucky to come here. I had nothing back in Fort Stockton—dead end job in a gas station, no education, no girlfriend, no family except a drunk mother and a father who beat her up." He looked around at the courtyard. The light that lit the walkway made shadows on the walls, and the cool breeze carried the scent of the late-blooming flowers. "Here I have a huge family who all care about me and want to take care of me. I have time to read about things I'm interested in, work out when I feel like it, and talk to my kids any time they need me."

I didn't say anything, but I was thinking about our apartment back in Bethesda, and Mom and Lorrie and even Sancho.

"I know it's harder for you because you miss your family," Hobart went on, his voice gentle, "but since you can't get back, you're better off here with my girls." He grinned even wider, the happy grin of a man who was pleased with life. "And besides, a man here gets sex every single night that he wants it."

Okay, that part sounded great, but I had already seen the down side of not being able to choose who I'd be in bed with.

That night, I lay fully dressed in my Makoron clothes and waited until I heard someone knock on Hobart's door. After it opened and closed again, I got up and put on my jeans, my tee shirt, and my denim jacket. I had to wear Makoron shoes, though, because my sneakers had worn out.

I took my supplies from my hiding place in the back of the closet. I had filched a knife from the kitchen, a piece of fabric from the sewing room, and, most importantly, a length of rope from the laundry room. When I had told Panya I was hungry, she had made me a sandwich, shaking her head at my odd food choices. I had wrapped the sandwich in a cloth napkin and stowed it away. I used the length of fabric to fashion a sort of padded sheath for the knife, so I wouldn't stab myself to death carrying it around in my pocket.

I wasn't sure if there was anywhere in Makoro that I could hide, but I planned to try—if I could get out of this house.

When I let myself out of my room, the house was quiet. I crept up the stairs as quietly as I could. I heard a low laugh when I passed Hobart's room, but luckily no one appeared on the landing. When I got to the door to the main wing it took me three tries to get the key code right. I was getting panicked when I finally heard a click, and then I opened the door.

I stepped through, still moving as quietly as I could, and walked down the corridor. I'd been there lots of times, in the daytime, but never this late. I didn't hear voices, but a light shone from under the door to the room Teleza shared with Panya and Ulu. I crept past it trying not to let my shoes make any noise.

Finally, I came to the end of the corridor and the tiny back stairs that led to the attic. No one had bothered to show it to me, but I had noticed that stairway on my own.

I put my foot on the first step and started to climb. As soon as I put my weight on the step, it creaked loudly. I froze.

Nothing. No sounds of inquiry, no lights from doors opening. I tried putting my foot on the far side of each step instead of in the middle. The stairs still creaked, but not as loudly. I made myself slow down, moving like I was in slow motion, and that helped more. It seemed like hours before I made it to the landing. Then, finally, I was at the top of the steps.

I put my hand on the latch of the attic door and tried to push down. It wouldn't budge. The door was locked.

"Fuck!" I whispered furiously.

I crouched on the top step and wedged the tip of the knife between the doorframe and the door. I took me awhile, especially because I kept looking over my shoulder, but eventually I was able to push the bolt back with the tip of the knife. I held it there with one hand and pushed the door open with the other.

I cringed when the hinges let out a long, painful squeal. I left the door open, partly so I'd have some light, but mostly so it wouldn't squeak again.

Moving through the attic felt spooky; it was full of dark corners and odd, shadowy shapes. The room, a big open space, ran the whole length of the house. Small gabled windows on either side of it let in a little bit of light. I looked around as I walked in. Boxes, trunks, and all kinds of assorted junk filled the floor space. At least the floor was solid; the walls were rough and there was no ceiling, just the roof joists.

I put the knife back in its homemade sheath and tiptoed over to the nearest window. It overlooked the courtyard. Not good. I checked the other side, but that overlooked the same busy street the gym did. Not much better. At the far end of the room I found a window that overlooked an alley at the back of the house.

Fortunately, the window lock was a simple twist latch. The wood squeaked when I opened it, but not as badly as the door had. I looked down. No sign of anyone or anything moving in the alley.

I set my shoulders and took a deep breath. Time to get going. I tucked the knife into a jacket pocket, checked that my sandwich was in the other jacket pocket, and then started to drag the largest trunk I could find over to the open window. The noise sounded deafening to me, but I told myself that was just because the house was so quiet and sound echoed in the open space of the attic. When I got the trunk close, I took the rope I'd stolen from the laundry room and tied one end to the handle of the trunk. I threw the other end out the window. When I looked down, it looked like the rope reached all the way to the ground, but it was hard to be sure.

I thought back to gym class, and every movie with a mountain climbing scene I'd ever seen. I'd finally managed to climb a rope in gym, but I'd never had to rappel down a wall before.

I figured there had to be a first time, so I wrapped the rope loosely around my left wrist and threw my right leg out the window. The window was small enough that I had to scrunch over, and it was a good thing I was so thin. I grabbed the rope a little farther down with my right hand, leaned away from the house to test my grip, and then pulled my other leg over the window ledge.

I damn near fell right there. The rope slid through my hands—I'd never thought about rope burns until then—for a few seconds, until I tightened my grip. Finally, I got both feet against the wall and stopped myself from sliding. I didn't so much rappel as inch my way down the side of the house. When I was still several feet from the ground, I realized the rope was slipping—not through my hands but from the window!

A loud screeching noise sounded a little like someone using power tools. I realized the trunk was scraping the floor, so I tried to go faster. There was a thunk like the trunk had hit an obstacle but the rope kept slipping. The knot had come untied! I pushed out from the wall with my feet, let go, and dropped to the ground with my knees bent.

The fall was enough that I fell over onto the pavement and scraped my knees just as the rope fell on my head. "Shit!"

"I don't know what that means," a woman's voice said in Neluan, "but I thought you'd never make it down."

I scrambled to my feet. For a second I thought it was Adeola or someone from her household, and then I realized the woman was a stranger, and she wasn't alone.

And then the two of them dropped a bag over my head and everything went black.

Ten

In spite of the fact that I couldn't see a thing through the bag that covered my head, the two women made me walk damn fast. They tugged me along by the rope they had tied my hands with, the same rope I had stolen from the laundry room. I could hear everything they said, but I couldn't talk because every time I tried to make any noise one of them would muffle my face with the bag until I couldn't breathe. After the third time I got the idea and kept quiet.

"I've been thinking, Esi," the first woman said after a few minutes. "It's not safe to take him past the camp."

The second woman snorted. "Very true." A hand patted my shoulder. "If we want to profit from this gift that dropped from heaven we need to keep him to ourselves until we can find a buyer."

A buyer? That didn't sound good. It made me feel like a used car.

"You're right," the first woman said. "Is it even safe to take him home?"

Esi must have pondered her answer because there was a pause before she spoke. "I think so. We're far enough from the camp that no one could hear him even if he screamed."

Why would I scream? What did they have in mind? I could feel my forehead sweating inside the bag.

"If we go the long way round no one will see us," the first woman said. "But we won't get any dinner."

"I'll go and fetch it after we're home," Esi said, "as soon as we get him safely tied up."

We walked for at least an hour after that. I had no idea what direction we went, but I could smell woodsy smells so I didn't think it was back toward the city. I kept tripping because I couldn't see where I was going. Every time I fell one of them would haul me to my feet. I was exhausted, and I still had no clue where they were taking me. All I learned was that the first woman's name was Marjani.

"Here we are," Esi said at last. "Let's get him inside."

"Mind your step, young man," Marjani added.

"I can't fucking see!" I had learned the Neluan version of the f-word only a week ago when Gyasi accidentally hit Hobart in the crotch during a *jin-weh* match. I hadn't expected to need to swear so badly so soon after I had learned how.

Esi chuckled. "You do speak Neluan. I wondered. Well, lift your feet, then. There's a step here."

I lifted my foot, wondering why neither of them seemed to be opening a door. I climbed a single uneven stair and then took a few hesitant steps with one of them pulling me along.

It got suddenly cooler and slightly damper.

"Sit here." Esi pushed down on my shoulder.

I sank down slowly and found myself sitting on something cold and hard. "Can you take the bag off, please?"

"What do you think, Marjani?"

"He won't fetch much of a price if he accidentally suffocates."

A few seconds later the bag was pulled off my head, but it was still so dark it didn't make much difference. Then I heard a sound like a match scratching, and all at once a bright flicker of light illuminated a bizarre scene.

The taller woman had lit a small lantern with a tin base and a glass chimney, kind of like a hurricane lamp. She held it up now, and I could see I was in some sort of cave, except that while some of the walls were dirt and rock, some were concrete.

It took me a second to put it together. We were probably under an overpass or a bridge. Boards and branches enclosed a space a little bigger than my mom's living room. An opening in the boards formed a doorway. There was no real door, but more boards and some pieces of paneling had been nailed together and stood propped up next to the opening. I could see a half moon in the night sky, and lots of stars.

I had been abducted by homeless people.

The woman standing next to me was as tall as Adeola but younger and a lot more buff; she looked like she worked out. "There now," she said as she put down the lantern, and I knew from her voice she was Marjani, "that's better."

She stood beside a battered wooden table where she had placed the lantern. I glanced around and saw the table was almost the only real furniture they had. A large mattress at the back of the cavern lay directly on the ground, and crates and boxes stood stacked on one side of the room—if it could be called a room. Boards laid across the crates served as shelves that held a lot of assorted junk—dishes, pots and pans, books, clothes, and even a bow and a quiver of arrows. There were two home-made stools but no chairs. I sat on a block of concrete near the middle of the room. It was a homeless squat—better than a cardboard box, but not much more perma-nent-looking.

"Welcome to our home," Esi said. Shorter than Marjani, and several years younger, she had a wiry build but still looked like she could take care of herself. Like Marjani, she wore a slightly tattered Egume pantsuit, but hers fit better and looked cleaner. Both of them were a little on the fragrant side.

I glared at her. "Fuck you!"

She laughed. "How kind of you to offer, but no thanks." She smiled at Marjani. "I gave up longing for a man years ago."

Marjani smiled back, and it came to me that they were more than friends.

"We need to tie him up," Esi said. "I won't leave you alone with him otherwise."

Marjani tisked with her tongue as if to suggest Esi was being overpro-tective, but she cut off an excess piece of the rope that bound my hands and then tied that snugly around my ankles.

"Looks good," Esi said, checking the knots, "but keep an eye on him."

"I will, dear." Marjani leaned over and gave the smaller woman a peck on the cheek. "Mind your way in the dark coming back."

Esi kissed her back, took two chipped dinner plates from a shelf, and then strode off.

I sat on my concrete block and glared at Marjani.

"Now, now," she said. "It could have been worse. If you'd tried run-ning away in the wrong part of the city, most likely you'd be locked in a brothel right now, fighting off your first customer."

The word brothel made a cold knot form in the pit of my stomach. Hobart had never mentioned such places.

"Tisk, tisk." Marjani shook her head. "Don't look like that. Esi and I will find a nice family without a son to barter, but with enough money to pay well for you." She tilted her head and looked me up and down. "Your clothes are very peculiar. Are you one of the *keesai* who come from another world and appear out of the air?"

I nodded. I didn't see any reason not to tell her, and pissing her off might make her less picky about who she sold me to.

She gave a sort of pleased chuckle. "That's good luck, that is. You *kee-sai* are more likely to have sons, so everyone will be eager to get you. And we won't have to worry about clan loyalty or incest rules."

I cleared my throat. I needed information, and just sitting there wouldn't get me any. "What clan are you and Esi in?"

An odd look crossed her face—not anger, but something almost as negative. "I was born a Rufaro, but I don't consider myself one now, any more than they worry about me."

"Why not?"

She turned toward the wall and picked up a brown glass jug. "Clans are made up of households, not individuals. Do you want some water?"

"Yes, please."

She poured water into a metal cup and brought it over to me. "Here." She tilted the cup to my lips, and I drank, steadying the cup with my bound hands.

"Thanks," I said when she moved the cup. I tried to think of a way I could get to the knife in my pocket and cut myself loose. "I'm really tired. Could I lie down for a while?"

She looked down at my bound ankles. "You won't be able to walk."

I got to my feet and teetered for a few seconds. "I could hop to the bed." I nodded at the mattress and took a tentative jump.

She bent down and picked me up over her shoulder. "Ow!" She set me down again. "What was that?"

"What was what?" But I was pretty sure I knew because the knife had jabbed me, too.

She didn't bother to answer me. Her hands moved up and down my body like a cop frisking a perp. One hand dove into my jeans pockets—not as much of a thrill as it could have been with the right woman—but she didn't find anything until she checked my jacket pockets and pulled out the knife.

"No wonder!" she said, pulling my makeshift sheath off of the blade. "That's a good knife—a little bonus for us."

She put it on the table and continued to search me. She found the sandwich in my other jacket pocket and put it on the table next to the knife.

"Not much to run away on," she said, finally letting go of me. She bent down and picked me up over her shoulder again, walked the few steps to the back of the cavern and tossed me onto the mattress.

I landed with a thud that nearly knocked the wind out of me, which wasn't entirely bad because the mattress smelled really musty.

It looked as if I had arrived in my second Makoron home. So far it was a downhill journey. Just as I had that thought, the ceiling started to shake.

"What the hell is that?" I shouted.

Marjani glanced over her shoulder at me. "What is what?"

The whole room seemed to be vibrating, and there was a weird noise—almost like being inside a kazoo. "That humming noise—and the vibration! Is it a cave-in?"

She grinned. "Oh, that. Don't worry it's just the train." She looked up. "We're under the track."

I knew Egume had an extensive network of magnetic levitation trains, but I had never seen one, and I had no idea how much noise they might make. Abruptly the sound and vibration stopped, and I went back to breathing normally.

A little while later, Esi came back with the two plates full of food. The two women sat down and ate, chatting all the while about what they would do with the money they would get for selling me. They decided that buying a small house would be best, but they couldn't agree on where it should be.

I lay on the mattress and remembered my first night alone on Gyasi's much more comfortable bed. If my mother had been there, she would have said I had jumped out of the frying pan and landed right in the fire.

I WOKE up with a stiff neck and stiffer arms. I was still lying on the mattress, trussed up hand and foot, but the two women were no longer lying on either side of me, as they had been when I finally fell asleep the night before.

"The trick will be delivering him once we make the sale," Esi's voice said. "Getting him out of here unseen won't be easy unless we go at night."

I stifled a groan and moved so I could see better. Sunlight streamed in through the cracks in the makeshift door Esi had put in place right before bedtime.

The two women sat on the two stools, drinking something from metal cups. The squat looked even more primitive in the daylight.

"We should work on a disguise," Marjani said. "He's a stick, but we could add padding in the right places with no trouble."

Esi made a gurgling nose, half snort and half laugh. "How will that help hide his beard?"

"We'll have to get a razor or some *tacha*."

"He'll still make a damned homely girl."

It was silly, but I felt a little insulted. And I wondered what *tacha* was.

Marjani got to her feet. "Stop being difficult, Esi. This is our very own miracle, and I won't have you putting obstacles in our way."

Esi stared into her cup. "I hope so. In the light of day, I'm wondering if it wouldn't have been better to knock on the door and ask for a reward for returning him."

Marjani paced the room and waved one arm, a wild sweeping gesture. "A reward? They'd have been as likely to accuse us of stealing him! No, a house that big wouldn't look kindly on the likes of you and me knocking on their door in the middle of the night."

Esi sighed. "You're right. I know you're right." She got to her feet and put one arm around Marjani. "This is our chance to finally have a place of our own, a real place with a roof and four walls."

Marjani threw both arms around her and hugged her tightly. "Don't forget a real door."

They laughed and kissed each other on the mouth. I know a lot of guys get hot watching women kiss each other, but probably those guys hadn't spent the night tied hand and foot on an old mattress. It sure didn't do anything for me.

I moved so I made some noise, and groaned when my stiff muscles protested. "Uh, hello. I need to pee."

Marjani let go of Esi. "Our little treasure is awake and needs to pee."

Esi picked up a metal can that was sitting on the floor by the concrete block. "Here. You can go in this."

I was horrified. "In front of you?"

They both laughed. They untied my ankles and hauled me to my feet, but Marjani didn't want to untie my hands. Only when she couldn't figure out how to unzip my jeans did she finally untie me and let me unzip myself. It wasn't easy with my fingers so stiff.

I insisted on standing at the far end of the cavern and turning my back on the two of them, before I even tried to pee. Just as I got a stream going, a shadow moved on the wall. I glanced over my shoulder and realized that Esi was watching me.

"It's not fair, Jani!" She sounded half amused and half resentful. "Not only can he stand up, he can aim!"

"Not that useful a job skill, but amusing to do, I'm sure." Marjani didn't sound nearly as intrigued.

After I zipped up, I turned around.

Esi was putting a bowl, a lump of soap, and the jug of water on the table. "Here, come wash your hands."

Her tone reminded me of my mother, even though she was probably more than ten years younger than Mom. Marjani looked fortyish, but Esi couldn't be more than thirty-one or maybe thirty-two. She wore her black hair short, like so many women in Egume, and when she smiled she was almost hot.

Marjani wasn't bad looking—she had a thick mane of black hair and dark eyes—but she didn't smile as much, and she was so solidly built it was hard to see her as anything but a threat. She picked up the half-full can and took it outside while I washed my hands. She moved the door out of the way to do it, which let in a lot more sunlight.

"You need to eat something so we can tie you up again," Esi said, turning toward the shelf. "We saved your bread and meat for you."

She had her back to me, and I suddenly realized I had a shot at getting away, so I jumped up and raced toward the doorway. I stumbled because I was so stiff, and Esi turned back and saw me.

"Stop!" She jumped in front of me with her hands out.

I kept going and knocked her down. I got to the doorway just as a dark shape blocked the light.

Marjani grabbed me by the throat and squeezed.

"Argh!" I could barely make any sound. I couldn't breathe, either.

Marjani dragged me farther back into the cavern. I had a brief glimpse of Esi lying on the ground with blood trickling from her head and then everything went black.

I HEARD voices when I came to. Esi and Marjani were arguing.

"I don't want to leave you alone with him." Marjani sounded angry and worried at the same time.

I stared at the concrete beams of the ceiling. I was lying on my back, but my arms were above me. They had to have put the door back. I could barely see in the dim light.

"We need money." Esi sounded okay, so I couldn't have hurt her badly. "We need to buy things for a disguise. The tower job is the only one that's hiring day laborers right now, and you know the job boss there." She chuckled. "And besides, you tied him up really well."

I tried to move and discovered Esi was right. My hands were tied above my head and my feet were tied down, too. I couldn't so much as roll over. I groaned when I tried.

Marjani's face loomed over me, scowling. "Listen to me, you stubble-faced scum! If you hurt Esi while I'm gone, I'll hunt you down and kill you." She patted my crotch. "These will be the first to go. I know men are very protective of them."

I tried to pull away from her, but I couldn't move an inch.

Esi's face leaned over me next to Marjani's face. She had a sort of makeshift band-aid on her forehead, but otherwise she looked fine. "Don't be so *shufaw*, Marjani. I promise I won't untie him. We'll be fine."

I wondered what *shufaw* meant. Maybe bloodthirsty.

Marjani hugged Esi and then went to the door and lifted it out of the way. She turned to look back at us. "I'll be back as soon as I can. Put the door in place and keep out of sight."

"Yes, First Mother." Esi said the words with something close to sarcasm.

Marjani didn't bother to answer but only vanished from the doorway.

Esi went over and shifted the heavy frame of boards so it covered the doorway. Sunlight shone in through the cracks, but it still got dimmer.

I tipped my head back and saw that my hands were bound together at the wrists and then tied to a stake driven into the ground. When I stretched my neck to look at my feet, they were staked down, too. The ground under me felt cold.

Esi went to the shelf and came back with a book. She pulled one of the stools closer to me. "I'm going to read. If you like, I can read out loud. Otherwise, I'll read to myself."

I thought she was being pretty nice considering I had knocked her down. "What's the book?"

She read from the front of it. "*My Life as a Soldier*, by Folame Urbi Kondo." She looked up and grinned at me. "It was very popular when it came out a few years ago, because it's partly about a famous scandal. But if you want something lighter, I could read from one of Marjani's love stories."

Something told me Marjani's love stories wouldn't have any men in them. "This book sounds fine. Go ahead and read out loud." I stretched my muscles as much as I could. "I'm not going anywhere."

Esi opened the book. "I'm already on chapter three. To fill you in, Folame Kondo was born into a large household, but by the time her father finally sired a son there was no way her family could barter a husband for the elder girls."

"What does that mean?" I interrupted. "Why did her brother's age matter? Wouldn't the older girls get priority?"

Esi gave me a look like she suspected me of asking facetiously. "Of course not. No one trades a son for a *future* husband; it's always for a man old enough to be married. A woman whose brother is twenty years or more younger than she is would be too old to be sure she could have children by the time he was of an age to marry. Unless she had a very well-paying job, no household would want her."

"Oh." I thought back to Teleza and her sisters. At least Kafele was only fourteen years younger than Zuwina. But with me gone, she might have to wait until she was over thirty to get married. No wonder they had wanted to jump start things by sucking me into their new household.

"Now, here's chapter three." Esi put her head down and began to read. Folame Kondo had a rather flowery way of expressing herself, for a soldier. She had never met a superlative she didn't like. Her situation always sounded dire, even when she was just looking for somewhere to live. I listened because there was nothing else to do, but it wasn't that interesting until Folame decided to enlist.

"Why did it help to join the army?" I interrupted. "Was it just because it gave her somewhere to live?"

Esi gave me an impatient glance. "Joining the army isn't like getting a job. If you join the army, you can never join a household—the army *is* your household. You join for life, and they take care of you when you get old."

I thought that over. An all-woman army still seemed totally weird. "What happens if a woman in the army gets pregnant?"

Esi laughed. "Most soldiers don't make enough money to afford insemination fees. But if one did, she'd have the baby and raise her in the barracks. I told you the army was like a household."

"What if she has a boy baby?"

Esi gave me an annoyed look. "Then her clan would take him when he was old enough to leave his mother—six or seven—and foster him in one of their households."

I couldn't imagine moving into Adeola and Hobart's house at six. I had a feeling Teleza would have looked a lot less hot if I'd grown up knowing her like I knew Lorrie.

Esi went back to her reading. I let her go on for quite a while, almost losing track of the story, until one sentence got my attention.

"'I met Bejida Urbi Siti when I was forty-five,'" Esi read.

Instantly, I recalled Mr. Walters' daughter saying her mother's name. It looked like I might find out what had happened to her.

"'I was old enough to know better,'" Esi read on, "'but still, her beauty, her charm, her *kufa* won me over. In spite of her youth, I became an ardent follower, and supported her in the Urbi elections.'"

"What's *kufa* mean?" I interrupted, opting for the safest reason to ask questions.

Esi let out an annoyed sound, almost a sigh. "It means that quality that some people have that persuades everyone around them to follow them."

"What did she mean by the Urbi elections?"

Esi rolled her eyes. "Clans in Dodomah are different than they are in Egume. Individuals vote, not households, and they elect a single leader instead of a council."

She went back to reading and I let her go on, still wondering how I could find out more about Bejida Urbi Siti.

Folame Kondo's career prospered, and she was made an officer. Folame recounted how she made many friends, in spite of often rejecting some of them as lovers.

"'Many officers found it comfortable to take lovers from their own companies, but I have never thought the practice a sound one. How can one give orders to a bed partner? Feelings so often obscure good sense, resulting in calamity and heartbreak.'"

It sounded reasonable to me. Considering all the soldiers were women, it also sounded a hundred and eighty degrees from the 'don't ask, don't tell' policy formerly in place in the U. S. military.

When Bejida Urbi Siti became the youngest Ocan Garun Dodomah had ever had, Folame was appointed as captain of her personal guard. The next sentence made me sit up and take notice.

"'I had thought Bejida shared my views, as she had never married and had never been known to take a lover, but when the *keesai* who would consume her life and annihilate her career arrived, it became clear she had other reasons for staying unattached.'"

Did 'the *keesai*' mean Mr. Walters? I craned my head to watch Esi read as if somehow it would help me follow the story.

"'The *keesai* appeared miraculously from thin air, as these men do, and was taken to the Ocan Garun. Bejida met him in a public audience, with another *keesai* present, a man who had married into the Urbi clan. However when the Urbi man was unable to speak to the new *keesai*, instead of seeking out another *keesai* for assistance, Bejida announced that she herself would teach the man to speak Neluan, as she had *kayel gazan*.'"

Apparently little Ruveka had inherited that spooky talent from her mother, along with her flawless skin.

Esi read on. Like most of the city, Folame Kondo had been horrified when Bejida Urbi Siti had refused to assign the strange man to a household, even one in her own clan. A few months later Bejida married the stranger—all by herself, no other brides—and Folame had felt the shock as strongly as if she had been struck a physical blow.

Esi's forehead wrinkled in concern as she read Folame's words. "'Of course I was amazed, but still I clung to my perception of Bejida as a woman of character, a leader among women. I waited anxiously for her to announce who else would join her in this new household. She had two unmarried younger sisters whom everyone expected would be the first, but in fact Bejida later arranged a marriage for them in a different household. As the months passed, the Urbi grew more and more puzzled as no clanswomen were invited by Bejida to share her husband.

"'And then the news broke that Bejida Urbi Siti was pregnant.'"

Esi let out a small sigh of regret, as if she had read something horrifying. "'She had the child, a girl whom she named Ruveka, and still she refused to take another woman into her household. She allowed her husband to care for the child, and even hired an unrelated woman to help him.'"

Folame's narrative veered off into her own life and problems, as her mother became ill, and Folame and her sisters quarreled about who should have what responsibility.

I fidgeted in my bonds, totally uninterested in Folame's problems. "Do you think you could untie me for a bit? I need to stretch."

Esi put the book down. "I'm sorry, no. I promised Marjani I wouldn't."

"What happens when I have to pee again?"

She grinned at me. "That depends on whether I can get your trousers open or not."

It wasn't that I didn't want to hear a woman talk about unzipping my pants, but on the other hand I didn't want to be tied up while she did it. "What about food? Don't I get any breakfast?"

Esi pursed her lips. "I suppose I could feed you." She glanced over at the shelf. "We saved your bread and meat."

I was hungry enough not to care how long my sandwich had been without refrigeration. "That would be good."

She put the book down and retrieved my only provisions from the shelf, then came over to sit down beside me. She tore the sandwich in half and held a piece just above my mouth.

I stretched enough to snatch a bite of it and chewed carefully, not wanting to choke from eating while lying down.

"Is it true your world has more men in it?" Esi asked.

I swallowed. "Yes. Lots more. In fact slightly more boy babies are born than girl babies."

She shook her head, and I couldn't tell if she didn't believe me or just found it amazing. "I can't imagine such a thing. Does that mean every woman has a husband to herself?"

"No." She had moved the sandwich, and I couldn't stretch enough to reach it. "Some people never get married. And some get married and then get—" I paused when I couldn't think of a word for divorced— "get the marriage dissolved."

"Dissolved?" She crinkled her nose. "But a marriage isn't a physical *thing* that can dissolve, like a lump of sugar left in the rain."

"Well, they ask a judge to make them not married anymore, and then they aren't." I stretched my neck but still couldn't reach. "Can you move that back, please?"

She looked at her hand in surprise, then moved it closer to my face. "Oh, sorry."

I took more bites and ate as fast as I dared. I had just choked down the last bite when something abruptly blocked the light from the cracks in the door.

Esi looked up, her eyes wide. "Who's there?"

She jumped for the doorway just as the makeshift door moved.

Eleven

I felt like the goat staked out for the T-rex in *Jurassic Park*—terrified and with no good options. I didn't even know if I should shout for help. For all I knew an axe murderer had come to call.

Esi was obviously in no doubt. She held the door with both hands and leaned all her weight against it.

A woman's voice spoke from the other side of the door. "It's Dorscha. Is anyone home?"

"I'm here, Dorscha," Esi said.

"Esi? Is that you?"

"Yes." Esi managed to sound only slightly agitated. She shifted her body so it almost touched the door, both hands still pressing it firmly in place. "I can't ask you in. I've come down with a fever."

"Are you sure you're all right?" The unseen visitor sounded concerned. "I saw Marjani leaving a while ago."

"I'll be fine." Esi twisted her head to glance at me over her shoulder and gave me a look that was half pleading and half grimacing. Probably she was afraid I would call for help. If I had thought I'd get help, I would have called for it, but Makoro had taught me otherwise.

"Marjani went to get me some soup," Esi said. "She'll be back soon."

Dorscha made a disapproving noise. "Why don't you leave that Rufaro trash? If you joined our household, you wouldn't have to pay for your dinner."

Esi frowned. "Don't speak that way about Marjani—not to me."

An audible sigh sounded through the door. "Are you sure you're all right, Esi?"

"I'll be fine." Esi pressed her body against the door like she was willing the other woman to leave—or perhaps she meant to keep her out bodily. "Really."

"Very well, then. I'll see you when you're feeling better."

Footsteps sounded and then faded away.

Esi's shoulders drooped with relief for a few seconds, and then she ran over to the concrete block and shoved it until it moved a few inches. She stopped to rest, panting, and then she pushed again. It took her a while, but she finally got the block wedged in front of the door.

"Who was that?" I asked, when Esi had dropped down onto one of the stools.

She poured herself a cup of water and drank it before she answered. "Dorscha—one of the women from the camp."

"Why did she call Marjani 'Rufaro trash'?"

Esi shrugged and looked away. "All the women at the camp are Kabaregas, like me. That's why they call themselves a household, even though they live in tents instead of a house." She paused, and then seemed to think that wasn't enough explanation. "They don't like that I use Marjani's last name. She's Marjani Rufaro Medwar, and I'm Esi Kabarega Medwar."

"Oh." It sounded more like a regular marriage than anything I'd seen on Makoro, and yet Esi seemed not to want to talk about it. "Are you going to read some more?"

"Not that book." She reached for the shelf. "I need something lighter."

I cleared my throat. "Well, if you're not going to finish the other book for a while, can you tell me what happened to Bejida Urbi Siti?"

Esi glanced up from the new book. "She died."

So Mr. Walters was a widower for real. "How?"

Esi pursed her lips like she was summing things up in her head. "When her child was six, Bejida Urbi Siti announced she was pregnant again. She still refused to share her husband or her child, so the women of Dodomah rose up and attacked her palace. After the palace guards joined the revolution, Bejida Urbi Siti was dragged from her apartment and killed by a mob." Esi blinked, like she was fighting tears. "They never found her husband or her child. No one knows what happened to them."

Of course they couldn't find them when Walters was standing in the middle of a highway in upstate New York clutching his six-year-old daughter.

"Why were they so angry at Bejida?" I asked.

Esi frowned as if the question surprised her. "She refused to share. There aren't enough men. No one gets one to herself, not even an Ocan Garun. It was not only selfish, it was an abuse of her power." She put her head down. "This book is called *Conquered by Love*. Do you want me to read it aloud?"

"No, thank you." I tried to stretch again and failed. It was going to be a long day.

IT was a horrible day—long bouts of boredom and pain, punctuated by periodic spurts of noise and vibration when a train passed overhead. The cold dampness of the cavern floor made the ache in my muscles even worse, but after a few hours, all I could think about was how badly I needed to take a leak.

Finally, I couldn't hold it any longer. "I have to pee."

Esi looked up from her book. "I'll get the can."

She brought it over and bent down to peer at the zipper on my pants. "How does this work?"

"Don't touch me." I tried to pull away from her but couldn't move. "Just untie one hand, and I'll take care of it."

She shook her head. "I promised Marjani I wouldn't undo even one knot."

"Never mind then."

"Foo!" She made a disapproving noise with her tongue. "Are you going to wet yourself and then spend the rest of today in damp, smelly trousers?"

She had a point. Cringing, I told her to hold the waistband of my jeans with one hand, grasp the zipper pull with the other, and tug it straight down.

It took Esi a couple of tugs to get the zipper pull to move, and I flinched both times. Finally, she got my pants unzipped. I shut my eyes when she took my penis out, but I could still hear her commenting on the things it reminded her of—a sausage, and some vegetables I didn't recognize—which embarrassed the heck out of me.

In spite of the relief it brought, taking a leak while Esi held the metal can under my dick were some of the worst minutes of my life.

"How do you clean it off?" Esi asked when I had finished.

"Just give it a shake."

She made a disapproving noise. "That's not very sanitary."

I gritted my teeth. Making someone mad right before she zipped up my package didn't seem like a good idea, so I didn't swear, but I wanted to. "Just do it, please."

She did, but then she got interested in the texture of my foreskin. I had always been a little embarrassed about not being circumcised—Mom didn't believe in it—but I had never been so completely mortified as when Esi decided to see how much the foreskin on my penis could stretch.

"Amazing!" she said. She looked like a kid playing with a Slinky for the first time.

I could feel right away that mortification wasn't enough to prevent a hard-on. "Will you stop that!"

Her face went suddenly red. "Oh, I am sorry!"

She put everything back and zipped me up, then went to empty the can. After she came back and got the concrete block in place again, she washed her hands and then came over and crouched down beside me. Her face still looked flushed. "I'm sorry. It's just I never got a chance to see a man's—I mean, I know I shouldn't have touched you like that."

I was surprised enough to get over being mad. "You mean you never— uh—you've never had sex with a man—ever?"

She shook her head. "I haven't even seen a man up close since I left home." She chortled. "And I certainly never saw *that part* of my father."

"Why did you leave home?"

Her face got a desolate look, like she was remembering something sad. "I didn't want to be a burden on anyone." She looked down at the dirt floor. "I was twenty-two and I wanted desperately to marry into a household, but I had no prospects—no brother and no dowry. I couldn't find work—I grew up in a small village fifty *darupau* away from the city—so I thought I'd go out into the world and earn my own bread."

Her story reminded me of a guy I had known who had graduated from Clara Barton and hit the road looking for something better. Last I had heard, he was working in a Wal-Mart in Kansas. Except he hadn't turned gay. "How did you meet Marjani?"

A warm smile lit her face. "I hired onto a construction job where she was the job boss. Some of the other women got me drunk after my first day of work, and Marjani took me home and let me sleep it off safely."

She said it very casually, but I had a feeling getting her drunk hadn't been a gesture of good will. "You mean Marjani brought you here?"

The smile slid from her face. "No, not here. Marjani—Marjani lived in a Rufaro household at the time."

The clan thing confused me. It seemed to matter a lot what clan someone was in. "So you two hit it off right away?"

Esi frowned. "You ask a lot of questions."

A sharp ache shot up my arms, and I got mad. "You've got me staked down so I can't even pee on my own. I'm bored to tears, and every muscle in my body hurts like hell. If you don't want to answer questions, I could scream my head off for a while instead."

She got up and paced a few steps, then sat down at the table. "All right. If you don't want to listen to that other love story, I'll tell you mine."

I felt bad for making her talk about personal stuff, but I was bored, and I needed information. "Fine. Let's hear it."

Esi knit her brow, not in a frown but more of a pensive expression. "I had never thought I could love another woman; I had never tried. When I met Marjani, I was *oopcha*. Marjani guessed that. She didn't press me to have sex right away." Esi smiled reflectively. "Instead she became my best friend—someone I could talk to about anything and everything."

I decided *oopcha* must mean virgin. I wondered whether Esi was gay or bi or just willing to settle. Maybe in this world it didn't matter, at least not for women.

"For a few months we worked together, ate and drank together, went on picnics and walks together. And just when I realized that Marjani had become the most important person in my life, she asked me if I would be willing to live with just her."

I waited, but Esi said nothing more. She just sat there with an intent look on her face.

"What did you answer?" I prompted.

She smiled, a bright, animated smile. "I said yes, and I've never been sorry." The smile faded a bit. "It was rough at first, not being able to find a place we could live together."

"What about Marjani's place?"

She shook her head despairingly, like Hobart used to do when I got an easy question wrong. "That was a Rufaro household, so I couldn't live there. And the Kabaregas wouldn't let a Rufaro—wouldn't let a woman who wasn't a Kabarega—live in one of their households, either."

I had the feeling Esi was leaving something out, but I had no clue what it could be. "So that's why you live here?"

She chuckled. "Yes, although this is much nicer than the first place we found. That was a cave with no door."

It was hard to imagine the crude space around me as nicer than somewhere else.

All at once the door shook. "Esi!"

Esi jumped up. "Marjani?"

The door shook again. "It's me," Marjani's voice said. "What's wrong with the door?"

"Wait, I've got it blocked." Esi darted to the doorway and shoved the concrete block a few inches, then lifted the door.

Light flooded the room, and outlined Marjani's silhouette in the doorway. I blinked as the bright light hit my eyes.

Marjani climbed over the block and stepped into the room. She had a bundle under one arm and a canvas bag in the other hand. She set them both down on the table and gave Esi a quick hug. "Why did you do that to the doorway?"

Esi hugged her back and then let go. "Dorscha came around, and it scared me. I didn't want anyone to open the door with him—" she stopped and looked at me in surprise. "What's your name?"

"Jason."

"Jayzoon what?" Esi asked.

"Jason Trouble," Marjani answered before I could say anything. She actually said my name correctly, which amazed me. "That was an Omdur household he climbed out of, and he's underage."

"Really?" Esi looked at me critically. "But he has a beard."

Marjani waved a hand in an impatient gesture. "Maybe he does, but he's still only sixteen. Everyone is talking about his escape. The Ocan Garun has offered a reward for his safe return."

Esi's eyes brightened, and she smiled a tentative smile. "How much?"

"Five thousand *corts*."

The smile vanished. "That's not very much—not near enough for a house." Esi sounded amazingly outraged considering she and Marjani had kidnapped me.

"I know." Marjani gave me a calculating look. "His age makes it harder, but we can still do a lot better than five thousand. We'll just have to use a *cortunna*."

"What's a *cortunna*?" I asked, alarmed. My arms ached, and I somehow felt even more helpless with Marjani in the room.

"A middlewoman," Esi said. "Someone who acts between two parties who don't know each other."

"And we need to move him." Marjani glanced around at the shelves like she was already mentally packing. "We can't stay here. I saw some Kabaregas from the camp roaming about on my way here. They might come snooping around." She opened the canvas bag and began to pull things out of it. "If I can get his disguise ready in time, we'll leave right before twilight tonight."

Esi put her hand on Marjani's shoulder. "Where can we go? Where is it safe to hide him?"

"The cave where we used to live," Marjani said.

Oh great, somewhere worse than a dump where the ceiling shook every hour.

Marjani patted Esi's hand. "None of the Kabaregas knows about it, do they?"

Esi shook her head. "I never mentioned it to them."

Marjani nodded. "Good." She glanced around again. "We'll take the blankets, the stew pot, and the water jug. I brought some food, but just in case, we'll take the snares and the bow and arrows." She grinned and pointed with her chin at the battered metal can I had been using to pee in. "And of course, we need the toilet."

"Speaking of what we need," I said, groaning as my muscles told me how unhappy they were, "how about letting me up?"

Marjani chewed her lip as she studied me.

"If you expect me to walk later, you'd better untie me now," I said, groaning for effect. "I'm going to be stiff for a while."

Marjani undid the knots on my ankles while Esi untied my wrists. As soon as my hands were free, I tried to move my arms. "Agh!"

"Shh!" Esi slipped her hand over my mouth. "Quiet!"

"Ack," I said more quietly when she moved her hand. "My arms hurt." I moved one leg tentatively. It was sore, but nowhere near as bad as my arms. I tried to sit up and nearly screamed again. "In fact my whole body hurts."

"Poor thing." Esi pushed me to a sitting position. "I'll have to give you a *koru ba*."

"A what?" I'd never heard the word before, so it alarmed me.

"Like this." Esi kneaded my neck muscles for a second, and I got it. A *koru ba* was a massage.

At Esi's direction, I sat cross-legged on the ground. Meanwhile Marjani put the door back in place and then sat down at the table. It seemed much dimmer in the room after that, and I realized it must be late in the day.

Marjani lit the lantern and began inspecting the things she had taken from the canvas bag, muttering to herself as she did it. She sounded like she was deciding the best way to assemble a disguise.

I watched Marjani thread a needle while Esi knelt behind me and put her hands on my shoulders. At first Esi just rubbed lightly, but after a while she dug her fingers into my shoulder muscles, and I let out an exclamation. "Agh!"

Esi moved her hands away.

"Don't stop." I twisted my head back and forth trying to get the kinks out of my neck. "It's painful at first, but it helps."

Marjani cut and stitched while Esi rubbed my back and my arms for me, kneading vigorously and even pounding on my back. I still hurt, but at least I could sit up without screaming. After Esi finished my arms, she told me to put my legs out straight, and then she began to massage my calves.

Marjani stood up and lifted something that looked sort of like a cross between a padded bra and those corset things women wore a long time ago. "Let's try this on him."

"I'm not wearing that," I said at once.

Marjani smiled, but it wasn't a warm smile. "Would you care to wager on that?"

"You have to, Jayzoon," Esi said in a rush, her face contorted into a distressed frown. "If people realize you're a man, you could be pulled to pieces."

Marjani came over to where I sat on the ground with my legs spread in front of me. "Hold out your arms, Jason."

I wondered again why Marjani could pronounce my name when no one else from Makoro could, but I had other concerns at the moment. I shook my head. "I don't think so."

One of Marjani's feet shot out in a swift kick to my groin.

I saw it coming just in time to move, so she got me in the thigh instead of the nuts, but it still hurt. "Ow!"

Esi screamed, but Marjani just grabbed my hair and yanked my head back. My hands were too busy shielding the family jewels for me to try to fight back.

"Don't make me do worse," Marjani said.

What did it matter if I wore a bra? No one I cared about was going to see me in it. I pulled off my shirt and held out my arms.

"Lace it in the back, Esi," Marjani said, slipping the thing over my arms.

Esi tied it on. It felt like a fucking corset.

"Do you really wear these?" I asked.

"Marjani does," Esi said, adjusting the straps. "I'm small, so I don't bother." She held up a high-necked gray tunic. "Now this."

I stood up to put on the tunic. The collar was too snug to be comfortable, but the bra was the worst part. I had fucking boobs. Small as they were, they got in the way when I moved my arms.

"I feel like an idiot," I said, tugging at the tight collar.

"Now the pants," Esi said, picking up the black trousers.

"This goes on first." Marjani held up something that looked like a girdle, but the seat had been padded.

I opened my mouth to say I wasn't going to wear it, but a glare from Marjani made me change my mind. I turned my back to the two of them, dropped my jeans, and pulled on the girdle. It fit snugly but wasn't uncomfortably tight except for the crotch where Marjani had fastened a round piece of plastic that flattened me out but good. It was almost like wearing a cup, but one that someone had stepped on first.

I pulled the pants up next. They fit tighter than the girdle, especially around the waist. I fastened them and turned around, feeling like I had been shrink-wrapped.

The disguise wasn't complete yet. My hair was cut in the short, distinctive Mr. Spock style that Hobart had insisted on. Esi put a long brown wig on my head and twitched it into place. It itched, and it felt really weird.

Marjani gave me a critical stare. "You look like a girl who grew too fast for her own good. But you're not so homely as I thought you'd be." She frowned and slapped my hands away from the collar. "Don't unbutton the tunic. That bump on your throat will give you away."

It took me a minute to realize she meant my Adam's apple.

"And the beard," Esi said.

I rubbed my hand across the stubble on my chin. I'd been shaving for over a year, but in the last few months my beard had started to come in much thicker.

"I've got some *tacha* for that," Marjani said. "It cost more than it should, but it's supposed to work."

When Marjani picked up a small jar and opened it, I realized *tacha* must mean lotion or cream. The stuff looked more like Mom's moisturizer than anything else.

Marjani held the jar to the lantern light and read the directions. "It's supposed to be quick."

It was quick. Marjani slathered some of the pale blue cream on my face while Esi went to fetch more water. The cream tingled a bit, but by the time Esi came back with the water, Marjani said it was time to wash it off.

Esi poured the water into the wash basin and I washed my face. My skin felt remarkably smooth—much smoother than I'd ever gotten it with a razor.

"There." Marjani sounded pleased. "That will do." She looked at the small jar. "Hopefully, we can sell him within the next day or two, or we'll need to buy more *tacha*."

Esi flinched, but she looked me up and down, too. "He does look better. But his hands are too masculine."

I looked down at my own hands—square, with long but blunt fingers and uneven fingernails. They reassured me; I might be wearing a wig and a bra and have a padded butt, but I wasn't really a girl. I tucked my hands behind me before Marjani could suggest using the cream to get rid of the hair on my knuckles.

"Hopefully no one will pay attention to his hands." Marjani tilted her head. "Should we make his *poorchai* bigger?"

When Esi patted my padded bra I figured the word must mean boobs.

"No," Esi said. "He would look out of proportion. He's slender, like me, so he should be a little small." She took a step closer and studied my butt. "You did a good job with the padding."

A wave of dizziness came over me. I was standing in a homeless squat, wearing a wig, a padded bra, and pants tight enough to make my mother frown. Not even the months I'd spent in Adeola's and Hobart's house had prepared me for the possibility of reality changing that much.

"He looks faint," Marjani said. "We had better feed him before we go."

Esi laid out the food while Marjani pushed the concrete block back over toward the table. I sat on the concrete, and they each took a stool.

Dinner was a lamb pie, that was more crust than meat, and an apple. I ate because I was ravenous, but the food tasted like ashes in my mouth. Sitting at a dinner table, even with two homeless kidnappers, reminded me of family dinners with Mom and Lorrie. Missing them brought a lump to my throat that made it hard to swallow.

I chewed the stringy lamb and prayed that my stay in Makoro wouldn't get any worse.

But I knew very well it could.

MARJANI blew out the lantern, screwed the lid to the fuel compartment shut, and then slipped the lantern into the pack on my back. She gripped my shoulder. "Remember, if you try to run, I'll tackle you and then put the bag over your head again."

I nodded. I knew it, but that didn't mean I wouldn't run if I got the chance.

"We should wait until it's darker," Esi said, shifting the bundle on her back. The bundle over my shoulder was even bigger, but Marjani had left her own arms free so she could keep me in line.

"I don't want to have to climb that hill in the dark," Marjani said. She gave me a shove. "Get moving."

I started forward, but as soon as I stepped outside I halted. It wasn't much lighter outside than it had been inside after Marjani blew out the lantern.

Esi stepped around me. "I'll go first. I know the way."

I started walking but took a moment to study the area, as best as I could see it in the approaching twilight. The maglev track, a thick concrete causeway on low pylons ran in a long gradual curve toward the city. Marjani and Esi's squat was built underneath it, where the pylons rose up to cross over the stream and meet a line of nearby hills. Off in the distance I could just see three dots of light and faint shapes moving around them. I realized the lights were campfires. I decided it was the Kabarega camp the two women had talked about.

We took a trail that led away from the camp, but we had only gone a dozen steps when I felt a faint vibration in the ground. I twisted my neck to look back and saw a sleek silver shape gliding effortlessly and incredibly swiftly on the track. The few dozen cars, lit up from inside, held women sitting at tables and half reclining in comfortable seats. From where I stood the train made very little sound. It was gone in a flash, leaving nothing in its wake but a faint glimmer on my retinas.

"The express from Dodomah," Marjani said. "It's right on time."

We went down a slope, and I heard running water. That explained how they could always get water so quickly. The stream looked deep, but we crossed where it was narrow, leaping from one bank to another, first Esi, then me, then Marjani.

I wanted to look around to get my bearings, but Marjani gave me another shove.

"Get going, Jason."

I walked as slowly as I could from sheer perversity, while it got darker and darker. I didn't think dawdling would do me any good if someone found us, but I was mad enough at Marjani to want to spoil her plans.

Marjani kept literally pushing me to keep up with Esi, who walked more briskly than I did. Even though Esi's stride was shorter, I managed to let her get ten or twelve yards in front of us before Marjani swatted at my head.

I ducked, but she caught me on my ear and it stung.

"Walk faster, or I'll make you sorry." Marjani said.

"I can't see where I'm going." It was partly true. It was getting hard to see. A half moon was up, but clouds obscured it so thoroughly it gave hardly any light. But even in the semidarkness I could see we were headed toward some hills, most likely the site of their cave. The ground was already hillier, and the trail had petered out to nothingness. "What happens if someone else is staying in this cave when we get there?"

Marjani snorted. "They'd have to be desperate for shelter."

I opened my mouth to point out that she and Esi had been desperate enough to find the cave the first time, but before I could say it, Esi let out a scream and I heard a thud.

"Esi!" Marjani pushed me out of the way and ran past me.

I dropped the pack and took off in the opposite direction, running as fast as I dared.

For a few seconds I heard Esi crying and Marjani talking at the same time, and then I heard nothing but the sound of my own feet thudding in the darkness, and my breath coming fast as I ran. I ran steadily, glad for all the time I had spent lifting weights and exercising in the gym.

I lost my bearings and had no real sense where I was going, but I kept moving anyway, as fast as I could manage. If I could find a place to hide overnight, I could travel early in the morning and try to get away from the city. Now that I had a disguise, I would be less noticeable, and that could buy me some time. There had to be somewhere on Makoro where I could live on my own, even if I had to turn into Mowgli the wolf boy to do it.

All at once, the ground seemed to disappear under my feet. I caught desperately at a scraggly bush and stopped myself from falling off a ledge. Just as I noticed moonlight glinting on water, I heard the sound of the stream.

I had to walk a little ways to find a place to cross, and then I set out again, still running as fast as I could. I tripped on a rock and fell, got up, and slowed to a walk. I stopped to listen, but I didn't hear any sound of pursuit or even running water.

My chest ached from running so long, and I unbuttoned my collar so I could breath better. I debated about taking off the itchy wig, but I knew I was better off with the disguise than without it.

I stared hard through the darkness and thought I could make out a white line running across the ground. It dawned on me that this must be the railroad track.

I looked at the small clump of trees that grew beside it and debated whether to look for a place to sleep for a few hours or to keep going. I didn't want daylight to overtake me in the open. Suddenly a vaguely familiar voice said, "Who the hell are you?"

Twelve

I nearly jumped out of my skin. I started to blurt out the same question, then remembered that I was dressed as a girl. "Who's there?" I said, pitching my voice just a little higher than usual. I didn't want to sound fake, but I didn't want to sound like a guy, either. I had never been so happy to be a tenor.

A woman stepped into the open from the trees. I could vaguely see her outline in the remnant of moonlight. She was shorter than me by a good bit, and almost as slender. "I asked first," she said.

I placed the voice. It was Dorscha, the unseen Kabarega who had come to check on Esi.

I knew my accent would give me away as a foreigner so I made a split-second decision. "My name is Teleza Urbi Kondo, and I come from Dodomah."

She took a step closer and turned on a flashlight that she shone in my general direction. "What are you doing here?"

"Looking for a place to sleep." I blinked as the light hit my eyes, and then gestured toward the trees. "I got lost. I've been in the city looking for work, but I don't have any money, so I thought I'd sleep in the woods where it's safer."

She nodded. "A wise decision. The city is no place for young girls on their own." She hesitated and then spoke again. "We're a Kabarega household, but you're welcome to a meal and a night's shelter in our camp."

I shook my head. "Thanks, but I won't trouble you."

Just then the clouds over the moon broke, and it got noticeably brighter. I could see that Dorscha wore her dark hair short, looked about forty, and was giving me a sharp glance.

"Well, I'll be on my way," I said.

"Dorscha?" a woman's voice called. "Dorscha, are you there?"

"Over here," Dorscha said, raising her voice and moving the flashlight back and forth in signal.

I inched away, prepared to make a run for it.

Three women appeared from the darkness, all of them younger than Dorscha. The plumpest one looked about twenty-five, the skinniest one a little younger. The third woman was almost as tall as me and looked like she worked out. I couldn't guess her age; she could have been anywhere from twenty-five to forty.

I froze. Outrunning all four of them would be tricky in the dark when I didn't know the lay of the land. I didn't want to run into a maglev pylon or a tree.

"Who is this?" the buff-looking woman asked.

"Her name is Teleza Urbi Kondo," Dorscha said, shining her light toward me. "She's lost. I just offered her a night's shelter."

The plump one smiled at me. "I don't mind sharing my tent."

The buff one laughed and slapped me on the back so hard I nearly fell over. "Don't mind our Vasha. And don't worry. The rest of us won't try to seduce you."

"Uh," I said, "it's really nice of you, but—"

"We insist," the buff one said. She put an arm around my shoulder and tugged me along. "Come along. Our camp is quite close."

It was close, less than fifty yards away behind the trees. I realized I must have run in a big semicircle around Esi and Marjani's squat, and come out by the camp.

A half dozen tents of various sizes stood on either side of three campfires. When we walked up to the center campfire I was conscious of being an impostor. I had no clue how to walk like a woman, so I walked as naturally as I could, except I shortened my stride.

Five women came out of the tents, four of them middle-aged or older, and Dorscha introduced me. No one shook hands; it was all just nods and polite greetings. None of them seemed to suspect the truth about me. Still, I was almost afraid to breathe for fear of doing something wrong.

At Dorscha's urging I took a seat on a stool, copying another woman's pose as best I could with a damn plastic plate over my crotch. The aroma of meat and vegetables wafting from a pot hanging over the coals made my mouth water, even though I had eaten recently. One of the younger women ladled a generous serving of lamb stew into a dish and added a thick slice of bread to it. When she handed it to me, I thanked her and started to eat.

Everyone else seemed to have eaten already, as no one else asked for food. Except for Dorscha, the four older women all went back to their tents, leaving Dorscha and the five younger women sitting around the campfire. I figured I would wait for my chance and slip away as soon as I could.

"So where is Esi tonight?" Vasha asked. "She hasn't come by to get dinner."

"I don't know," Dorscha said. "I went by there, but neither of them was home." She frowned into the campfire. "It looked almost like they had moved. Some of their things were gone."

"Could be thieves," the buff woman said.

Dorscha smiled grimly. "Hardly worth a thief's trouble."

Vasha laughed. "Esi should leave that incuharu and join our household."

I wondered what incuharu meant, but I didn't dare ask.

"Household?" The buff woman shook her head. "Tent-hold is more like it." She sighed.

"We do the best we can with what we have," Dorscha said.

"We've been together for four years now," Vasha said. "When will the Kabaregas recognize us as a household?"

Dorscha frowned. "We shouldn't talk about clan business in front of a guest."

They all looked at me just as I was taking a bite of bread. I choked, and the buff woman slapped me on the back.

"Oh, dear," she said, slapping me again. "You've got something caught in your throat."

Horrified, I remembered unbuttoning the collar of my tunic. My Adam's apple must have been in plain sight.

Dorscha's eyes widened. She stared at my hands, and then she jumped up. "He's a man! Grab him, Oni!"

The buff woman froze for a second, then stared at me.

I dropped my plate and started to run, but I hadn't gone three steps when the buff woman brought me down in a flying tackle.

Suddenly I was the piñata at a birthday party. Hands grabbed my clothes and pulled; other hands tugged and patted relevant body parts. The older women poured from their tents to join the feeding frenzy. In a very short time I was lying on the ground, damn near naked. All I had on were my briefs and what was left of that fucking bra.

"Careful with him, Oni!" Dorscha said. "Don't injure him."

Oni hauled me to my feet, and I stood nearly naked in a circle of ten women.

"She's a man!" Oni said.

"A boy, I think," Dorscha said. "Do you remember the Ocan Garun's announcement?"

Oni unlaced the bra and pulled it off. "We can get the reward."

Dorscha's smile sent a chill up my spine. "I don't think we want to claim so small a reward when something much better is in our grasp."

I sighed to myself. Now instead of two women who wanted to sell me, I was in the hands of ten.

"What do you mean, Dorscha?" Vasha said.

Dorscha laughed. "Why should we give up what we've all been hoping for—all but you, anyway, Vasha."

Oni looked from me to Dorscha. "What have we been hoping for?"

Dorscha held one arm out to point at me in a triumphant gesture. "I'd like you all to meet our new husband."

My jaw dropped. Out of the frying pan into fucking hell.

THE quarreling started almost immediately, just as soon as they got me tied up.

"Why do you get to be the senior wife?" a gray-haired woman demanded. "I'm the eldest."

"You're too old," Dorscha said brutally. "And you haven't worked in years."

"We can't marry him," Oni said. "He's only sixteen. We could all be arrested."

"It happens all the time," Dorscha said. "People get impatient." When no one spoke she added a qualification. "We just have to keep his age a secret." She surveyed me critically. "I'm sure we could make him look older."

"Why do we need a husband?" Vasha asked. "We're doing fine without one."

"Fine?" Dorscha waved a hand. "Do you see any children running around the camp?"

"We don't need a man for that." Vasha frowned. "If we just had the money for the fees—"

"Well we don't." Dorscha practically snapped out the words. "And even if we turned him in for the reward, it wouldn't pay for more than a few visits to an insemination site." She glanced at the assembled women standing and sitting around the fire. "Which of us would get them? And if none of them took, we'd be right where we were before." She gave me a hard glance. "Now that we have our very own husband, we can keep him on the job until every one of us who wants a baby has one—or more."

I felt a cold chill in my stomach. Dorscha looked like she was pushing forty, but I was pretty sure she would be in line with the others. Somehow even Zuwina looked good by comparison. At least she only wanted one child right away, while Dorscha wanted to make me a father many times over as soon as humanly possible.

"But why do you get to be senior?" one of the other gray-haired women said.

"Because I'm the leader," Dorscha said. "I earn the most, I've helped you all from time to time, and it was my idea."

There was some grumbling at this, but no one said anything out loud.

"Take him to my tent." Dorscha jerked her head toward the largest canvas structure. "Make sure he can't get away."

"What about the ceremony?" Oni said. "You can't just take him off to your bed without a marriage taking place."

"The ceremony will be tomorrow."

"We can't get an elder to come here so quickly," the gray-haired woman said, "especially not on *Wahlau.*"

"I'll perform the ceremony." Dorscha glanced around like she was daring anyone to object. "But first Oni will go into the city and see if she can find a pharmacy that's open during the holiday. We need a good supply of *puojao.*"

Several women snickered.

Oni frowned. "That doesn't seem right." She looked at me with something close to pity. "He's only sixteen."

"If you feel that way, you can wait a year for your turn." Angry derision filled Dorscha's voice. "*I* don't intend to miss my last chance at motherhood because of a scruple."

I really wanted to know what *puojao* was, but I was afraid to ask. A couple of the women took hold of the rope Dorscha had used to tie my wrists and tugged me toward the tent. I tried to set my heels, but they just pulled harder.

Dorscha came up behind me and pushed. "Go inside, little one. No one will hurt you. Tomorrow you will be our husband. Tonight will be your last night sleeping alone."

I gave up the struggle. I was damn tired, and I figured I needed a good night's sleep.

A bunch of them followed as I was escorted into the tent. They trussed me up like a rolled roast, wrapping my whole body in rope that they tied off behind my back where I couldn't reach any of the knots. They laid me down on a straw pallet, and Dorscha threw a blanket over me.

"I'll sleep in your tent tonight, Vasha," Dorscha said. "It may be the last time for awhile." She pointed at three of the younger women, Oni and two others. "You three bring your blankets and sleep across the doorway to keep guard. No one touches him until after he's our husband."

She went off and left me alone with three of my fiancées.

"Well," Oni said, "I hope we don't all live to regret this decision."

One of us was already regretting it.

MY wedding day dawned clear. When Dorscha lifted the tent flap the next morning, the sky behind her was a beautiful blue.

"All right, everyone," Dorscha said to the three women standing guard. "Get him cleaned up. I've found some clothes for him."

She left a pile of clothing on the ground and whirled away like she had a lot to do.

Oni and the other two women untied me, wrapped me in a blanket, and walked me to their latrine. They wouldn't leave me alone, but at least it was better than using a tin can.

Next they took me to a spot where a metal bathtub had been enclosed by canvas walls, a sort of tent without a roof. The tub was already filled with water, and a lump of soap and a towel waited on the stand next to it.

"Hop in," Oni said.

I was feeling grubby, but not eager to wash in front of them.

"Or we could give you a bath?" Oni said.

I stripped off my briefs and stepped into the tub. The water was freezing. I soaped myself all over and then plunged in for a quick rinse that left my teeth chattering.

Once I was clean and dry they gave me the clothes Dorscha had brought. The pants were too short, but at least I was clothed—and not wearing a bra. They gave me my shoes back, but they took my underwear— to wash, they said—so the shoes were the only things I wore that had come from Hobart's house.

Oni looked me up and down as she led me out to the center of the camp. "I'll look for a *thrya* in the city. A man can't get married without a decent *thrya*."

"What's *puojao*?" I asked.

She grinned. "You'll find out tonight." She turned to go and looked back over her shoulder. "There are eight of us, not counting me and Vasha, so you'll need it."

The two women guarding me pushed me down on a stool, and I watched Oni walk away from the camp with a brisk step.

Every time I thought I'd had my worst day on Makoro, I turned out to be wrong. I spent that day sitting, my ankles bound tightly to the legs of the stool, while two women guarded me. I would have killed for twenty minutes of decent jazz—even the new fusion stuff. Instead, I had nothing to do but observe the camp and dread the coming of night.

The camp was pretty spread out. A half dozen canvas tents of various sizes—some gray and newer-looking, some tan that were patched and tattered—had been pitched in two straggling lines. Near the bathing area, several clotheslines had been strung from tall posts, and trousers and tunics flapped in the breeze. A ring of stools and logs around the central campfire made a sort of outdoor dining room. The well worn paths between the tents, the weathered wooden posts, the absence of any grass near the campfires, showed that the Kabaregas had lived there for a good while.

I watched the women busily tidying up and decorating the tents with greenery and flowers, singing as they cooked, and calling out to each other to admire their efforts. They were having a party, and I was the main course. I had hit a new low.

They offered me food, but somehow I wasn't hungry. After they had the camp ready, they all lined up to take turns bathing. The two women guarding me got their turn with two other women taking their place. When the first two guards came back, they looked dressed up. One of them, the skinny woman who had come looking for Dorscha the night before, wore the gray tunic that had been part of my disguise. It looked better on her than it had on me.

And then Oni came striding into camp, whistling a cheerful tune.

"The place looks nice," she said to my guards. She handed me a bundle of folded cloth. "Here. Your wedding *thrya*."

I unfolded the bundle. The *thrya* was ankle-length and made of silvery fabric.

"Excellent!" Dorscha said, coming up behind Oni. "Did you get the *puojao?*"

Oni turned and handed her a small package tied up in brown paper.

"You're sure it's genuine?" Dorscha said. She gave me a measured look. "I wouldn't want to poison him or anything."

"I got it from a pharmacist," Oni said. "I told her my brother had turned shy, and we needed it for his wedding. She was very sympathetic. She even put something in it to keep him from getting anxious."

Dorscha smiled a pleased smile and twitched the *thrya* out of my hands. "We'll have him put this on after we get the *puojao* into him. Wouldn't want to get it dirty."

She walked off with the *thrya* and the brown paper packet.

I wanted to puke. If I hadn't been tied to the stool I was sitting on, I would have tried to run, even with all of them right there.

Oni gave me a pitying look. "Cheer up, Jayzoon. Every man gets wedding jitters. You'll get over it."

I remembered she had had qualms about my age. "I'm only sixteen!"

She shook her head. "I asked around in the city. They said you claimed to be sixteen when you arrived, but no one knows for sure how old you are."

The skinny woman laughed. "Does that mean you're going to want your turn, Oni?"

Oni shrugged. "No, not tonight. I'll give him a few months. By then he'll be older and more used to the idea."

She walked off without even a backward look at me.

It was late in the afternoon by then, and in spite of the cold lump of fear in my throat I was hungry. My guards gave me some food, but before I could finish it, Vasha came running into camp.

"Quick!" she shouted. "Hide him! The Rufaro is coming!"

Oni raced out from a tent. "What's going on?"

"Marjani is coming!" Vasha said, panting. "We have to hide him."

Oni grabbed one of my arms. "Vasha, you take the other arm." She waved a hand at the skinny guard. "We'll drag him into a tent. You cover up the marks, Kambo."

Oni and Vasha tilted me backwards and then pulled. The stool came with me, and left two deep grooves in the dirt as they dragged me toward a tent. The skinny woman took a piece of greenery and rapidly brushed the grooves away while the other guard sat down and began to eat from my plate.

Once we were in the tent, Vasha closed the tent flaps and started to tie them shut.

Oni clapped one hand over my mouth. "Keep quiet."

I pulled her hand away and drew a breath to scream, but before I got more than an abortive sound out, Oni knocked the stool over and jumped on my chest, straddling my torso with her legs. My head hit the ground, the air left my lungs, and my feet, still tied to the stool, stuck up into the air.

"Shut up!" Oni put a hand on my throat and pressed down.

I tried to push Oni's hand away, but Vasha grabbed both my hands with her own and held them.

I pulled my hands loose and tried to swat at Oni, but I couldn't breathe. The tent swam around me for a few seconds. When I came to, Vasha was tying my wrists to the sides of the stool.

Oni had moved off of me but still held one hand over my throat. "Hold still," she whispered fiercely. "If you make a sound, I'll cut off your air."

I hesitated. From nearby I could hear a murmured conversation. It faded quickly.

Oni didn't move her hand until a few minutes later, when the tent flaps twitched.

"Just a moment." Vasha rushed to untie the tent flaps.

Dorscha stepped into the tent and glanced at me. She smiled. "I see you have him in hand, Oni."

"Is it safe to let him up?" Oni asked.

Dorscha nodded. "She's gone. She just came to get food and some pain killer for Esi, who has a badly broken ankle."

I felt a twinge of remorse for having left Esi with a broken ankle, but not much, because she had helped to kidnap me.

Dorscha made a sweeping motion with one hand. "Get him up out of the dirt. We don't want a dirty husband."

Oni and Vasha pulled me upright, my wrists and ankles still tied to the stool.

"My legs ache," I said.

Dorscha chortled. "You won't have to stand long, and then you'll be lying down all night."

"It would be better if he could walk to the campfire," Oni said. "Let's untie him now and walk him around for a bit."

"First we give him this." Dorscha pulled a small bottle from her pocket. "It takes at least an hour to work, it says. That should be about right."

I stared at the bottle in her hand. It was about the size of a travel-size bottle of mouthwash, but I was pretty sure the pale green liquid in it wasn't Scope or Listerine.

Dorscha took off the cap and stepped up to me. "Open your mouth."

I clamped my mouth shut.

Vasha reached over and pinched my nostrils closed. I tried to pull my head away, but Oni came up behind me and got me in a headlock that would have done Doofie Slater proud. I held my breath as long as I could and then I opened my mouth and gasped for breath.

Dorscha poured the liquid into my mouth, and before I could spit it out Oni tilted my head back and pulled my jaw shut.

"Swallow!" Dorscha ordered.

I tried not to, but Dorscha stroked my throat like Mom used to do to Sancho when he had to take a pill, and then Oni closed my nostrils again.

"Swallow!" Dorscha ordered, and I did.

They let me go, and I spit what was left in my mouth onto the ground, but it wasn't much.

"Do you think you got enough into him?" Vasha asked.

"I don't know if it will be enough for all of us," Dorscha said. "But it will be enough for me."

I wasn't sure what she meant. I really didn't want to think about what she meant.

They untied me after that, and Oni and another woman walked me around the camp. Every woman we met smiled at me and said my name, although all of them said it Jayzoon.

After about an hour, the light started to fail. They fed the main camp-fire until it flared up into a bonfire, and then Dorscha brought me the silver *thrya*.

"Put this on," she said, holding it out.

I didn't move. "I don't want to get married."

Dorscha handed the *thrya* to the four women now acting as my guards. "Put this on him. We're ready to start."

"I don't want to get married!" I shouted as they forced my arms into the sleeves. "I don't want to be one woman's husband, let alone ten."

Dorscha stepped up to me and scowled. "Do you think you're the first reluctant groom in the world?" She waved a hand at the fire behind her. "Why do you think there's a version of the wedding ceremony that doesn't require you to speak?"

"I don't fucking want to get married!"

For a second I thought she was going to slap me, but she didn't. "We all have to do things we don't want to do."

She turned and walked toward the fire.

My guards pushed me forward.

Dorscha started the ceremony by announcing that the household had chosen a husband. She gave my name, but she called me Jayzoon Kabarega Miller.

"That's not my name!" I shouted. "I'm not in the Kabarega clan."

"Hush!" Oni swatted at the back of my head. "Be quiet. This is a solemn moment. Show some reverence."

I started to feel suddenly strange, not quite light-headed but weird.

Dorscha called each woman's full name in turn, and asked each one if she wished to marry Jayzoon Kabarega Miller or leave the household. One by one they all said they wanted to marry me—even Oni and Vasha.

"The household is united," Dorscha said. She held out her hands and all the women did the same, holding hands to form a circle with me and the fire inside it.

It was dusk, and the firelight flickered on all their eager faces. I knew I should try to run, but all I could do was stand there.

Dorscha went around the circle, asking each of them to vow faithfulness—not to be intimate with a man other than me—and they did. She asked them to vow affection and kindness, to me and to each other, and they did. She asked them to promise to shelter me, to feed me, and to protect me, and they all did. She asked them to care for each other's children as their own, and they agreed.

"And so we bring Jayzoon Kabarega Miller into our hearth and into our household," Dorscha intoned. "He is now our husband, to cherish and to love." She let go of the other women's hands and held her own up in the air. "We are married!"

They lifted their arms and shouted, then all rushed in to kiss me. I stood there, reeling, and realized I was now married to ten total strangers, and I had the father of all hard-ons.

APPARENTLY, there was to be no delay in the honeymoon. The whole lot of them swarmed around me and then pushed me into Dorscha's tent. They stripped off the silver *thrya*, then my shoes, and then every stitch of clothing I had on. Unlike Dorscha's flashlight, the lanterns they carried each had an actual flame, much like the one Marjani and Esi had used. The flickering lights cast spooky shadows on the grimy gray tent walls.

"He's very thin," one of the gray-haired women said, holding up her lantern to stare at my erection, which even the presence of a horde of women I had no desire for couldn't seem to weaken.

"He'll fill out with time," Dorscha said, taking the lantern away from her. "Get him ready and then you can all leave."

'Ready' seemed to mean 'unable to resist,' as they laid me down on my back on the pallet and tied my arms and legs to the stakes already pounded into the ground. I wasn't confined as much as I had been in the cavern; I could move each limb a foot or more, but I couldn't reach any of the knots. My head was to one end of the tent, and my feet to the other, with the doorway on my left side.

The horde stepped back and all stared down at me.

I was feeling really odd, like I was watching this happen to someone else. I knew I should be terrified, but I felt too detached to work up any real fear.

Dorscha made herding motions toward the doorway "Go. I'll come out when I'm done, and it's Obax's turn."

I wasn't sure which one was Obax. I wasn't sure it mattered.

The others left. Dorscha set the lantern onto the ground near my right foot. She straightened up and began to undress, one garment at a time. I watched her, mesmerized, not because I was turned on by her, but because her actions were so deliberate. Finally, she was naked. She came over to where I lay on the ground and looked down at me.

A look of rapture lit her face, as if she were undergoing a religious experience. "I've waited a long time for this."

I swallowed hard but didn't say anything. I felt sick, not because she was horrible looking—she wasn't really—but because I was powerless. I had never thought rape could happen to me. Even my weird feeling of detachment wasn't enough to make this moment any less terrible.

A rustling sound outside the tent entrance made Dorscha look up and frown. It occurred to me that the lantern must be lighting up the tent walls so that everyone outside could see her standing there. It must have occurred to her, too, because she stepped over to the doorway. "Go away," she said in a loud voice. And then she began to tie the tent flaps closed, finishing each one with a satisfied yank.

I closed my eyes and wished I was more scared so I could Turn. I wouldn't have cared where I went so long as it was out of Dorscha's tent. But whatever they had poured down my throat had made me too calm for panic.

And then I heard a tiny sound, like fabric tearing.

Thirteen

I opened my eyes and saw Dorscha still working on the last door tie. I turned my head away from the doorway and noticed something small and pointed sticking through the opposite tent wall, about three feet up from the ground. As I watched, the thing moved downward, leaving a straight line behind it. It took me a second to realize it was the tip of a knife cutting a slit in the canvas wall.

I held my breath, not sure what I could hope for.

Just as a woman's hands widened the slit into a gap, I realized who it had to be. Instantly, I kicked as hard as I could and knocked the lantern over.

It hit the ground, the flame went out, and the inside of the tent went dark.

Dorscha let out a word I didn't recognize, but she sounded mad. "Little fool! You could start a fire." She bent over the lantern, muttering to herself about my stupidity.

A dark, shadowy shape slipped through the hole in the wall and loomed over Dorscha. One quick tap with the hilt of the knife and Dorscha crumpled onto the ground.

"Marjani?" I whispered.

She came close and whispered back. "Are you all right, Jason?"

Except for still having a damn hard-on. "Yes. Can you cut me loose?"

She slit the bindings in seconds. "Come. We don't have much time."

"I'm naked!" I whispered furiously. I might be too calm for panic, but I could still be mortified.

"I have your own clothes a little ways away."

I decided not to argue. I had nine other brides waiting, and even Marjani couldn't deal with all of them.

I grabbed my shoes and followed her through the hole in the canvas and into the darkness. The moon was up, so I could see a little, but that wasn't entirely a good thing. A naked man was pretty damn conspicuous in that place, especially with his flag pole up.

Marjani ducked down and darted through the brush around the camp, then circled back toward the railroad line. I followed her as fast as I could and almost ran into her when she straightened up and stopped suddenly.

"Your clothes are here," she said, still speaking in a low voice as she indicated a bundle on a boulder. "But put them on quickly."

The bundle included pants but no underwear. I damn near injured myself zipping up, but I got my pants on and pulled on my shoes. Before I could put on the shirt and belt, I heard a shout from back at the camp.

"Let's go!" Marjani grabbed my arm and pulled.

I ran with her, as fast as I could, holding my pants up with one hand and clutching my belt and shirt in the other. I was pretty sure we went past her squat, but we were moving so fast I couldn't tell for sure. We definitely ran under the railroad and leapt across the stream, so it seemed likely.

Just as we got to a small clump of trees and bushes, Marjani stopped again. This time I did run into her. I didn't knock her over, but it was close.

"Idiot!" she said, pushing me away. "Be careful or you'll break my ankle, too."

I didn't have a hand free to balance so I fell against a pine tree. The needles scratched my arms, and the scent reminded me of Christmas. "Sorry."

"Marjani?" a voice called.

"Here, Esi," Marjani said, looking around anxiously. "Where are you?"

A pale face bobbed up and down in the moonlight as Esi hopped out of the trees on one foot. "Did you get to him in time?"

"Barely." Marjani jerked her head at me while I put my belt on. "They had him staked out and primed with *puojao*, but Dorscha was just making her move when I came through the tent wall." She gave me a second glance. "He had the sense to knock over the lantern. Dorscha must have wanted a good view."

I had just buckled my belt when I heard a howl of rage from a short distance away, the sound of women's voices raised in a primal scream of fury.

"They found our place empty," Marjani said. "Time to get moving." She bent down and picked Esi up over her shoulder in a fireman's carry, then turned toward me. "Come with us or go on your own, as you choose. I promised Esi I'd try to save you from the Kabaregas, but that's all."

Marjani set off without waiting for an answer, Esi's head bouncing with every step the older woman took.

It took two seconds for me to make up my mind. I could still hear angry whoops from the other side of the stream, and I didn't want to take a chance on running into any Kabaregas by wandering around on my own. "Wait for me!" I pulled my shirt on and ran to catch up.

The moonlight flashed on Esi's face as she looked up and grinned at me. Her dark hair swung back and forth. "Did you have a wedding ceremony?"

I shuddered as I recalled the event, and then tried to walk where I could see Esi's and Marjani's faces at the same time. There wasn't really a good spot for that, so I walked a little behind Marjani so I could see Esi. "Yes. How did you know I was there?"

"Kambo was wearing the tunic I got for your disguise," Marjani said over her shoulder. "Except for that I might have believed the decorations were for the holiday like they said. But once I knew they had found you, I figured they planned to have a wedding." She chuckled. "Luckily for you, I had time to get back there after I got Esi out of our house."

When I recalled how close Marjani had cut it, it gave me the shivers, even doped up like I was. "Where are we going?"

"The cave." Marjani gave me another over-the-shoulder glance. "You probably shouldn't stay there more than a few days. The Kabaregas will keep looking."

It was a grim thought. Where could I go? If the alternative was gang rape by random groups of women, would I be better off giving up and going back to Hobart's house? At least I'd have a few months before I got forced into marriage.

I pondered as I walked. I wasn't ready to give up yet. There had to be wilderness somewhere on this world where I could live off the land while I tried to figure out a way to get home.

I just had to find it.

WE stopped to pick up the supplies and the other things Marjani had stashed away for the stay in the cave. I ended up shouldering most of the bundles, but I didn't complain. Marjani carried Esi, and Esi had sent her back for me. I followed the two of them for almost an hour.

"There's the trail," Marjani finally said, a few minutes after our third rest stop. She grunted as she shifted Esi on her shoulder and started climbing upward. "We're almost home."

We climbed about a hundred yards up a fairly steep incline, until we came to a yawning black opening in the side of the hill. It didn't look like home. It looked more like a dank, dark pit. And then the clouds covered the moon, and the opening to the cave became just inky black on murky gray.

"Get the lantern from the pack," Marjani said. "I don't want to trip and drop Esi."

"You can put me down," Esi said. "I can hop a little ways."

"Not on this hill," Marjani said.

I put the pack down and felt around for the tin lantern. As soon as I found it, Marjani handed me some matches, and I struck one. She had to tell me how to adjust the wick, but I got the thing lit. The glass chimney had a long crack in it that I didn't remember being there, but at least the lantern gave enough light that I could see a little better.

"Go inside quickly," Marjani said. "We don't want anyone to see that light."

I cupped my hand around the lantern chimney and stepped into the blackness. The cave walls sparkled, like they had quartz or some other shiny mineral in them. I walked a dozen steps and realized the cave wasn't very deep, not more than thirty feet at its deepest point. I held the light up over my head, but I couldn't see a ceiling.

"Put the lantern down and help me with Esi," Marjani called.

I put the lantern on a sort of natural ledge about chest high on the left wall of the cave, and then I helped Marjani set Esi down on the ground.

"Ow!" Esi flinched as her left foot touched the rock floor.

I looked at her ankle. Even in the flickering light I could see it was red and swollen inside the wooden splints on either side of it, with deep scratches in the skin. She must have bled for a while, too. "You should take her to the doctor tomorrow."

"I'll be fine," Esi said. "Marjani set the bone. She's done it before."

"I never set an ankle bone before," Marjani said. "Feet and ankles are complicated."

"You did fine," Esi said. "I'll be better tomorrow." Her face looked very pale.

Marjani didn't say anything, but her expression said she didn't believe Esi. She took the lantern and searched until she found a part of the cave floor that was dirt instead of stone, and then she spread some blankets on it and carried Esi to it.

"You need to get some sleep," Marjani said. "We all do."

I needed something even more than I needed sleep. Walking that last mile had been incredibly painful. Whatever was in *puojao* could give Viagra a run for its money, and I really needed to do something about my hard-on.

"I'm going to go for a little walk." I held up both hands in a 'don't worry' gesture. "I'm not going far, believe me."

Esi looked anxious. "Don't fall on the trail. I wouldn't want all Marjani's hard work in saving you to go to waste."

"Neither would I." It occurred to me that I hadn't thanked them. "I appreciate that you asked Marjani to rescue me, Esi. Thank you. I'm grateful for that."

"If you mean it, there's something you could do for Esi." Marjani got to her feet.

I was half a head taller, but somehow I still felt intimidated. "What?"

"Marjani!" Esi tugged on the other woman's pant leg. "No, don't! It's not fair to Jayzoon to ask him that."

"Why not?" Marjani bent down and patted Esi's shoulder reassuringly. "It won't cost him anything. Why do you think he's going outside?" Her eyes raked me up and down, stopping right at my crotch. "He can't pee in that condition."

For a horrible moment I thought I was right back in Dorscha's tent.

Then Marjani reached over to the pack of supplies and fumbled around for a moment. She took out a small tin drinking cup and handed it to me. "Here. You can use this."

I stared at the cup and then I understood. I wasn't sure I liked the idea, but it was certainly better than being staked out for a tribe of Amazons.

"No!" Esi tried to drag herself across the floor. "No, it's not fair, Marjani." She winced. "I won't let you ask him."

"When will you have another chance, Esi?" Marjani's tone bordered on brutal. "I know you want a child. How could we ever afford the fee?" Her face softened, and she knelt down next to Esi. "If we're not to have our own house, you should at least have a child of your own. Your clan would provide for her, if we can't, and you could see her from time to time."

I took a step closer and took the cup from Marjani's hand. "I'll do it."

They both turned astonished faces toward me.

"Why?" Esi said.

I shrugged. "I have my reasons." One of them was I really didn't think they had a hope of getting Esi knocked up without the kind of equipment a fertility clinic used. I'd heard stories of lesbians using those giant eyedropper-shaped turkey basters to do it, but I was pretty sure Marjani and Esi didn't have a turkey baster in their supplies.

But also, Esi had made Marjani rescue me. Even in pain and at risk herself, she had been unwilling to leave me to my fate among the Kabaregas.

That deserved some reward, and on Makoro, it seemed unlikely anyone else would be in a position to do Esi the favor Marjani was asking of me.

I headed out the cave entrance and down the hill before I could change my mind.

I really, really had to do something soon, or I would explode.

WHEN I came back into the cave, Esi had propped herself up on the pack of supplies and sat with her injured leg stretched out in front of her. Marjani sat cross-legged next to her. The lantern on the ground between them lit both women's faces from below, almost like a haunted house display.

I held out the tin cup.

Marjani got up to take it, but it was Esi who spoke.

"Thank you, Jayzoon." Her face glowed in the lantern light. I had never seen a human being radiate happiness like that. She seemed to exude an aura of pure delight. "Thank you very much."

I was feeling pretty pleased with myself until Marjani handed me a blanket.

"I'm sure you understand," she said, "that Esi and I need to be alone to make our child."

I did understand. I didn't particularly want to be a witness, but I didn't look forward to sleeping on the hillside, either.

"I'll call you when we're done," Marjani said.

I went outside and sat for a while, trying not to think about what implement they could be using for artificial insemination by lantern light in a cave. After a few minutes I was glad they had sent me outside. *Puojao* was powerful stuff.

"CAREFUL!" Marjani sounded on edge.

I shifted Esi's arm on my shoulder and tried to help Marjani maneuver her toward the front of the cave without bumping her injured ankle.

Esi's face looked pale in the muted sunlight, but she smiled. "I'm fine, Jani. You don't need to fuss at Jayzoon."

Marjani lowered the younger woman onto the small boulder that she had already padded with a folded blanket. "I do so. He'll have to care for you while I go to find food."

"We'll manage by ourselves very well," Esi said. "We have an agreement, remember."

Marjani gave me a stern look. "I remember. See that you do, too, Jason."

I gave her a sour grimace. "Well, since the Kabaregas are still out hunting me, I think staying here and taking care of Esi is the safest thing I can do right now." I looked down at Esi's ankle. It didn't look any better to me. If anything, it looked more swollen, the scratches even redder. "Are you sure you don't want to take Esi to a doctor?"

Esi made a brushing away gesture with both hands, as if to shoo away my concern. "Nonsense. I'll be better in a few days. Meanwhile Marjani needs to find something for us to eat. We're all hungry."

After two days stuck in that cave, I was ravenous. We had eaten the last of the bread and cheese the day before, and there hadn't been that much of it.

"I'll do my best." Marjani gathered up her collection of snares, the bow, and the quiver of metal-tipped arrows, and put them into the canvas bag. "See that you do yours."

She embraced Esi, gave me a stern look, and headed down the trail.

Esi and I sat near the mouth of the cave, her on the padded boulder and me on a blanket on the ground, and watched Marjani climb down the hillside. Off in the distance I could see the silvery glints of the stream as it meandered through the countryside, and the white and gray train tracks making a much straighter line toward the city. A train whizzed along, a freight train this time, with several dozen cars, at least. It was coming from Egume and headed north.

"That one must be going to Dodomah." Esi let out a sigh. "I wish Marjani had thought to bring some books."

I would have loved to have a book to read over the last two days. Instead I had spent interminable hours listening to Esi and Marjani going back and forth between telling each other how wonderful it would be if Esi were pregnant and reassuring each other that even if she wasn't pregnant, they still had each other. Every time they had mentioned the possibility of a pregnancy, I flinched.

I really didn't want to be a father, even without child support coming into it. The idea that a child of mine could grow up without my ever seeing her creeped me out. She would probably wonder about me—about who I was, and why I wasn't around for her—and I wouldn't be there to tell her my side of things. And what if, against the odds, it was a boy? What kind of life could he possibly lead on Makoro?

It came to me that making a decision under the combined influence of Valium and Viagra was a bad idea.

Esi still had some of that happy glow, but the pain in her ankle had dimmed it noticeably. She let out a sigh. "Tell me about your world, Jayzoon."

I was bored enough to comply. I rambled on about my family, about school, about Ryan, and even about Sancho. By the time I had filled Esi in on the details, I had made myself thoroughly homesick.

"Your family sounds so small." Esi wrinkled her nose. "Only the three of you. Did someone steal your father?"

I snorted. "No. He left my mother when I was seven."

Her eyes opened wide. "Your mother let him go out?"

I laughed at the idea. What little I could remember of my dad was that he hated being told what to do. "No one locks guys up where I live—not unless they're criminals. My parents split up—got their marriage dissolved—and then Dad decided life was simpler without kids, and we never saw him again."

Esi let out a strange sigh, half regret and half apprehension. "It sounds very strange."

I couldn't let that one pass. "Not nearly as strange as listening to a woman old enough to be my mother announce that she and nine other women were married to me."

Esi frowned. "Do you mean Dorscha performed the ceremony herself?"

I nodded. "Isn't that normal?"

Her mouth twisted in a disapproving grimace. "Oh, no. I doubt it's even legal. A Kabarega elder should have performed the ceremony, and I know Dorscha's not an elder."

I figured elder meant something specific, not just an old woman. "So I'm not really married, then?"

She shook her head and then gave me an appraising glance. "Not yet. They might have gotten away with your being so young since there's no actual proof of your age, but a marriage is only legal if it's recognized by the women's clan."

"And they all have to be in the same clan?"

She waved a hand as if the matter were obvious. "Of course." She shifted on her padded seat and looked genuinely interested. "Can men and women in different clans marry on your world?"

I started to say there were no clans and then remembered that there were. "Well, they don't have clans at all where I live, and I don't know what the rules are in the parts of the world that do have them."

She frowned and stared off into the distance. "What's that?"

I looked out at the expanse of hills, grassland, and clumps of trees, the distant suburbs, and the towers of downtown Egume. "What's what?"

She lifted one hand and pointed at a faint black line against the blue sky. "That."

I looked again, and the line blossomed to a plume. "Smoke!"

"It's coming from our place." Esi sounded desolate.

I recalled the scraps of wood stacked to make shelves, the battered wooden table, the patched-together door. It didn't seem like that much to lose, until I remembered it was all Esi and Marjani had. "I'm sorry."

She shook her head. "It's not your fault. It must be Dorscha and the others, taking revenge."

The thought made me shiver. How angry could the Kabarega women be to still want vengeance after two days? The smoke billowed out now, in a thick black pillar. They must have set fire to all the contents of the squat.

Esi let her head droop; her chin rested on her chest. "It doesn't matter. We'd have to find a new place anyway. We couldn't stay near the camp."

I suppressed an urge to pat her shoulder like Mom always did when I felt bad. "Maybe you'll find somewhere better."

"Maybe."

She didn't sound like she thought it was likely. I decided to change the subject. "So, how many wives did your father have?"

She turned her head and looked at me skeptically, like she suspected my motives. "Eight."

"And that's not a big family?"

She shook her head. "Not especially. How many Omdur women were there in the household you left?"

"Seven."

Esi tilted her head as if she were appraising me. "Why did you leave? Were they unkind to you?"

I recalled the time I had spent with Teleza, especially our afternoon in bed. If she had been the eldest and not Zuwina I might still be there. "No, not unkind, but they clearly had plans for my future that I didn't have any say in."

"Hmph." She sounded a lot like Mom when I confessed to breaking a school rule. "Is it that important to you to be able to decide which household you marry into?"

"Fuck, yes!" I slammed one fist into the other hand. "I don't want to marry into a household at all."

She flinched like I had offended her, so I tried for a softer tone.

"Look, you wouldn't want to be told you had to leave Marjani, would you?"

"Fuck, no." She grinned after she said it.

I grinned back. "Well, it's the same for me. I want to be the one to decide who I spend my life with—if I spend it with anyone."

She shifted on her padding again.

"Are you in pain?" I asked.

She had a decent tan, but it looked to me like she flushed just a bit. "No, I just need to—that is, I have to pee."

Esi hadn't seemed to mind when Marjani had helped her to pee, but then I had always made it a point to duck outside for a minute. I had a weird sense of *deja vu* when I got the can, and I realized it came from having been the one who needed assistance in this situation.

We got through it without too much trouble, and then I brought her soap and water to wash with.

"We're out of water," I said, emptying the jug over her hands. "I'll have to run down to the creek."

She nodded but gave me an anxious look as she waved her hands in the air to dry them. "Be careful."

"I will." I started for the entrance.

"Jayzoon!" Esi called before I had gone two steps.

I turned. "Yes?"

She smiled at me. "I'm sorry we forced you to come with us."

I shrugged. "It could have been worse. Dorscha could have been walking in that street."

Esi laughed, and I headed out of the cave.

I picked my way down the hill carefully and walked to the stream. The cave was a good ways downstream from the place where we had crossed on our way from the squat, and the water was deeper here. I walked a ways looking for a place where the bank sloped, so I could reach the water without falling in. I had just rounded a bend in the stream when I heard voices raised and realized two women were shouting at each other. Their voices got louder and louder, like they were coming closer.

I dove into the nearest shrubbery and waited, trying not to breathe too loud or make any noise, even when the branches scratched me.

A second later, Dorscha and Oni came down the path toward the stream. Oni strode along at a rapid pace, shouting, while Dorscha hung back like she was reluctant to move in the same direction as Oni.

"How *jochir* long do we have to keep this up?" Oni said. She stopped and turned, hands on her hips, to face Dorscha. "It's foolish! The boy is gone."

Dorscha lifted her chin. I half expected steam to come out of her ears, she looked so mad. "He can't have got far. We could still find him—if we keep looking."

"Maybe," Oni said. "But if Marjani and Esi have him, they could be holed up in the hills or they could have headed out onto the plains. They might even have taken him into the city to sell."

Dorscha cast a glance around the area like she expected to find me sitting on a rock waiting for her. "I don't think they could take him into the city. Too many people are looking for him there."

Oni threw up her hands. "It doesn't matter! If I don't go back to work soon I'll lose my job, and so will you."

I inched backwards out of the shrubbery, trying to keep the two women in sight and get farther away at the same time. I froze when a twig cracked under my foot, but they didn't seem to notice.

And then a hand came from behind me and closed over my mouth.

Fourteen

I grabbed the hand, and tried to wrench it away, but then a voice whispered in my ear.

"Quiet, Jason."

Except for Hobart, only Marjani had ever gotten my name right. I stopped struggling.

We waited, frozen, while Dorscha and Oni moved away, arguing the whole time.

"You nearly gave me heart failure," I whispered as soon as the other two women were across the stream and out of earshot. It occurred to me that if I'd managed to get aroused by listening to Dorscha and Oni's argument, I probably would have Turned when Marjani grabbed me. It seemed a waste of a good scare.

"You were about to step into one of my snares." She knelt down and brushed the leaves and dirt off of a loop of twine, then unhooked the gizmo from the fallen log next to it. "I came to collect it."

I noticed a bulge in the canvas bag. "Did you kill something?"

She looked up and grinned at me. "I got two rabbits, and I picked some berries."

I thought about the furry bunny my grandma had given me for Easter when I was five. We had had to give him away when we moved out of the house after Dad left us. Mr. Wiggles had been cute, but I was damn hungry. "Great."

She looked at the water jug in my hand. "Did you come out for water?"

I recalled my errand with a start. "Oh, yeah. I forgot."

She handed me the bag, and then reached for the jug. "Here, you take this back to the cave while I get the water. You shouldn't be out any more than necessary."

Especially not if Dorscha was on the prowl. "Fine."

I scrambled up the hill as fast as I could, keeping low to the ground, and crawling when there was no cover. I looked back for any sign of Dorscha or Oni, but I didn't see them.

Esi smiled at me as I came tumbling into the cave, but the smile slipped into a puzzled look. "Where's the jug?" She got it in a second when I tossed the canvas bag onto the ground. "You met Marjani?"

"In a way." I recalled the situation, my panic when Marjani had grabbed me. "I almost tripped over Dorscha and Oni, too. They were out looking for me."

Esi nodded. "Dorscha won't give up easily. She's wanted a child for years."

"So have you, and you never tried to rape me."

She clicked her tongue at the same time she let out a sigh, producing a sound that was disapproving and regretful at the same time. "Don't judge her too harshly. She's had to fight for what she's got."

I remembered Dorscha standing over me in the lantern-lit tent. I didn't say anything, but I wasn't prepared to forgive what she had tried to do to me just because she wanted a kid so badly.

"Where is Marjani now?" Esi asked.

"Getting water." I pointed at the bag. "She got two rabbits."

Esi's face brightened, but I could see dark circles under her eyes. She looked like she was in pain.

"You should go to a doctor." I crouched down next to her and inspected her ankle. It looked puffier than ever. "That still looks bad."

She set her jaw. "We don't have money for a doctor."

"Don't they have charity hospitals in Egume?"

A muffled snort escaped her. "They do, but no one goes there if they can help it."

"All too true," Marjani's voice said from behind me. "They would probably amputate to fix a broken ankle." She moved into the cave, cast a swift glance at Esi, and handed me the water jug. "Here, put this away."

I put the jug on the stone shelf.

When I turned, Marjani had opened the canvas bag and taken out two dead rabbits, and a bundle of blackberries tied up in a piece of cloth. She handed Esi the berries. "Eat some of these while I clean the rabbits. We'll start the fire as soon as it's too dark for the smoke to show."

Esi ate a couple of berries but she didn't seem all that hungry.

I was ravenous. Unfortunately, wolfing down all the blackberries Marjani gave me only made me hungrier. After I had built a low wall of rocks as a shield, I laid a fire just like they had taught me in scouts, and then watched Marjani skin and gut the rabbits. The grisly sight didn't make me any less eager to devour them.

"Once the fire is lit, we'll need to wait for it to go to coals if we want to cook the rabbits without burning them," Marjani said, skewering a carcass on a long, sharpened stick. She propped it up against the wall and repeated the trick on the other carcass.

I walked to the cave entrance and looked outside. In the west the sun was dipping toward the horizon, lighting the landscape with dramatic shadows. Glints of light hit the white strip of maglev track, making it look like a trail of pixie dust. Off in the distance I could see a forest of *janullos* at the city's edge, their clan flags all taken in for the night, their red signal lights already blinking. Beyond that, a few lights sparkled amid the tall towers of the center of Egume.

I turned back toward the cave. "We can't light the fire yet. It's not entirely dark."

Marjani came up and handed me the two skewers. "Hold them while I take all the *jaruk* outside and bury it."

When she gathered up all the rabbit guts and skin, I figured that *jaruk* meant either garbage or offal. I held the two carcasses until she got back; I had never in my life been so tempted by raw meat.

After Marjani came back, I went outside again, so I wouldn't have to smell the raw meat. The sky went from dark azure to charcoal. The faint clouds became smudges on the sky. I could barely see the train track now.

I went back in and saw that Marjani had lit the fire. It burned brightly, so I sat down and watched it, making sure none of the flames went higher than my wall of stones. I watched the blue flickers and thought about how hungry I was. After a while the flames died down considerably.

"The coals should be ready in a few minutes," Marjani said.

She must have been hungry, too because after she put the rabbits over the coals, she sat across from me and watched them cook.

Once the meat had roasted for a while, the smell drove me wild. To distract myself, I asked Marjani a question. "How is it you can pronounce my name properly when no one else here can?"

She looked up and grinned at me. "My father was *keesai*. He taught me some words of his own language."

I had never considered that there were adults walking around whose fathers were from my world, not just girls like Hobart's daughters. "What's his name, and where is he from?"

"His name was Edward Rufaro Kowalski, and he said he was from Baltimore." She said the city name as clearly as she said mine and her father's.

"Can you speak English?" I asked in that language.

She shook her head and spoke a few halting words in English. "I not know many words. Forget much." She shrugged and switched to Neluan. "But Father wanted someone to talk to in his language. He taught us all, but my brothers learned best."

"You have brothers?" Somehow I was surprised. I had assumed her story mirrored Esi's—no brother meant no dowry to marry into a household.

"I have three brothers and six sisters." She said the words with a reluctant pride in her voice, like she didn't like the fact that having brothers was sure to be seen as an accomplishment.

My jaw dropped. "Doesn't that make your family rich, in a way?"

Marjani didn't answer right away. She poked the coals with a stick and watched the embers spark, and then finally she spoke. "It did make us well off, once my brothers came of age. With three boys and only seven girls, we could even borrow against their future dowries."

"But still you didn't get married?"

Marjani glanced over at Esi, and lowered her voice. "I did, actually. My family wanted me to marry into a household with my sisters. My sisters said they wouldn't mind that I didn't want to share their husband's bed or have children, so when my youngest sister was old enough, we found a husband and we all married him."

I stared. "I thought—from what Esi said, I thought you couldn't get out of a marriage once you were in it."

She nodded and dropped the stick. "You can't. I'm still legally married."

I cleared my throat. "I don't get it. What happened?"

Marjani crossed her arms over her chest and stared into the coals. "I thought I could be happy living just as *haru* to my sisters, and only sometimes finding women for sex. But then I met Esi."

I didn't say anything.

After a moment, Marjani went on. "When I decided I wanted to share my life with her, I left my household." She stopped abruptly like the memory was painful.

"Is that illegal or something?" I didn't want to pry, but I needed to understand what had happened.

"No." Marjani finally looked up from the coals and met my eyes. "It's not against Egume law, but it is against clan custom. And so the Rufaro disowned me. I lost my job as a construction engineer and had to take work as a laborer."

"What happened to your brothers?"

She looked confused. "Nothing happened. They all married. So far as I know they're happy enough in their households. The youngest has seven wives, the other two five, and they each have at least four sons. My youngest is my full brother; we have the same mother. After I left my sisters, he persuaded his senior wife to let me and Esi stay with them for a few weeks." Her expression got bleaker. "But even my brother urged me to return to my *haru* and leave Esi, so we didn't stay long."

It sounded rather sad. But it was interesting, too. Her brothers had married into small households by Egume standards, so most likely their wives were well off.

I cleared my throat. "Were any of your brothers like you?"

She lifted her brows. "What do you mean like me?"

I wished I knew the Neluan word for gay. "Did all your bothers want to get married to women, or did any of them want to be with another man instead?"

Her mouth twisted in a wry smile. "No, none of them were like me." Her shoulders dropped a little, like she'd been tensing up but now she was relaxed. "Although with three of them, if one of them had been, the family would probably have let him go to an insemination site."

That got my attention. "What?"

She grinned. "Who do you think supplies insemination sites? It's men who don't want to make children with women, that's who. The fees provide for the upkeep on their compounds and for a staff to care for them. That's why it's so expensive to use their services."

The way she said 'care for them' it made it sound like men were children or mental patients, unable to care for themselves. Then I remembered how quickly I had been snatched up when I arrived in Egume. A compound of gay guys might feel safer behind walls than loose in the streets of a city full of women—very aggressive women.

"I think the meat is cooked," Marjani said.

I lost all interest in Egume customs. I wolfed down my share of rabbit without even a thought for Mr. Wiggles.

Esi didn't eat much. Marjani coaxed her into eating a few bites, but she couldn't get Esi to show any real interest in the food. Marjani put Esi's share aside with a comment that she could eat it in the morning.

"I'm cold," Esi said suddenly. "Can I have a blanket, please?"

Marjani and I exchanged glances. It was quite comfortable in the cave with the embers of fire so near to where we sat. Marjani got up and fetched a blanket, but after she draped it over Esi, she pressed her hand to Esi's forehead.

"You're burning up with fever," Marjani said. "Jason is right. You need to see a doctor."

"She would just say I need to keep off the ankle for a few weeks," Esi said, clutching the blanket around her. "Besides, we don't have any money."

"I could ask my family for money," Marjani said. She tossed a few small pieces of wood onto the fire, and it flared up again.

"No!" Esi shifted her weight like she couldn't get comfortable. "They might help if you were hurt, but they would never help me. They would probably make me promise never to see you again or something."

Marjani didn't answer, but she moved closer to Esi's injured ankle and pushed up her pant leg.

Even in the flickering light, I could see the red streaks running up Esi's leg. I recalled my first aid class from scouts. Blood poisoning—septicemia, to use a fancier word. Not good.

Marjani looked Esi in the face. "I have to take you to a hospital."

Esi jerked her foot back. "Ow! No! No, Marjani! I won't let them cut off my leg." Her eyes welled up. "Especially now, when—" She broke off and looked at me.

Especially when she might be pregnant.

"Excuse me, but I need to pee." More than willing to give them some privacy, I got up and scrambled for the cave opening, then started down the hillside carefully. I really did have to take a leak, but I didn't want to break a limb doing it.

After I took care of business, I sat down a ways from the cave entrance and surveyed the countryside.

In the far distance, the lights of the Kabarega camp flickered and winked in and out as the women there moved about, having their dinner. I watched for a while, remembering the position of the camp fires and the tents, wondering who it was walking between me and the firelight. If I'd had binoculars or a telescope, I might have been able to see their faces.

I didn't have to see her face to know Dorscha was there. I shivered in my denim jacket, but it wasn't from the cold. I knew exactly what Dorscha would do if she found me.

I looked back over my shoulder at the cave, wondering if Esi and Marjani were through arguing. To my horror, the cave entrance shimmered. Even with the stones to block the actual fire, the firelight sparkled on the quartz in the cave walls and the whole place glowed like a giant night light.

I jumped up and rushed up the hill.

"Put the fire out!" I ordered as I dashed inside.

"What?" Marjani had been holding Esi. She let her go and stood up. "What's wrong?"

I frantically scooped up dirt and tossed it onto the fire. "The damn place is glowing from the firelight! You can probably see the cave entrance for miles."

I got the fire out, but it began to smoke.

Esi coughed. At least I thought it was Esi. I couldn't see well in the dark.

Marjani fumbled around and in a moment I heard the scritch of a match lighting and then I saw Marjani was holding the lantern. It looked pathetic with its glass chimney tied together with twine, but the dim light was better than total gloom.

Marjani cranked the flame down as low as it could go without going out. "We'll have to be sure we don't have a fire after dark anymore."

I thought about the view from the plain. If I could see them, they could see me. Realistically, I couldn't expect to hide here any longer. Between the Kabaregas and the city police, my chances of getting caught were darn good, and I'd much rather get caught by the police.

Esi let out a tiny moan.

"I don't think it will be a problem," I said. "I don't think I should stay here."

"Where will you go?" Marjani asked.

I hesitated, not sure I really wanted to say out loud what I had decided. Once I had said it, it would be hard to take it back.

"It's not safe for you on your own, Jayzoon," Esi said. "You can stay with us." She looked around. "Why is it so dark? Marjani, turn up the lantern." She shifted her position. "My leg hurts."

I wondered if she was out of her head. "Marjani, do you think you could get me into the city without us getting caught on the way?"

Marjani stared at me. "I thought you wanted to get away from the city?"

I swallowed hard, then set my shoulders and made myself speak. "I don't think that's a practical thing to hope for. I think I'm going to have to settle for going back to Hobart's house—the Omdur house where you found me."

"So you want me to take you there?"

I shook my head. "No, I think we should go to City Hall—or whatever it's called—so you can claim the reward for finding me."

Esi didn't seem to understand, but Marjani got to her feet. She held out her hand. "I thank you, Jason, for what you're offering."

I let out a long breath of regret as I shook her hand. If I had to go back, I might as well make sure Esi could afford a doctor before her leg got any worse. "I just hope you can get me there."

Marjani glanced down at Esi and then up at me. "I'll get you there."

The resolution in her voice reassured me. If I could have been sure I'd made the right choice, I would have been much happier.

"We'll have to leave in the middle of the night," Marjani said. "That way we can arrive at the Ocan Garun's palace when the streets are still empty."

Always assuming we made it past Dorscha and the other Kabaregas.

We left almost right away. I didn't have anything to pack, so it was just a matter of making Esi comfortable before we left. Once we were ready, I said goodbye and gave Esi a hug, but I wasn't sure she understood what was going on.

Marjani kissed her on the forehead and embraced her tightly. "Stay still, Esi. Keep quiet."

"I'm fine," Esi said. "Except my leg hurts."

"Try not to move it." Marjani kissed her again, and then stood up. "I'll be back as soon as I can."

I took a quick look around the gloom. This was one place I'd be happy never to see again.

Esi looked up at Marjani. "Are you going somewhere?"

Marjani knelt down and stroked her forehead. "I'm just taking Jason into the city. I'll be back in the morning."

Esi half sat up and clutched her arm. "I love you, Marjani."

"I love you, too." Marjani pulled herself free gently. "Go to sleep now. I'll be back before you know it."

Esi lay down, and Marjani turned to go.

I waited for her to lead the way, and took one last look at the cave.

I really hoped we made it to the city so I could go back to Hobart's house. If I continued my trend of leaving a place for somewhere much worse, I'd end up in a pit.

Fifteen

I hadn't enjoyed being dragged along through the streets of Egume with a bag over my head. It wasn't much fun without the bag, either. Marjani set a wicked pace to begin with, and then she pulled me by my arm whenever I lagged behind. After we passed through the suburbs, it didn't take more than an hour before we were well into the downtown area.

We cut through an alley. It was dark, and I was walking with one hand on the crumbling, uneven wall to guide me, when I heard a laugh that turned into a snort. It sounded damn close. I saw a shadowy cluster of people about twenty feet ahead of us, and I froze.

Marjani muffled a curse and shoved me backwards into a crevice in the wall. I hit my head on the bricks, but I didn't dare protest. Marjani pressed herself against me like she wanted to make out—or maybe she was just trying to blend in with the wall. I could feel her breathing really fast.

Barely able to breathe myself, I waited until the sounds of drunken women arguing got farther and farther away. "Ow!" I said, trying to rub my head.

Marjani grunted and moved away from me. "Sorry. I didn't realize the opening was shorter than you."

I hunched my shoulders and bent my knees to get a little room between the top of my head and the bricks of the crevice. "That's all right. I didn't want to be out in the open with those women around."

I had a feeling Marjani was nodding, but I really couldn't see her well enough to say.

"They're gone," she said. "I don't hear anyone else."

I stepped out carefully and listened. The city of Egume seemed quiet, which was a relief.

I was exhausted. It was probably after four in the morning, and I had walked damn fast for several hours with no sleep and little rest. "How close are we?"

"Hmm." She paused. "Very close, I think." Her shadowy shape darted back and forth in the alley. "This way."

She tugged on me again, and I let her pull me along. We came out onto a broad boulevard, much more brightly lit than any part of the city we had seen so far. Across the street I saw the tall steps of the imposing building I had been taken to months ago when I first arrived in Egume—the Ocan Garun's Palace.

I stepped into the lighted street, but Marjani pulled me back.

"Wait!" She looked up and down the street. It was empty. "It's clear. Let's go."

I felt like a kid being walked across the street for the first time—except we didn't walk, we ran. Once we set foot on the Palace grounds, I felt suddenly exposed. A series of flood lights on the lawn illuminated the walkway, the grounds, and the building itself. It made me want to run like hell the other way.

When we got to the bottom of the steps, two women stepped out from the shadows of the portico. They stood at the top of the flight of stairs and leveled weapons at us. "Stop where you are!"

I froze with one foot in the air.

"Don't shoot!" Marjani said. "We're not armed."

"Who are you, and what's your business at the Ocan Garun's Palace?" The first woman aimed her gun at Marjani.

The second woman aimed at me. In the stark spotlights that shone onto the porch from the lawn I could see her eyes widen as she stared at me. "She—he's a man!"

"His name is Jason Omdur Miller," Marjani said. "He wandered away from an Omdur household, and I've come to claim the Ocan Garun's reward for finding him."

"Wandered?" The first woman looked me over and grinned. "I heard he climbed out the attic window."

"The reward is the same, no matter how he got out." Marjani sounded on edge. The harsh light made her face look older, her clothes more ragged.

"True." The woman gestured with the point of what I hoped was only a stun gun. "Come up, then."

The other soldier was talking into a radio or a cell phone or something. They took us into a sort of guard room which soon filled up with women, some in uniform, some not. A tall brown-haired woman who wore a pale blue bathrobe over striped pajamas seemed to be in charge.

Except for looking me over closely, they didn't pay much attention to me. No one even asked me any questions. They had Marjani fill out an electronic form on a sort of oversized iPhone, sign her name, and press her thumb onto the screen, but all they did with me was park me on a bench and assign two armed women to watch me.

After they had asked Marjani where she found me—she told them I had been running loose in the countryside—the woman in the bathrobe told her she could go.

Marjani frowned. "When do I get the reward?"

The woman tapped the iPhone thing. "The funds should be available to you at any bank in the city as soon as they open this morning. Just identify yourself."

Marjani gave me a last look. I couldn't tell what it meant, exactly. Her expression looked grim, like she was warning me against giving the authorities too much information, but it could have just been worry for Esi. "Good fortune to you, Jason," she said, and then she turned and went out the door.

I swallowed, feeling suddenly more alone.

And then they all jumped to attention as another woman came into the room, a woman in a charcoal gray pantsuit. I recognized the braid in her hair first, and her face second. It was the Ocan Garun.

I could tell right away she was pissed at me. She glared at me in exactly the same way the principal at Clara Barton had glared when I got hauled into her office for bringing a tiny Swiss Army knife to school. I had caused the Ocan Garun trouble, and she wasn't happy about it.

"Has he been fed?" she asked, as if I were a stray dog.

The woman in the bathrobe shook her head. "He hasn't been here that long."

The Ocan Garun nodded. "Take him to a guest room and get him cleaned up and fed—but keep guards in the room—while I decide what to do with him."

"But—" I wasn't sure it was smart to speak, but I couldn't hold back. "But, won't you send me back to Ho—to Adeola Omdur Hamad's house?"

The Ocan Garun looked surprised, perhaps because she hadn't realized I had learned to speak Neluan. "Your foster family lost their rights to you when they allowed you to escape."

The floor seemed to shift under me. It had never occurred to me that they didn't have to send me to live with Hobart and Teleza and the others. "Where else would you send me?"

She paused and looked me up and down. "I don't know yet. Perhaps to an insemination site—although you're young for that. Or perhaps to a more secure household." She smiled like she was pleased with herself. "Now that you speak our language, I'm less limited in my choices."

She turned without any further words to me and swept out of the room. A moment later, two soldiers took me by the arms and marched me through the corridors of the Palace to a small second floor room, where they waited while I cleaned up in the adjacent bathroom.

The shower felt great after days without one, but as I let the warm water run down my back all I could think about was where the hell would I end up next.

"WAKE up!" The voice sounded annoyed.

I had my own problems. The principal was mad at me, and I might get expelled. Mom would be furious and upset at the same time.

It came to me that I was dreaming. I opened my eyes to find myself lying fully clothed in my own grubby clothes, on a fancy bed in a strange room.

When I sat up, a man moved away from the bed to open the thick purple drapes. Light flooded the room and illuminated the elaborate carpet and posh furniture. I flinched at the sudden change. The shadows on the floor matched the pattern of the bars on the window and suggested it was late afternoon, which meant I had slept most of the day. Just then it dawned on me the man had spoken English.

It was Max, the first guy I had met in Egume.

"What are you doing here?" I said.

He gave me a sour grin. "Visiting you. I had to beg to be allowed to see you, but I promised Hobart I would try."

I didn't know what to say. I swung my feet to the floor and tried to bring myself fully awake. "How is Hobart?" It sounded lame, even to me.

"He's well enough." Max threw himself into a chair. "You do realize how badly you hurt him, don't you?"

I wasn't sure what he meant. "I'm sorry if I hurt Hobart's feelings—"

Max snorted before I could finish. "Hurt his feelings? Hobart's daughters have had their futures put on hold." His volume rose with every word, and his face was turning red. "Adeola locks Hobart and his boys up much more securely now. In fact, every senior wife in Egume is looking closely at security in her household because of you."

It was hard to believe a guy had never escaped from a household before. But then I thought about all the things that had happened to me since I left Hobart's house, and I understood why it was likely to be a rare event.

I thought about Teleza and our one time in bed. I had liked her a lot, but not enough to stick around and become another Hobart.

Max was glaring at me like he expected me to answer him.

It made me damn mad that he was so angry at me. "Look, I didn't ask to come to Egume. I didn't even ask to go to Hobart's house."

Max jumped out of his chair. "None of us asked to come here, but we're here and we have to make the best of it."

"I don't want to make the best of it."

He held both hands up like he was fed up. "It doesn't matter what you want."

"I know that." I had found it out the hard way. "That's why I hate it here, because it doesn't matter what I want." I got to my feet so I was looking down at him and not up. "Ten women tied me down in the dirt and tried to rape me just because I was the only man available. Maybe you're prepared to go along with that, but I'm not."

He flinched and turned his head away. When he turned back toward me he looked calmer. "What happened?"

I told him about Marjani and Esi kidnapping me—without using their names—and about the Kabaregas catching me.

"Kabaregas?" He said the clan name with distaste. "Was the senior wife named Dorscha?"

I blinked. How had he known that? "Yes."

A look of revulsion crossed his face. "You won't have to worry about her again. She's just been arrested for killing another Kabarega."

For a second I thought I'd heard him wrong. Dorscha had seemed fanatical but not homicidal. Had she snapped and turned on Oni for arguing with her? "Who was it?"

Max cleared his throat. "It wasn't anyone from her own household," he said, as if that somehow made the crime less horrible. "It was some homeless Kabarega who lived nearby. She had been injured already and couldn't run away."

Esi! Dorscha had killed Esi! But why?

Because of me. Dorscha must have found the cave and killed Esi, maybe because Esi told her I was out of her reach forever, or maybe just because I wasn't there.

"Are you all right?"

Max sounded worried so I must have looked as sick as I felt. I couldn't believe Esi was dead. I had seen her—spoken with her—less than twen-

ty-four hours before, and now she was dead. It seemed impossible. "Yeah."
I sank down onto the edge of the bed. "I'm fine."

Except I still felt like I'd been hit by a truck. Poor Esi! And poor Marjani. I thought about Marjani heading back to the cave with the reward
money, ready to carry Esi all the way into the city for medical care. Had Esi
been dead already when we climbed the steps of the Ocan Garun's Palace?
It was hard to believe Dorscha could have succeeded if Marjani had been
there. "When did this happen?"

"Early this morning." He cleared his throat. "Apparently her *haru* were
horrified. They turned her in themselves."

Oni would certainly be able to take Dorscha in a fight, and she must
have had help. So Marjani would have arrived back at the cave to find Esi
dead or dying, or maybe missing altogether if they had already moved the
body. I swallowed hard and tasted bile. Esi had been a good person. Compared to most of Egume, she'd been remarkably sensitive and kindhearted.
She hadn't deserved what had happened to her. I remembered how happy
she had been at the idea of having a baby. She would never have that chance
now. My eyes welled up.

"Maybe you should eat something?" Max nodded at the door. "You
can ask the guards for food anytime. You're not being punished—not that
way, anyway."

I was ravenous, but his comment brought to mind a further question.
Max was married to the Ocan Garun. "Where are they going to send me?
Do you know?"

His face looked glum. "Not back to Hobart's. I tried arguing, but I
got nowhere. Right now it's still undecided, but you're definitely not going
there."

It looked like Teleza and her sisters would have to find someone else.
I hoped it was someone they liked. And I hoped Teleza didn't hate me. I
wasn't at all worried about what Zuwina thought.

A knock on the door signaled an end to Max's visit. I asked him to
tell Hobart I was okay, and to give him and everyone else at the house my
thanks for everything they had done for me. Max nodded, shook my hand,
and left.

The guards brought me dinner, and I ate it. Even hungry as I was, it
was hard to enjoy the food. I knew how a prisoner on trial felt waiting for
the jury to come back in.

After a woman took the tray away, I lay on the bed and stared at the
ceiling until I fell asleep again.

When I woke up, morning light streamed in the windows. The woman who had worn the bathrobe stood beside my bed, except now she wore a uniform.

"Get up," she said in Neluan. She nodded at a chair where some clothes were laid out. "Get dressed. You're leaving today."

I scrambled to my feet and looked at the clothes—underclothes, gray button-up trousers, a white shirt, and a red *thrya*. "Where am I going."

She grinned without a trace of humor. "You'll find out when you get there."

Sixteen

Whoever the woman who had worn the bathrobe was, she was efficient and short-tempered. When I came out of the bathroom wearing the Makoron clothes she had brought me, I found her waiting, all but tapping her foot. My jeans, tee shirt, and jacket had disappeared.

"Where are my clothes?" I asked.

She frowned. "They've been disposed of. You don't need them anymore, and they were in bad shape."

Maybe they were worn and grubby, but they were also mine. Before I could protest, she called in the guards from the corridor.

Four women came in carrying the same sort of straitjacket affair that I had been wrapped up in when I first arrived.

"What's going on?" I said.

Bathrobe Woman just smiled. "The Ocan Garun doesn't care to take any chances during your journey to your new home."

I tried to put up a fight, but those four women knew what they were doing. The shortest of them got my wrist in a grip that hurt like hell.

"Ow!"

"Hold still, then," Shortie said.

They had me trussed up in seconds.

"He's ready, madam," Shortie said, pulling the last strap tight.

Bathrobe Woman nodded. "Let's go."

She led the way, and my guards pushed me along behind her. We went out into a huge courtyard where what looked like an armored truck waited; it ran partly on wheels and partly on tracks like a tank. I had never seen a vehicle like it before except in old war movies.

Shortie shoved me into the back seat and then got in beside me and yanked me upright. Another guard got in on the other side, and then Bathrobe Woman opened the front passenger door and sat down next to the driver.

Bathrobe Woman took a quick glance at me and then spoke to the driver. "We're ready. Let's go."

The truck started up, and then I had my second ride through the streets of Egume. The blocks and blocks that Marjani and I had trudged through sped past at a high rate. I noted that the truck had little banners flying from both the front bumpers. They flapped briskly as we whizzed along, but I could see they included the green, gold, and red pattern that made up the Omdur flag, along with the Egume seal.

Other traffic made way for us, as if we had been an ambulance or a motorcade, so I figured the banners were the Ocan Garun's personal flag. We left the downtown area quickly and entered a suburban neighborhood much like the one where Hobart's house was, except these houses were even bigger—mostly three stories high and a full city block on a side—each with a tall *janullo* flying a clan banner above it. All the houses were built around squares, with a small garden or park in the center of each square.

"Where are we?" I asked.

Shortie looked to Bathrobe Woman, who glanced over her shoulder at me.

Bathrobe Woman lifted her brows. "If it matters to you, we just came into the Rufaro Grove area."

I glanced at the flags flying above the houses. I didn't know the Rufaro clan symbol, but all the nearby *janullos* flew the same flag, a blue field with a black border and some kind of gold emblem in the middle.

Shortly after that the hovercar pulled up at a huge, block-like house with almost no windows. The gate didn't swing open like the double gate on Monica's grandfather's estate, or like the single gates at Hobart's house. Instead a spiked steel grid, rather like the portcullis in a medieval castle, rose up into the roof of the tunnel that went through the wall. We drove past that and stopped. The first portcullis lowered to the ground with a clang before a second one lifted and we could drive into the courtyard.

If Hobart's house had been a minimum security prison, I was in maximum security now. I wondered what the guys in this place had done to deserve such treatment, and then I saw a whole cluster of boys—eight of them, aged three to nine or so—running from the doorway into the courtyard.

That explained it.

FOR a few minutes I thought it might have been a school for boys or something, but a bunch of women and girls joined the boys, and then the one adult guy, just like the day I had met Hobart and his family.

This man was much younger than Hobart, and both stockier and taller. He looked liked he worked out. He wore his black hair in that same Mr. Spock pointy sideburns haircut that Hobart had worn, but he also had a slight beard—more of a 5:00 shadow than a real beard.

They all waited for me, mimicking the welcome I had gotten from Adeola's household, but this time Shortie had to drag me out of the truck because I couldn't climb out myself. Once they got me out and standing, Bathrobe Woman waited while Shortie and the others undid the straps and set me loose.

"Why is he all tied up, *Daida*?" one of the younger boys asked.

"Hush!" The man bent down and said something else, and the boy ducked his head like he had been scolded.

"Welcome, madam," a woman in a green and brown suit said to Bathrobe Woman. She looked about thirty-five or so, only a couple years older than the man, and she had a pleasant expression. "We're happy to be able to oblige the Ocan Garun."

Bathrobe Woman nodded and glanced up at the blue flag flying at the top of the *janullo*. "Hopefully, we will do a better job of keeping the boy safe than the Omdur did."

I figured that meant she was in the same clan as this household. How did everyone know what clan someone was in? Or did it only matter in marriages and stuff like that?

The woman in the green and brown suit smiled at me. "Welcome, Jayzoon. My name is Lisha Rufaro Vai, and I'm the senior wife here." She indicated the man next to her. "And this is our husband, David Rufaro Medwar."

The first name caught my attention at once. "Are you—"

He shook his head even while he held out his hand. "I was born here in Egume. But my father was *keesai*."

I shook hands with a weird sense of *deja vu*. It felt like I should know the guy, which was impossible. And then the name clicked in my memory. "What was your father's name?" I asked.

"Edward Rufaro Kowalski."

I was shaking hands with Marjani's brother.

MY first day at the Rufaro house was a lot like my first day at Hobart's house except this time I could talk to everyone, and I wasn't as homesick. I was even more depressed, though, because I didn't get a room of my own. Except for David's suite, the men's space was like a dorm at a boarding school. All but the two youngest of David's eight sons lived there. The little ones slept in their mothers' rooms, but the six older ones shared two rooms on the ground floor, below David's suite. David explained I would have a lower bunk in the room occupied by his three oldest boys. When David and I walked into the room, the radio console was tuned to a station that sounded like someone was torturing small animals while thumping a steel drum with a stick.

Even David winced. "I'm sorry you have to share, but at least you won't be lonely."

But I was lonely. And I was also damn mad. I was fed up with being treated like a criminal or a mental patient. And I was really peeved that none of David's ten daughters was older than eleven.

David, on the other hand, seemed glad to have me there. He fell all over himself offering fencing lessons and *jin-weh* lessons. I took him up on it, partly for something to do, and partly because I figured either skill could come in handy.

I found out with my first lesson that David had Hobart beat at both fencing and *jin-weh*. He could disarm me in seconds or toss me to the floor at the same rate, even though I was two inches taller and had a longer reach. Usually, though, David let me stay armed or upright so I could practice. I noticed he did the same with his sons, and his daughters, too, when they joined us. Even the little ones could disarm me in fencing, so they all had fun at my expense.

In addition to PE, I spent a few hours each day in the family school—two rooms in the main part of the house. While one of David's wives taught the younger children, the family had hired a professional teacher for the older boys. Her name was Irna. I liked her because she was twenty-six and hot, and she was kind to me. David's seven wives treated me like I was a parolee on work release, but Irna seemed to see me more as a special needs kid who could be helped by extra attention.

"You need to read more, Jayzoon," she said on my third day in her class. "When you meet prospective brides, you need to be able to converse about history and current events."

"I don't think that's much of a consideration here," I said. "It seems to me all I have to be is male."

She shook her head as if despairing my attitude, and reached across the hi-tech desk, which was part furniture and part computer, to change the monitor so it displayed the local news. "Read!" she said, and then she moved off to deal with the other boys.

I did read, but mostly it was because I saw a familiar face. Dorscha had been arraigned for killing Esi. A picture showed her standing in the same kind of straitjacket I had worn, outside an official-looking building. Several uniformed women marched her along and kept back a crowd of onlookers.

I tapped the screen and the still photo moved, showing Dorscha flinching as the women in the crowd shouted at her, her guards pushing her to keep walking. I saw Oni waiting, not shouting, not moving at all, just watching, and a couple other faces familiar from the Kabarega camp. I didn't see Marjani anywhere.

The clip ended, and I read the article posted with it. Esi had been beaten to death, battered with a heavy flashlight until it cracked her skull. The report mentioned the cause of Dorscha's rage as her attempt to marry a young escaped *keesai* whom Esi and a companion had captured. It didn't give my name, just 'a young escaped *keesai*.' It reported that Marjani had properly turned me in for the reward, and described Dorscha's attempt at marriage as 'an example of the desperation the current economic climate has created, where unemployed and underemployed women don't have the means to form viable households.'

I wondered if they would call me as a witness at the trial, which was set to start in a week. It seemed incredibly quick compared to the U.S., but maybe Makoron courts were more efficient. On a hunch, I searched through the news database. I found only twelve murders reported over the past year in Egume. It seemed a low number for a city that size, and then it occurred to me that that might have been because the men were all locked up. The thought depressed me even further.

When class ended, I tried hanging around to talk to Irna, but Lisha showed up and took her off for a conversation about the boys' progress in social studies. Unlike Adeola, Lisha seemed to be home all the time. She also watched me a lot, which creeped me out. Since even the oldest girl in the house couldn't marry for several years, I was pretty sure Lisha wasn't sizing me up as a prospective son-in-law.

I walked into the courtyard and looked up at the sky. This courtyard wasn't completely open like the one in Hobart's house. A giant spider web of steel cables covered the entire opening. The hummingbirds that flitted and zoomed around the giant red flowers got through just fine, but I'd have a hard time. And even the attic windows were just narrow slits, too skinny for me to ever get out that way.

I let out a ragged sigh, half despair and half anger.

"You sound like you could use some exercise?"

I turned and found David standing there wearing white, loose-fitting *jin-weh* workout clothes, almost like they wore for karate back home.

"All right," I said, without any real enthusiasm. I didn't want that kind of exercise—jumping around a big empty room or even lifting weights. What I really wanted was to start walking to the bus stop and find Ryan waiting to give me a ride; I wanted to do pushups in my room and have my little sister burst in to call me to breakfast; I even wanted to help Mom with the laundry.

As we started for the men's quarters, it occurred to me that Marjani had said her brothers knew English.

"Is your father still alive?" I asked in that language.

David turned his head, an astonished look on his face, and answered in passable English. "No. He died several years ago, from—from bad lungs. He said that when he was young he had too many bad habits."

Probably smoking, which no one seemed to do on Makoro. "But he taught you his language?"

"Yes, but I have not spoken it since he died, except a few times to my brothers." He cocked his head. "How did you know I speak it?"

"Your sister told me."

He stopped dead. "Marjani?"

I nodded and stopped, too. We were right outside the door to the men's quarters.

"I knew she was the one who had found you," David said, switching to Neluan. "I didn't realize you knew she was my sister—or that you had conversed with her." He grinned as he opened the door. "It seems very like her to make conversation with a delinquent. How is Marjani?"

I followed him inside. "She's healthy, but probably not happy."

David led the way to the gym. He had a better gym than Hobart did—more equipment and more room. "You mean because Esi was killed?"

I recalled Marjani saying that she and Esi had stayed a few weeks with her youngest brother. She must have meant David. "Marjani loved her very much."

David nodded. "I know that. Marjani never loved any man except her blood relations. It made life much harder for her." He sort of sighed and tisked at the same time, like he was out of patience and disgusted. "When I heard she had turned you in, I hoped it meant she was more accepting of social conventions, but perhaps I was wrong. It was a great tragedy that

Esi was a Kabarega. If she had been an Omdur, my sisters could have welcomed her as *haru* and Marjani would never have disgraced herself."

Another example of clans mattering more than anything else. It was fine for a woman to be gay as long as she could invite her lover into her household.

"I wonder what Marjani will do now? I think my sisters would allow her to return to their household but— David stopped like he had just realized he was talking to a stranger and waved a hand at the dressing room. "Get changed, and we'll get started."

We spent over an hour practicing *jin-weh* moves. After that I lifted weights for another hour. The exercise did help, but I still felt a restless energy.

I lay in my lower bunk that night listening to the kid above me muttering in his sleep, and tried to think of a way to get home. Making the Turn was the only way. But I'd need to be in danger, and I'd need to be turned on, and in this house, neither one would be easy to do.

IT was only two days later that David stuck his head into the classroom and called out my name.

I looked up from my desk. "Yes?"

He grinned at me. "There's someone here to see you."

I started to ask who would come to see me—who would be allowed in to see me—when it came to me.

It had to be Marjani.

DAVID had parked his sister in a sitting room on the ground floor. Lisha sat there, too, planted firmly in an armchair. Her resolute air said she wasn't going anywhere anytime soon. Apparently I was allowed a visitor, but not a solo visit.

Marjani looked well scrubbed but a little haggard, like she had cleaned herself up but hadn't been sleeping well. Her thick black hair looked clean and recently trimmed, and her black pantsuit looked new.

"Hello, Jason," she said in Neluan.

"Hello, Marjani." I looked at Lisha and wondered if there was anything I could say to get her to leave.

"Sit down, Jayzoon," Lisha said.

Apparently there wasn't. I sat. "How are you?" I asked Marjani.

"Well enough." She glanced around the well furnished room. "You must be comfortable here. It's a beautiful house."

It occurred to me that Lisha might be so firmly settled in because she mistrusted Marjani more than she mistrusted me. "It's comfortable except they have me sleeping in a bunk bed with the older boys." With Lisha sitting there, I didn't want to mention her son's horrible taste in music.

Marjani grinned. "Well, they could hardly let you sleep with the older girls."

I smiled back, but Lisha didn't looked amused.

"I was sorry to hear about Esi," I said, because it had to be said. "Very sorry."

A spasm of pain crossed Marjani's face, but it was gone in seconds. "Thank you. I appreciate that you tried your best to help her."

I cleared my throat and wondered what else I could say. "Will you attend the trial?"

The spasm came back, stronger this time. "No, probably not." She stared out the window like she had never seen flowers and grass and hummingbirds. "The Kabaregas seem to be taking responsibility. No one is trying to get Dorscha off."

"What do you think her sentence will be?"

"Life in a work camp," Marjani said firmly, like she was convincing herself. "I hear the other prisoners treat murderers badly." She turned back to look at me. "How strange that you should end up in my brother's house!"

"An amazing coincidence," I said.

Marjani shook her head. "Not that amazing. David has more sons than any man in Egume, so of course his house is more secure than most. And since his daughters are too young for you to marry, the Ocan Garun doesn't mind that this is a Rufaro household, not an Omdur one."

Lisha frowned. I wasn't sure if it was actual bad manners to mention the politics of my incarceration, or just plainer speaking than she liked, but clearly she was put out.

"I thought this house was a school at first," I said, hoping to lighten the atmosphere.

Marjani smiled the most natural smile I had seen from her that day. "Not a school, only a family." The smile faded a little. "Family is very important. I should have visited David before this."

It sounded like maybe she'd had a chance to talk with her brother. Hopefully, Lisha hadn't stayed in the room for that, too.

Marjani interrupted my thoughts by asking me about my fencing and *jin-weh* lessons with David.

I rattled on about it while Lisha sat silent and disapproving.

After about fifteen minutes, it was like a timer went off in Lisha's head because she suddenly stood up. "Time for you to go, Marjani."

I jumped up, too, as Marjani got to her feet. She surprised me by offering her hand.

"Goodbye, Jason."

I reached out to shake Marjani's hand and as I clasped it, I felt something solid in her palm.

She gripped my hand tightly. "As my father used to say to me, study well, and you'll be sure to prosper."

I managed to grasp whatever it was when she let go of me. "Thank you. I will."

Lisha made it clear that she was going to be the one to walk Marjani to the gate, not me, which was fine with me. I went straight to the men's quarters and locked myself in the bathroom so I could see what Marjani had slipped me.

It was just a piece of paper folded several times. I unfolded it, and found a rough floor plan of David's house. Right at the base of the *janullo* Marjani had drawn an arrow with a notation. 'Access panel on second floor' it said.

Underneath the drawing was a brief note:

> Jason—
>
> Find a saw that can cut metal. You will
> need it to cut through the vents. You can get
> outside once you are above the house. Please
> destroy this note.

That was it—just those four sentences with no signature. But it was enough. Marjani had given me a way out!

Seventeen

I wasted no time looking for the access panel in Marjani's drawing. The older girls' rooms occupied that part of the second floor, so I waited until the next morning when they had all left for school and my classes hadn't started yet. A tapestry hung over the wall between the window and the nearest bedroom, but whether the panel was hidden for security reasons or for aesthetics, I didn't know.

When I pulled the tapestry back, I could see the panel was more of a door, made of wood, about four feet high and two feet wide. It had hinges on one side and a lock with a keyhole on the other. I didn't think I could pick the lock, so I checked the screws that secured the hinges to the wall, to see what kind of tool I would need to take them off. The screw heads had a three-legged groove rather than a single flat groove or a crossed one, so a knife wouldn't work.

I went to class trying to think where I could find the right tools. I couldn't recall seeing any tools in the house. Over the course of the day I went looking, but there I was balked. No one seemed to have any, and unlike Hobart's house, I wasn't welcome in the kitchen. The wife who cooked the meals didn't look happy when she caught me pulling open drawers later that afternoon.

"Aren't you supposed to be in class?" she asked.

"Irna is giving the boys a lesson on plants, in the courtyard," I said. "And I'm hungry."

She frowned at the drawer full of eating utensils I had just opened. "You won't find any food in there."

She fetched some crackers from a cupboard and shooed me firmly away.

I ate the crackers and then went to join the boys in the courtyard. Irna smiled at me as she expounded on the various types of plants growing in the flower beds and hanging planters, and then we all trooped back to the schoolroom for a quiz, which I failed because I hadn't been paying attention.

"Don't worry, Jayzoon," Irna said. "You'll catch up soon."

I didn't want to catch up; I wanted to go home.

And then, that afternoon I found help in the most unlikely place.

DAVID'S oldest daughter was an eleven-year-old named Nuri. She had pretty much ignored me since my arrival, and I hadn't had a reason to pay much attention to her.

But that afternoon I was watching out the window of the dorm when Nuri pushed a funny-looking wobbly bicycle into the courtyard. I had seen bikes in the street, and in pictures in my schoolbooks, but not up close. No one in Hobart's house had used one. Nuri propped the bike up against one of the benches and set a wooden toolbox down on the ground next to it.

I got up and went outside. I tried to look casual as I walked over to where Nuri had opened the toolbox and was laying out tools. "What are you doing?" I asked.

She looked up at me and squinted. I realized the sun was behind me, and she must be looking up at it. "None of your business."

I was much too hopeful about the toolbox to take the hint. I crouched down next to her and inspected the bike. It had two wheels, but no chain that I could see. I wasn't sure if it was supposed to have a chain or not. It didn't look like any bicycle I had ever ridden. It had a steering wheel instead of handlebars, and the seat was almost a chair. "Is it broken?"

She made a dismissive noise. "Yes. Why else would someone have thrown it away?"

That surprised me. "I thought your family was too rich to worry about fixing broken things."

Nuri gave me a disdainful grimace, like I had made a stupid suggestion. "I'm not fixing it because I *need* to fix it. I'm fixing it because I like fixing things."

Just the kind of person I needed. I felt better than I had in days. "So what's broken?"

She screwed her face up into a look of intent interest. "I'm not sure. I never fixed anything as big as a bicycle before."

I glanced down at the toolbox and the tools spread out on the grass. Among them was an assortment of different-sized screwdrivers and what looked like a hacksaw. Yes! "Do you have any books on how bicycles work?"

She lifted her face in a more thoughtful expression. "Books?"

I had a sudden wrenching sense of homesickness because it reminded me of helping Lorrie with her middle school science project. "Yeah. Sometimes when something is broken it helps to find a book on how it's supposed to work."

She mulled that over for a bit, and then scrambled to her feet. "Don't touch anything! I'll be right back."

She turned and ran for the girls' wing. I got up and reviewed the courtyard as I slid onto the bench. A couple of the boys were playing a game of marbles in one corner, four girls were jumping rope—two turning the ends and the other two jumping in turn to a rhyme—and one of the wives was sitting in the sun knitting a scarf, but no one seemed to be paying any attention to me.

And then I noticed Lisha in the sitting room window. She was leaning on her elbows and looking right at me. I leaned back and stretched my legs out in front of me, like I didn't have a care in the world.

I might have found some tools, but they were a long way from in my hands. I'd have to watch my step.

NURI and I worked on the broken bicycle for two days. At the end of each day she carefully packed up her tools and took away the toolbox, which frustrated me no end, but I was still hopeful, because I at least knew the right tools were in the house.

Nuri was much more mechanically inclined than I was, but sometimes she needed an extra pair of hands, so she tolerated me. Her mother had bought her all the missing bike parts and found her a book on bicycle repair, and with that help, it seemed likely Nuri could get everything working again.

On the third day, I was sitting on the grass watching while Nuri fastened the gearshift back onto the frame when I saw a shadow on the grass next to us. I turned and saw David looking down at us.

"How is it going?" he asked.

"Almost done," Nuri said. She grinned. "Did you think I couldn't fix it, *Daida*?"

David shook his head. "Never." He nodded at me. "But I didn't expect you would have help."

Nuri frowned.

"I'm just the assistant," I said. "I hand her things, and sometimes I help her tighten bolts and things."

This seemed to mollify Nuri. "Jayzoon has been helpful."

David looked the bike over and then looked at Nuri. "Is it too big for you?"

It was a little big. Nuri had tried it out the day before and her tiptoes could barely touch the ground when she sat on the seat. "It's fine," she said.

David glanced around the courtyard. "You'll have to take it outside to really try it out. Not enough room here."

Nuri tightened the last nut, gave the pedals a spin, and stood up. "I wish you could come watch me, *Daida*."

"I wish I could, too." David sounded a little wistful. "But your mother will be home from work soon."

"I don't need *help*." Nuri's tone reeked of indignation. "I can ride it, but I wish you could watch me."

"I can watch from the window," he said. "Your mother's room is on the side of the house that overlooks the park."

I knew the room he meant. I had scoped out every window in the house. The ones that overlooked the street next to the park were all tall but very narrow, only about eight inches wide.

Nuri tossed her wrench into the toolbox and shut the lid. "I'll put this away, and then you and Jayzoon can go watch me."

I started to offer to take the toolbox but David was too quick for me. He took the box from Nuri's hand. "I'll take care of it. You take your bike outside."

She grinned and pushed the bike along. It rolled smoothly, without a squeak or a wobble.

"She's very good with her hands," I said.

"Her mother is an engineer," David said. "Nuri comes by the talent from her." He waved the toolbox toward the house. "Come on. Let's go see how she does."

I followed. I would have followed that toolbox anywhere in the house.

David led the way to the second floor in the main part of the house. He pushed the door to Nuri's mother's room open without knocking, but then he knew the occupant wasn't there. We moved to the two narrow windows set into the wall, without drapes or curtains obscuring them.

David stood at one window, and I stood at the other. Down in the street I could see Nuri waiting by her bicycle, looking up at the house. When David waved, she smiled and waved back.

She tilted the bike and swung one leg over the bar.

"Does she even know how to ride?" I asked.

"She's had a bike for years, but it's smaller," David said. "I hope this one isn't too much for her."

Nuri had got herself upright on the bike. She pushed off quickly, wobbled once, then straightened out and took off at a brisk pace, speeding down the street and turning the corner to circle the park.

"She's doing fine," David said, as if I were the only one who had doubted Nuri could handle the bike. He put the toolbox down on the table between the windows and stood with his hands on his hips, watching out the window.

In a few seconds, Nuri came around the corner of the park and headed back toward the house. She was doing well until a dog ran into the street in front of her.

Nuri braked, but she wasn't able to get her foot down in time to stop herself from falling. Just as David shouted a warning that Nuri could never have heard, a hovercar pulled out from an adjacent house.

Nuri went down, and I couldn't see whether the hovercar went over her or not.

"Nuri!" David turned and raced from the room at a dead run.

I felt terrible for not running just as fast, but I didn't know how many chances I would get. I ripped open the toolbox, found the screwdriver and the hacksaw, closed the box, and only then left the room. I didn't go straight to the courtyard, though. I ran to the corridor with the tapestry and stuck the tools behind it. I made sure they didn't show at all and then, finally, I raced downstairs and outside.

David was pacing by the steel door next to the hovercar entrance.

"What happened?" I demanded before he could ask where I had been. "I couldn't see well. What happened?"

"Nuri fell," he said, running one hand through his black hair. He looked pale, and he had a portable phone clenched in one hand. "Lisha is checking on her."

The phone blipped, and David lifted it to eye level. "What?"

I couldn't see Lisha's face but I heard her voice from where I stood. She sounded concerned. "She hit her head. And her arm looks odd. I think she'll be all right, but I've called an ambulance."

Shoulders hunched, David kept his head down as he asked a few questions. He got incomplete answers because Lisha wasn't a doctor. In a few minutes we heard the wail of a siren. David tried to see out the steel gates of the car entrance, but it didn't show much except the ambulance passing in a blur.

More of David's wives, sons, and daughters gathered at the gate as they heard what had happened. Finally, Lisha called to say she was at the hospital, and Nuri would be fine, but two of her ribs were cracked and her arm was broken. They were keeping her overnight to be sure nothing more serious was wrong. Lisha said Nuri's mother was on her way, and that Lisha would come home only after Nuri's mother had arrived.

David's shoulders finally relaxed, and some color returned to his face.

"I feel bad for helping Nuri fix the bike," I said.

He blinked. "What? Oh, no, it wasn't you. I let her ride it." He shook his head like he was coming awake. "Her mother will kill me."

The rest of them clustered around David and reassured him. I took the opportunity to slink off alone.

I had the tools in place. Now I just needed a chance to use them.

Eighteen

Nuri came home the next day, a very chastened Nuri, who had to stay in bed because she had a concussion—I'd had to look up the meaning of the Neluan word for that when I heard it—along with a broken arm and two cracked ribs. They had shaved a small patch of her short brown hair off to apply the bandage that wrapped around her head, and that and her pale face gave her a dismal look. The cast on her right arm didn't help either.

I waited until all her brothers and sisters had visited to go to see her. "You look pretty awful," I said with the same frankness I would have used with Lorrie. "How do you feel?"

"Not too bad," she said. They had her lying flat on her back, but someone had propped up the head of the bed so she could talk to people, and she fidgeted like she wasn't comfortable. "But my mother won't let me keep the bicycle."

"You'd grow into it in a year or so," I said. "They could just keep it for you. No one else would need it until then."

She was the tallest kid in the house unless you counted me.

Apparently, Nuri did count me, because she looked suddenly grave and said, "It's too bad you're a boy. If you were a girl you could ride it."

"If I were a girl I wouldn't be here." That was one thing Hobart had been sure of. No girls had ever come through from my world to Makoro.

Nuri cocked her head and looked at me. "I was always glad I wasn't a boy, because I wanted to do things and not have to stay in the house all day. But I never thought how unfair it all was, until now."

It was the first time I could remember someone from Egume admitting boys weren't treated fairly. "Thanks, but I'd just as soon not be a girl."

She nodded, her eyes so solemn and her expression so serious that she looked sort of like a patched-together, very small Buddha. "You shouldn't have to be a girl to do stuff."

I leaned over and gave her hair a quick rub, not pressing hard and avoiding the sore part of her head. "I agree."

She scrunched her face up. "When I'm grown up, I'm going to fight to make new laws so that men and boys can't be locked up."

I smiled at her fierceness, but I took her comment seriously. She had the kind of determination that got things done, and if she stuck to her inclination, she really might be able to change this world one day. "That's not enough, hot shot. You have to make sure they don't get kidnapped or forced into households if they walk out in the street."

She sighed and shook her head. "I'll have to think about it."

Well, she was only eleven. It wasn't fair to expect an instant solution. "Don't think too hard. You have a concussion, remember."

"I know." She sounded even more unhappy. "And cracked ribs. I can't even fix things for at least a week."

Which meant it would be a week before she would open her toolbox and possibly notice some of her tools were missing. I felt like a total louse for being glad I had those seven days.

FOUR days went by without anything resembling a chance to use my escape route. The problem was, I was almost never alone. I ate with the family, went to school in a group, exercised with David, and slept in a virtual dorm room. Except for the bathroom, I had no privacy and no chance to slip away unnoticed.

I was leaning back on a bench in the courtyard during a break from school when David walked outside. I could tell right away something was up. He walked fast, and he looked grim.

I sat up as he got close.

"I need to tell you something," he said without any kind of greeting. "They're coming for you today. They might even be on their way now."

"Who?" I stood up so fast I felt dizzy. "Who's coming, and where are they taking me?"

"To your new house—your own house."

I tried to sort that out. "You mean . . ." I couldn't make myself say it.

David nodded. "The Ocan Garun has declared you legally of age and granted a brand new Omdur household the right to claim you as a husband." He let out a sigh. "Congratulations, Jason. Today is your wedding day."

Between *deja vu* and standing up too fast, it was all I could do to stay on my feet. "How—how many women are there?"

"Seven." His grim look eased. "At least the oldest one is only twenty-six."

I was tempted to ask for more details, but I didn't want to waste the time. This was it. If I was going to get out of here, it would have to be now—right now. "I—I think I'd like to go say goodbye to Nuri, if you don't mind."

"Of course." He shot a quick glance over his shoulder at the school-room window. "I'll tell Irna and the others you won't be coming back. I'm sure they'll come see you off when—when the Omdur delegation gets here." He looked me up and down. "I'll find you a *thrya* to wear, too, so you make a good impression."

"Thanks." I headed for the door to the bedroom wing. It wasn't Nuri I wanted to get to so quickly, it was my tools—and the access panel.

I climbed the stairs two at a time. In a way it was a good time for this to happen. Except for Nuri, everyone who went to school or a job was busy, and Lisha was out of the house for once, doing some shopping.

I went straight to the tapestry and pulled it back. The tools were still there. I pulled a nearby chair over to hold the tapestry out of the way while I started working on the hinges. The need for haste made my stomach do flip-flops, but I forced myself to stay cool. I got the first hinge unscrewed quickly, but just as I was starting on the second one I heard a sound.

I turned, and Nuri stood there in her pajamas.

I didn't know what to say. There I was kneeling on the floor unscrewing a hinge from the wall—with her screw driver! What was there to say?

"Is something broken?" Nuri asked in a hopeful tone.

I was tempted to say yes, but then she would never have left. "No."

"Then what are you doing?"

I took a deep breath. There was no way I could hurt her, not even to save myself. And in her condition, there was no safe way to put her out of commission. "I'm trying to get out of the house so I can go home to my own world and my own family."

She didn't say anything for a minute. And then she nodded. "I think you should go home." She glanced down at the hacksaw—her hacksaw—and then up at me. She didn't say anything for a moment, and then she took two steps, bent over and kissed my forehead. "Goodbye, Jayzoon." She turned to go and then grimaced. "I think I'll go to bed and pretend to sleep. If anyone asks me, I'll say you read to me until I fell asleep, and I don't know where you are now."

I was touched. I didn't know if it would help me any, but it was nice she was trying. "Goodbye, Nuri, and thank you."

She padded down the hall to her own doorway, and I went back to unscrewing the hinge.

I got the door off and then put the chair back so the tapestry hung down over the panel again. Just as I came back, Nuri came out of her room. She held a coiled-up jump rope in one hand.

"You'll need this," she said.

She was right. If I'd been able to find one, I would have stolen a rope. "Thank you."

She handed it to me, glanced down the hall, and whispered, "Hurry!"

I didn't need any reminder. I ducked inside, and then I heard Nuri push the panel back in place.

As soon as she did, it got really dark.

I hadn't thought about bringing a light. Well, I hadn't had enough time to plan. I remembered the Omdur women on their way to the house, and it made me not worry about how dark it was or how funky it smelled—sort of musty, like an attic that had been closed up a long time.

I felt around the walls and discovered a series of rungs, like a built-in ladder. I put the screwdriver in my pocket, just in case I needed it again, slipped the coil of rope around my neck and one arm, bandoleer-style, tucked the hacksaw carefully inside my shirt, and started to climb. After about twenty rungs my head bumped something very solid.

"Fuck!" I held on with one hand and felt above me with the other. It was a sort of trapdoor, made of steel or some other hard metal, with hinges on one side. I found a bolt and pushed it back, but the trap door wouldn't open.

I was afraid it had a lock that needed a key, until my hand found a second bolt. I undid that one, and sure enough the latch turned. I pushed the trapdoor upward.

Light flooded the space and temporarily blinded me. When I could see I looked up; I was inside the *janullo*. It was a little like a church steeple, only it was lit by periodic shafts of light every six or seven feet. A cable ran up one wall, and I figured that must be the wiring for the blinking red lights that shone from the *janullo* at night. But the important thing was, the rungs kept going. I started to climb, carefully closing the heavy steel trapdoor behind me.

In just a little bit I came to a vent about two feet square. It was sort of like an ornamental metal grate, all curlicues and curvy lines. When I peered through it, I could see the roof and the city skyline, and I felt a breeze moving past my face.

I hooked my right arm around the rung of the ladder and pulled the hacksaw out of my shirt.

"Ow!" I hadn't meant to yell, but I hadn't meant to cut myself on the chest, either.

I ignored the blood and worked on wedging the tip of the hacksaw between the curlicues. It was a tight fit, but I got it at a decent angle and began to saw. It felt like it took hours but probably it was just minutes before I cut through the first curlicue. I bent the metal piece back to make the hole bigger. This gave me room to work and I sawed faster after that. Eventually I cut through all the metal pieces on the bottom and started working my way up the sides. It didn't take long for each piece, but there were a lot of them.

Finally, I stopped. I tried to put the hacksaw back into my shirt but it fell and landed on the trapdoor with a loud clang that reverberated in the tower.

I flinched and braced myself for shouts or other sounds of pursuit, but I heard nothing. I tightened my grip on the rung with my right hand and pushed as hard as I could on the bottom of the grate with my left. It bent slowly outward. I got my breath and pushed again. It bent more. I leaned out through the opening. I could see an unfamiliar hovercar pulling into the house through the portcullis.

No time! I pushed with all my strength, and the bottom of the grate bent outward a good two feet away from the tower.

I climbed up a few rungs, and then stuck my feet through the hole. I kept my grip on the rung as I lowered myself down and only let go when I had to. I started to drop, and then my shirt caught on the grate. I fought panic and managed to pull free, and finally slid downward. After a moment my feet hit the shingles. I slithered out the rest of the way and stood triumphantly on the roof for about three seconds. I was out!

And then I started to slide.

I WISHED I had learned to skateboard. As it was, I lost my balance and tumbled down the slope of the roof until I came to a gable. I grabbed it and stopped myself from falling. I crawled on my hands and knees along the edge of the roof to the back of the house expecting any second that someone would come into the street, look up, and see me creeping along like a burglar.

When I came to an exposed truss under the eaves, I tied off one end of Nuri's jump rope, gripped the rope a few feet below the knot, and then swung down. I could hear shouting from inside the house. They must have realized I was missing.

Damn! If I had known how many times I'd need to climb down a rope I would have paid more attention in gym. The rope burned my hands as I half climbed and half slid down it. When I got to the end, I was still ten feet in the air. I bent my knees and let go.

I landed hard. My butt hit the pavement.

"Ow!"

"Be quiet, Jason!"

I twisted around. "Marjani!"

She stood there grinning at me. She wore her old clothes, not the fancy new suit, but she looked less haggard. "This way!"

When she turned and sprinted across the street, I followed as fast as I could. Behind me I heard the steel door open and the portcullis start to lift.

Marjani had run into an alley lined on either side with garage doors. She pulled open a door and beckoned to me. After I raced inside, she followed me in and pulled the door shut behind her.

We were completely in the dark.

"What is this place?" I whispered.

"A garage I rented for the month." I heard the laughter in her voice even if I couldn't see her smile. "I was beginning to wonder if you were ever going to get out of that house."

"Me, too."

My eyes were getting used to the dark. I heard shouting again, women's voices raised, calling to each other.

"Come on!" Marjani said, and she raced over to a large, bulky shape. When she opened the door I realized it was a hovercar. I opened the other door and got in.

"How did you get this car?" I asked as she started the engine.

"This is where most of the reward money went." She looked at me and I could see her eyes gleaming in a thin crack of light coming in through the shutters of the windows. "Hold on."

The front end of the car nudged the doors open, revealing four formally dressed women standing in the alley with their backs to us, tugging on the garage doors on the other side of the street.

"Get down!" Marjani ordered.

I had already crouched down so low I could no longer see what was happening.

Marjani made a sharp right and sped out into the alley. I heard someone shout for us to stop, but Marjani paid no attention.

After a few seconds, I started to sit up, but Marjani put a hand on my shoulder. "Stay down! If people see a man riding in a car, they'll pay attention."

I felt like a pretzel, scrunched down in the seat with my knees against the dash and my torso twisted to fit into the seat without letting my head show above the bottom of the window, but I did as she said. Marjani drove like a maniac. I could see houses and trees flash past, flags flying from *janullos*, and patches of sky. I began to worry that I would get carsick.

"I didn't know you planned to wait outside to help me," I said as a distraction. "Your note didn't mention it."

"I didn't decide to do it until two days after I wrote the note." She flashed a smile in my direction. "I realized getting you out of Lisha's house didn't do much good by itself."

I thought about it. "If I had known you were waiting for me, I would have been worried you'd give up."

"I almost did give up. But I had nothing better to do, and I wanted to help you like you tried to help Esi. So I bought the car, and I waited." She glanced over her shoulder and let out a sigh. "There. I don't think anyone is following us. Where do you want to go, Jason?"

At last, some help that didn't involve walking for hours. I tried to stretch without sitting up, but I couldn't. "I want to go to your place—the place you took me to first, not the cave."

She shot me a quick glance, her eyes opened wide in surprise. "Why? The Kabaregas burned everything. There's nothing left there."

"I know that."

She kept both eyes on the road and frowned. "Then why do you want to go there?"

I told her why.

Marjani shook her head. "You're crazy, Jason."

"Does that mean you won't help me?"

"No." There was a long pause. "No, if that's what you want, I'll take you there."

IN the failing light of twilight, the squat looked pretty dismal with the pile of ashes and blackened chunks of wood strewn about in front of it. The gaping hole the Kabaregas had made by pulling down Esi and Marjani's front wall didn't help.

Marjani's face looked dismal, too, when she stared at the place where she and Esi had lived.

I hadn't realized that asking to come back here would bring back so many memories for her. It wasn't the squat I needed, really, it was the access to the train track.

I surveyed the slope the squat was built into. The maglev track was raised on low pylons two to three feet high, but as it approached the hill where the squat was, the pylons grew taller and taller. Where the ground sloped down toward the creek, the pylons turned the track into a bridge that had to be twenty feet in the air.

"How long have we got until a train comes?"

She shrugged. "Soon. Ten minutes or so."

Not much time! Even with Makoron minutes being longer, it still gave me just under fifteen real minutes.

I'd have to hurry if I was going to have time to work myself up into a turned-on state. I looked at Marjani. I didn't think she'd be much help in that department. She'd never attracted me that way, and I knew quite well that I wasn't what she was looking for. I'd have to manage with mental stimulation and whatever else it took.

"I don't think this is a good idea, Jason," Marjani said. "You don't sound very sure you can make the Turn, and if you can't, you'll be stuck on the track. The next train is an express."

An express meant it would be going at least two hundred fifty miles an hour, which would make it hard for the engineer to stop if she saw me. All the better. "It's the only shot I've got."

Marjani put a hand on my shoulder like she meant to hold me back. "You're risking your life."

I thought about Mom and Lorrie and Sancho and Ryan and Clara Barton High School. I even thought about Monica Martin. I considered what life would be like if I stayed on Makoro, and added that to how much I missed everyone and everything at home. "If you could get Esi back—if you could go somewhere and know that Esi would be there waiting for you—would you risk your life to get there?"

Her eyes met mine. Her hand dropped from my shoulder. I could tell from her face she was wishing there was a way to do what I had said. "Yes, I would." She looked at the track. "I'd be right there with you."

I set my shoulders. "All right, then. Here I go."

We hurried around the slope to where the pylons were still short. I pulled myself up on top of the pylon and crouched there. The maglev track was a single raised strip about five or six feet across. The magnets were probably in the underneath part, which was wider than the raised strip by a foot or so on either side.

I waved goodbye to Marjani and then turned back toward the tracks. I wished I had paid more attention to how maglevs worked. I was pretty sure it wasn't like the Metro back home, where the train got power from a live third rail down the middle of the tracks. But still, it felt kind of creepy stepping from the pylon out onto the middle of the track. I glanced around. To be terrified enough to Turn, I'd need to have no way out. I walked up the track a good ways, walking over the squat and up the track until I was a lot higher up in the air. I stopped when I was at the peak, over the creek and halfway between two pylons. It gave me a great view, even in the twilight. I could see the lights of the city in the distance,

"Jason!" Marjani shouted. She had walked beside the track but stopped at the edge of the creek. I could still see her, but the light was going. "You won't be able to get down from up there if you change your mind."

"That's the idea," I shouted back. "I'll be fine. Thanks for your help."

She waved back, a big sweeping wave. "Good luck."

I suddenly remembered David's wish that she return to their sisters' household. "What will you do now? Will you go back to your sisters?"

She shook her head. "Even if they would take me back, I couldn't live like that again."

It occurred to me she could get in trouble if they caught her. "Will they punish you for helping me escape?"

I could barely see her oversized shrug. "I don't know if they'll figure out it was me. But anyway, I feel like starting over. I'll take the car and head north to Dodomah, or even farther."

"Good luck to you, too, then."

She waved again but didn't move. I set my shoulders. The thing was, standing there in the gathering darkness, I was the opposite of turned on. The scared part was easy. I was already scared. But girls were the last thing on my mind.

I took a deep breath and let it out slowly. I wished I'd gone in for yoga or something. After a few more deep breaths, I felt calmer. I closed my eyes and remembered going back to my room at Hobart's house and finding Teleza waiting for me. I remembered the way Teleza had unbuttoned her shirt so slowly and deliberately, one button at a time. I could see her slipping her shirt off, see her naked from the waist up, smiling at me.

I remembered ripping my own clothes off, lying down with her on Gyasi's bed, with the sunlight coming through the curtains and making patterns on Teleza's skin. I recalled the feel of her fingernails stroking my sides, making me burn.

I could feel myself getting into it. It wasn't that difficult, really, to think about something that had felt so good. In fact once I had started thinking about it, it was difficult to think of anything else. I let myself dwell on the very pleasant details of what had happened next.

And then I felt a tremor through my feet, a faint vibration that ran up my legs. I opened my eyes and saw a light in the distance, a bright light that seemed to be coming right at me.

I stood frozen. I really wanted to run down the slope and jump off the tracks, but I didn't. I made myself stand there, and at the same time I tried to think about how badly I wanted to be home, back on my own version of the Earth where my family was. I had thought about trying for our apartment, but I didn't want to risk giving Mom heart failure. Instead I pictured the most open space I could think of that I knew really well—Ryan's backyard. I wished really hard to be in Ryan's backyard.

I could see the train now, a dark shadowy shape behind the light that hurtled toward me like a comet. The bottom of the train engine curved around the raised strip of the track. It almost looked like a giant lighted zipper pull rushing along a huge zipper.

The track under me thrummed with a vibration that raced up my body. It felt like an earthquake and a sexual climax at the same time.

The train was so close and the light so bright that I couldn't watch it any longer. I lifted my eyes and saw the horrified face of the engineer. She waved both her arms frantically, like she wanted me to jump down.

God, I was crazy to do this! What had I been thinking? I just wanted to go home, and now I was going to die. I twisted to one side and shut my eyes.

Nineteen

I felt dizzy, and then suddenly it felt like I was falling.

I opened my eyes and saw treetops rushing past. I was falling! Before I could figure out where I was, I landed feet first in a pool of water.

I must have landed in the creek somehow. Water splashed everywhere, and my feet hit bottom quickly and hard, followed by the rest of me. I sat stunned for a second, holding my breath, and not seeing much but bubbles and churning water and my own knees. I pushed myself up to gasp for air and splashed even more.

I couldn't be in the creek. The water felt very warm, hot really. I was glad I didn't need to take a leak.

"Shit!" someone yelled in English.

I stood up, staggering, and found myself staring down at Ryan and Allie. Ryan had his arm around Allie, who wore a pink bikini. I couldn't tell if Ryan had anything on until he stood up and I saw his swim suit.

"Jason!" Ryan shouted.

I felt a little like I'd been through the spin cycle on Mom's washer. On top of it all, what had been open lawn now had a deck with lights, benches, and a five-person hot tub. "When did your folks put in a hot tub?" was all I could think of to say. I didn't want to comment on how hot Allie looked in a bikini.

Ryan threw his arms around me and slapped me on the back. "You're alive!"

I was alive but shivering. It was December in Maryland, and I was dripping wet.

Ryan let go, but he kept grinning. "You made it back!"

I nodded and glanced around at his backyard. The swing set his little brother still used stood next to the azalea bushes his mother had planted. The row of pine trees that blocked the neighbors from view gave off a familiar scent.

Ryan gave me his beach towel while Allie went inside to tell Ryan's parents I had dropped from the sky into their hot tub.

"Do your folks know about Makoro?" I asked, clutching the towel around me.

Ryan wrapped himself in the damp towel Allie had used before she went inside. "I told them, but I don't think they believed it." He grinned. "Not like the suits. They believed it."

"What suits?"

He tugged a corner of the towel loose and rubbed his wet hair. "A few days after the accident, some guys in dark suits showed up and started asking a lot of questions. They had badges from some government agency no one had ever heard of, and they never smiled."

"It sounds like *Person of Interest*."

He nodded. "I think it kind of is. They took Mr. Walters away for a few days, and then they let him go."

"You told them about Walters?"

Ryan looked a little guilty. "Dude, you vanished. That flaky driver's ed teacher swore you had disappeared *before* the crash, and the forensics guys backed him up—no human remains. It was in the news once, and then suddenly no one talked about it anymore."

I had almost forgotten about Mr. Aiyuku. "So Mr. Aiyuku lived through the accident?"

"Yeah, but right after he got out of the hospital they deported him." Ryan's guilty expression changed to a pensive frown. "I'm not sure if that was the suits' doing or not that he was deported, but it turned out he had lied to get into the U.S. His name wasn't really Aiyuku, he was from the Netherlands, not Rwanda, and he had a record."

That explained the odd accent.

The back door opened, and Ryan's mother stood there staring. "Jason Miller," she said after a long moment, "get in here before you freeze to death!"

We trooped inside. Allie was wearing a fluffy, too-big-for-her white bathrobe over her wet bikini, and Ryan's dad was on the phone.

He held the phone out to me. "Someone would like to talk to you, Jason."

I knew who it had to be.

"Jason?" Mom's voice said, cracking. "Jason, are you there?"

"Yeah, Mom," I said. For some reason, I seemed to have something caught in my throat. "It's me. I'm back."

I could hear her crying. "Are you all right?"

"I'm fine, Mom."

I heard Lorrie's voice in the background. "Is he okay? Can I talk to him?"

There were a couple of sobs, and then Lorrie's voice said, "Jason?"

"Hi, Squirt."

She laughed. "Mom's crying too much to talk. I'm glad you're back, Jason."

My eyes were welling up. I swallowed. "I'm glad I'm back, too."

"I'll drive you home," Ryan's dad said. "Tell your mom you'll be there in half an hour."

I relayed the message, and Lorrie told Mom.

After I hung up, Ryan's mom told Ryan to find me some dry clothes and sent us both upstairs to change. The shirt Ryan gave me was okay, but I could tell from looking at them the pants were too going to be too short, and the only shoes he had that fit me were bedroom slippers.

"Dude," Ryan said when I had stripped off the Makoron shirt, "you been working out?"

"There wasn't a whole lot else to do," I said. "They never let me go out."

A look of intense curiosity spread over his face, but he didn't say anything.

"The only recreation I got was lifting weights and having sex," I said as casually as I could.

He snorted and laughed at the same time. "Really? You're not making that up, are you?"

I shook my head. "Five times, five girls."

"Dude!" Curiosity changed to astonishment. "Awesome!"

"Some of it was," I said. And some of it wasn't, but I didn't want to go into that just then. Still, it felt great to have a guy my own age to talk to about girls and sex. I hadn't realized how much I had missed that until that moment.

And then his dad called out for us to come downstairs, and I didn't get to ask Ryan about him and Allie.

I felt a little silly getting into his dad's Lexus looking like I was wearing a nerd costume for Halloween. I even clutched a grocery bag full of wet Makoron clothes like a trick-or-treat bag. On the other hand, it was great not to worry about getting snatched.

And then right after we parked in front of the Westmoreland Apartments, two guys in dark gray suits jumped out of an SUV with smoked windows.

"Jason Miller?" the taller one said to me.

"Yeah," I said.

"Come with us, please."

AT least they let me see Mom and Lorrie first. Mom wanted to come with us, but they wouldn't let her. Another guy in a more expensive suit showed up and waved a paper at her and quoted the PATRIOT Act. Mom was shouting when they took me away, but at least she just looked angry instead of sad.

They took me somewhere in Virginia; I'm not sure where. I spent most of the next day talking into a video recorder about everything that had happened in Makoro—almost everything. I didn't tell them everything about me and Teleza and her sisters. It was none of their business.

They were definitely interested in Makoro—they even kept the Makoron clothes—but mostly they wanted to hear about how I got back. It seemed they had figured out the pattern of guys disappearing—they had even talked to a few guys who made a full Turn and seen Makoro for a few seconds. But they hadn't ever found any guys who had spent time there and then come back, except me and Mr. Walters. They hadn't realized Walters had been to Makoro until Ryan had told them.

I couldn't tell for sure, but it seemed to me they were looking for a way to use teleporting through Makoro as a weapon, or maybe a way to spy on people. It struck me as a risky thing to do. It would have to be a guy who went, and once a guy was in Makoro, he was no longer in charge of anything.

Finally, they let me go, but they told me they didn't want me to tell anyone about Makoro who didn't already know about it. They even concocted a story for me, about how I'd been thrown from the driver's ed car, wandered away in a daze, and accidentally hitchhiked to Pennsylvania where I'd lapsed into a coma and spent months in a hospital as a John Doe.

It was a crazy story, but I knew I'd be happier telling it than telling the truth.

And then finally, they let me go home.

I SPENT the first day and a half eating, sleeping, and listening to jazz in my room. My iPod was gone, but fortunately, I had lot of stuff on CDs. After I put them into chronological order, I played one disc after the other until I got up to Coltrane. I felt a lot better by then, and I decided I needed to come up for air, so I went out to the kitchen to talk to Mom.

She didn't ask me what had happened—not about the coma story or anything. Instead she focused on school. "There are only twelve days until the end of the semester, Jason, so I think it's just as well if you wait and go back to school after winter break."

"Okay." She seemed deliberately cheerful, which surprised me. "Don't you want to know what really happened to me?"

A flash of pain crossed her face. "Only if you need to tell me about it."

I got it. She thought I'd been abused or tortured or something, and she was afraid to hear about it. So I ignored the orders of the Super Secret Government Agency, sat her down at the kitchen table, and told her about Makoro, and about making the Turn.

Her eyes got big, and I could see she had a hard time believing it, but she never said anything to contradict me. I didn't tell her about me and Teleza and what it took to restore *haru*, but I did tell her what almost happened with Dorscha and the Kabarega women.

Mom glanced into the living room where Lorrie was lying on the floor watching TV. I could hear a newscaster relating an account of my miraculous appearance after I had come out of the coma and told the doctors in Pennsylvania who I was. "Don't tell Lorrie about this," Mom said. "Not until she's older."

"I won't."

Her hand grasped mine. "I was so afraid I'd never see you again."

I nodded. "I was afraid, too."

She started to talk about how I'd need to go to summer school, and how many credits I had to make up.

I figured I had twelve days to think about that, so I cleared my throat. "I think I'll go for a walk now."

Her forehead crinkled. "A walk?"

"Yeah." I hadn't been out alone since I had been back. "Just around the neighborhood." I wanted to walk outside and know that no one was going to grab me off the street. I wanted to be an inconspicuous bystander and not a treasured possession to be hidden away. And I needed to see Mr. Walters.

Mom hesitated. Her hand clutched mine again, and then she let go. She picked up her knitting basket. "All right, but don't be too late."

I noticed, as I promised her that I'd be home by 9:00, that she was still working on the same yellow sweater.

I remembered the way to Walters' house with no trouble. Ruveka opened the door to my knock.

"Will you tell your father I'm here, please?" I said in Neluan.

Her surprise showed on her face, but she nodded and held the door open.

I stepped inside. Same Ikea-looking sofa and chairs. Same prints on the walls.

"Ruveka, who—" Mr. Walters stopped in the doorway from the kitchen.

"He's here to see you, *Daida*," Ruveka said in Neluan. She slipped past him into the kitchen and I heard water running, like she had turned on the faucet.

Mr. Walters shut the door very carefully and then turned to face me. "Sit down, Mr. Miller."

I sat on one of the chairs.

Walters seemed reluctant to come to the point. He stood by the door for a moment, and then he crossed the room and sat on the sofa. "I'm happy to see you again."

"I'm glad to be back," I said in Neluan.

He shifted to the edge of the sofa, his eyes locked on me. "You were in Dodomah?" he said in the same language.

I shook my head. "Egume."

His expression went neutral, like he wasn't sure if that was good news or not. "Did you ever hear what happened to Bejida?"

I nodded. "She died."

His shoulders dropped, and he hung his head. I thought for a moment he was going to cry. "I—I never dared hope too much. The mob sounded very angry."

"She refused to share you."

He looked away. "It's ironic. If I tried to have ten wives here, they'd lock me up. And yet on Makoro it's monogamy that's seen as criminal."

To me, the real irony was that the one other guy in the world who spoke Neluan had never experienced Makoro the way the rest of the *keesai* did. Bejida Urbi Siti had sheltered him from that. "It's a different world."

"Yes." He looked me up and down like he expected to see physical evidence of my adventures. "How did you get back?"

I told him about the maglev tracks.

He shook his head just like Marjani had. "You're nuts."

"I'm here, aren't I?"

A small grin started. "I suppose so." He ran one hand through his hair. I noticed it was getting thinner, and I noticed he had stopped wearing his wedding ring. "At least now I can stop wondering if I should try to go back to Dodomah."

I barely held back a snort. "I don't recommend it."

Mr. Walters glanced at the closed kitchen door. "Some time when we can talk more freely, we'll have to compare notes on our experiences in Makoro."

"All right." I got to my feet. "I'd better get going."

He walked me to the door. "Will I see you in school?"

"Not until next semester." I offered my hand. "So long."

We shook hands, and then he opened the door for me.

I started walking home. I passed a middle-aged woman who was letting a pug lift his leg on a light pole while a mixed-breed terrier on another leash looked bored. The terrier came over to sniff my pant leg, but the woman never even looked at me. It felt great.

I lengthened my stride. Summer school would be a pain, but I could do it. I could catch up, graduate with Ryan, and get into a decent college if one would give me a scholarship. Whatever I became in life would be up to me.

I was halfway home when a red Prius pulled up next to me and the driver's window rolled down. A pretty girl with silvery blonde hair smiled at me. "Need a ride, Jason?"

It took me a second to recognize her without the blue hair. "Monica?"

She laughed. "Hop in."

I walked around to the passenger side and got in. Monica waited until I had fastened my seat belt to pull back onto the roadway. I stared at her, fascinated by how different she looked with her hair blonde instead of blue. She had been attractive before, but now she was really cute. "You changed your hair color."

She grinned. "I did it as a birthday present for my grandfather."

Probably the old man's favorite present.

She shot me a glance, and I realized I was staring.

"It's still me," she said. "Not a big deal."

"I like it."

She made a face. "I'm trying to decide if I care. You stood me up for homecoming."

I'd forgotten about that. "I'm sorry. I was in a coma."

She shot me another glance. "That was the best you could do? A coma?" She shook her head. "*Days of Our Lives* called. They want their plot back."

I knew better than to defend a lame story, so I just grinned.

Her eyes slid to my torso and then went back to the road. "I never heard of anyone coming out of a coma buffer than when they went into it."

I hadn't thought about that. She really was pretty smart. And she noticed things—she noticed me. "That's my story, and I'm sticking with it."

"Probably just as well." Her hands gripped the wheel a little tighter. "Do you think you can make it to prom without disappearing again?"

Her question surprised the heck out of me. "I'm not going anywhere if I can help it." I cleared my throat. "Are you asking me to prom?"

A slightly sour smile tugged at her mouth. "I know it's months away, but I don't want to take a chance on having to go to another dance with Doug."

"Doug?"

"Douglas Slater."

My jaw nearly dropped. "You went to homecoming with Doofie Slater?"

She nodded. "I had just started tutoring him in Spanish, and he asked me a week after you disappeared. I told him if he could ask me in Spanish, I'd go with him. Just my luck he'd been practicing."

I had to laugh. In fact, I howled.

"It's not that funny," Monica said.

"No, it's not." I felt kind of bad for laughing so hard. "I didn't know Doofie had such good taste in women."

This time the smile was pure delight. "So are we on for prom or not?"

"We're on," I said, "if I can afford the tickets by then."

She nodded. "Where do you want to go now? Home?"

I leaned back in the seat. Where did I want to go? Not home—at least, not right away. "I'm not picky. Why don't you just drive somewhere where we can talk."

She drove to the Bethesda Swim Club and pulled the Prius into a secluded corner of the deserted parking lot. When she put the ignition on accessory and turned on the CD player, Dave Matthews came on; I figured it could have been worse; she could have liked bubblegum pop or something.

We talked for a while about her life in Costa Rica and what it had been like to move to Maryland, and then the changer put on the next CD, and Wynton Marsalis' "Green Chimneys" started to play.

A sudden rush of elation washed over me. Finally, I'd found someone else who shared my passion. "You like jazz, too?"

An odd look crossed her face, and then she shook her head. "Not really. It's Grandpa's CD. I gave him a ride the other day."

I realized she had been tempted to lie but had told the truth. "Oh."

She got a really earnest expression on her face. "Grandpa loves jazz. He says listening to jazz is like watching an artist paint a picture—you never know how it will come out."

I hadn't ever thought about it that way, but it wasn't a bad description of the way jazz made me feel. Still, it was mortifying that it was her grandfather who shared my taste in music.

"I don't *dislike* jazz," she went on. "It's just not my thing."

That was probably about as good as I was going to get in a girl my age. Suddenly I noticed the time on the dash said 9:05. "Can I borrow your phone? Mine burned up in the crash."

She said sure, and handed me the phone.

Mom answered on the first ring. "Jason?" I could hear a sharp edge of panic in her voice.

"I'm fine, Mom." I glanced at Monica. "I met a friend, and we went for a ride. I'll be home soon."

Her voice quavered, but she said okay, so I hung up and gave Monica her phone back.

"How's your mom doing?" she asked.

I noticed she had let the Marsalis CD keep playing. That was a good sign. "She's okay now that I'm back."

She nodded, but she didn't say anything. The moon was up, and the moonlight shone on Monica's hair and on the gold chain around her neck. It occurred to me I was alone in a car with a girl I liked, and so I leaned over and kissed her.

She kissed me back. We made out for a while—not easy in bucket seats, but I didn't want to suggest moving to the back when we hadn't even been on a real date yet.

Right after I got to second base, Monica sighed and turned the ignition on. "We'd better get back before your mom freaks again."

"Okay." And it was okay. In fact, it was more than okay, it was great. And then Monica drove me home. It all felt wonderfully normal.

Mom looked relieved when I walked through the door. She hugged me like I'd been gone for a week instead of a few hours. Then Lorrie came into my room to give me a hug and a kiss before she went to bed. Even Sancho came and rubbed against my ankles while I brushed my teeth.

When I was ready for bed I put on a Dave Brubeck CD, because I was in a Brubeck mood. I lay down, alone but content, and spared a thought for Marjani, whom I had left waiting by the maglev tracks, and for Esi, who had been kind to me and had suffered for it, for Nuri who had helped me escape, and for Hobart and Teleza and all the others I had met in Makoro. Their lives would all go on without me.

I had liked some of them more than others, of course, but I knew that spending the rest of my life without seeing any of them again was going to be much easier to do than if I hadn't been able to come home.

Still, it was spooky to know there were two versions—or maybe more— of the world. It wasn't like I had merely traveled to a foreign country. When I left Makoro, I had disconnected from it. No postcards from Egume would ever land in our mailbox. I couldn't e-mail Nuri to ask how she was doing. I couldn't call Marjani to see if she got away safely, or text Teleza to find out if she and her sisters had found another guy to marry. In a way the past few months were like a dream or a delusion, especially because I couldn't tell anyone about that time who didn't already know about it, not even Monica.

Would I ever want to go back to Makoro? The suits might well figure out how to go to there and back without having to stand in front of a speeding train. If they did, though, they'd have to find another traveler. It might sound really cool to be able to go from one place to another in the blink of any eye, but I prefer to stay in my own world. And if I wanted to travel anywhere, I'd buy a damn ticket.

THE END

Acknowledgements

Thanks, as always, to the members of the Writers' Group from Hell for their critiques. Thanks also to my copy editor Risa Stewart. I appreciate her efforts very much!

And thanks to you, dear reader, for finishing the book!

I do have more books, you know, if you're still looking for something to read.

Carmen Webster Buxton

Made in the USA
Middletown, DE
31 January 2019